THE GIRL IN THE ATTIC

JOHN NICHOLL

Boldwood

First published in Great Britain in 2026 by Boldwood Books Ltd.

Cover Design by Head Design Ltd.

Cover Images: iStock and Shutterstock

A CIP catalogue record for this book is available from the British Library.

Paperback ISBN 978-1-80656-472-9

Large Print ISBN 978-1-80656-466-8

Hardback ISBN 978-1-80656-456-9

Trade Paperback ISBN 978-1-80656-467-5

Ebook ISBN 978-1-80656-460-6

Kindle ISBN 978-1-80656-458-3

Audio CD ISBN 978-1-80656-462-0

MP3 CD ISBN 978-1-80656-461-3

Digital audio download ISBN 978-1-80656-468-2

This book is printed on certified sustainable paper. Boldwood Books is dedicated to putting sustainability at the heart of our business. For more information please visit https://www.boldwoodbooks.com/about-us/sustainability/

Boldwood Books Ltd, 23 Bowerdean Street, London, SW6 3TN

www.boldwoodbooks.com

For Dianne

1

Joe, my boyfriend back then, all sunburnt charm and perfect teeth, told me once, half-laughing, eyes alive with a kind of reckless glee, that every time I came, a tiny earthquake rippled through some far-flung corner of the world. Like my sexual pleasure had the power to fracture tectonic plates, disturb the very bones of the earth. And I believed him. Not completely. But enough. Just enough for the thought to bury itself like a seed in the soft, damaged soil of my psyche: the part that still ached to feel something close to powerful. The part that wanted to believe I wasn't just another disposable girl. Another sad statistic. Passed from hand to hand by parents too high to remember my birthday, too wired to care who was paying to touch their daughter, so long as the notes were real and the dealer didn't skimp.

That lie, that lovely, glittering lie, I wore it like a second skin. Let it tighten around my ribs and lodge in my throat like a secret only I could taste. It gave me a kind of armour. Made me feel untouchable. For a while. But power, real power, doesn't come wrapped in silk and promises. It doesn't whisper sweet nothings into the darkness and vanish come morning. It was never real. Just another illusion: bright as glass, fragile as sugar; and illusions only hold their shape so long. Then they splinter.

The man who rewrote the script of my life proved that, the moment

Joe's affection soured and his gaze wandered. A man who never courted: he infiltrated. He crept beneath the skin with practised charm, laying siege with a smile that masked the rot. Politeness was his armour. Civility, his camouflage. A predator dressed as a gentleman, every gesture rehearsed, every word calculated.

There were no raised voices, no fists; not at first. He chose subtler weapons. Poison wrapped in honey. Empty praise dressed as devotion. He told me what I ached to hear, flattering my brittle ego until I mistook manipulation for love. Then he rationed out morsels of approval: crumbs dangled like currency. And I, naïve, desperate girl that I was, scrambled for them, hungry, foolish, blind: like a starving dog snapping.

He didn't tear me apart in one brutal motion. He unravelled me. Carefully. Methodically. Like he enjoyed the process. One layer at a time. Until I no longer recognised my own reflection. Until the sound of my own laughter startled me. Until my thoughts were no longer mine, but his, threaded into my brain like mould in bread. He hollowed me out. Turned me into a shadow of myself. And made me thank him for the darkness he wrapped around me.

By the time I realised what he was, what I'd become, it was too late. I wasn't me any more. Just an echo of the girl I used to be. A whisper in someone else's nightmare.

There were no earthquakes. No storms tearing across the sky. No power surging through forgotten lines. Just silence: the dying echo of a girl who once believed she could live a worthwhile life. A girl who dared to think she mattered. Who thought her voice might carry weight. That someone might listen. That she could make a difference.

But dreams die quietly. And he stood at the centre of the wreckage. Still. Poised. Serene, like the eye of a storm that never came. He smiled: softly, disarmingly, like none of it had ever touched him. Like the chaos and carnage were nothing more than background noise. As if he hadn't destroyed everything. As if he wasn't the monster behind the mask.

Because that's what he was: a man who sowed ruin with a whisper and watched the aftermath unfold with clinical detachment. He gave nothing but pain. Took everything, piece by piece, until I was hollowed out and barely human. And that's where I find myself now as I write this.

Of course, my words are only a glimpse of my new reality. A single thread plucked from a vast, suffocating web that still clings to me, tight and unrelenting. The kind of web you don't untangle. I've barely scratched the surface. Just grazed the rotting skin of something far more malignant, something that festers in the silence and refuses to die.

There's more to tell. So much more. Things I haven't said. Things I can't say; not yet. Not because I don't remember, but because some memories bite back when you touch them.

Still, I'll keep writing. Keep bleeding on to the page. Not just to make sense of it, though I ache for that, more than I care to admit. But because I'm desperate.

Desperate for someone, anyone, to read these words and look beyond the neat lines and tidy paragraphs. To see past the careful structure and find what's really there: the bruises beneath the ink. The scream buried in the spaces between sentences. To see me. To understand what was done. What's still being done. To help.

And if they don't, if no one hears me through this static, then I'm lost. Because this place I'm in, this cage wrapped in wallpaper and pleasantries, isn't just walls and locks. It's him. His shadow. His echo. His voice still whispering in the back of my skull, even when I think I'm alone. If no one reaches in soon... I won't survive it. Not whole. Not sane. Not alive. Above all, more than anything, this is a cry for help.

2

Lying locked in the narrow bed of my attic prison last night, I realised I'd neglected the most basic courtesy: I didn't even share who I am. The urgency to speak, to warn, overtook me. I launched into my story like a woman on fire, desperate for oxygen, and forgot the simplest thing. My name. My identity. And that matters. Because how can anyone save me if they don't know who I am? So let me put that right.

My name is Olivia Ashford. I'm eighteen years old. Small, five foot two on a good day, and fading fast. My body's wasting away, inch by inch. I'm little more than a whisper of the girl I used to be. He doesn't feed me properly. Starves me slowly. A cruel trickle of calories just enough to keep me alive. For now.

But I'm racing too far ahead: galloping through the horror without giving you the foundation. That's not how this works. Not if you're going to understand. Not if you're going to believe me. You need context. You need the truth, laid out like pieces of broken glass, sharp and glinting in the light.

So let me go back. All the way back. To the beginning. Only then will you see how I ended up here, in this place. In this hell. And maybe, just maybe, if someone out there takes the time to listen, if they care enough, if they don't dismiss me as another sad voice lost in the void, then there's a chance. A flicker of hope. If you like me, if you see me and if you can find me, maybe then I won't die in this room. Maybe then I'll live.

So here we go. Buckle up, tight. This won't be a gentle stroll down memory lane. It's more of a white-knuckle crawl through the wreckage. I'll give you a glimpse: just a fleeting look through a cracked window into the chaos that was my childhood. Just enough for the shadows to move. Just enough for you to feel the cold draft of what it was like. You don't need the full autopsy. The bones of it are enough.

My parents? Shit. They had no business raising a dog, let alone a child. They were the kind of people you cross the street to avoid. Broken people. Dangerous in their indifference. And I was the collateral damage. Innocent. Invisible. Unwanted.

That's all you need to know. That's all I can give you right now. So let's move on, shall we? Before the past drags us down. Before he slams the door on the attic and plunges it all into blackness again. Trust me, it's better that way.

I was ten when they took me. On a hot summer day in June. Ten years old and already half-broken. A Place of Safety Order, they called it. Like I was a misfiled document someone finally noticed. A mistake that needed processing.

It was a well-meaning social worker in his twenties who came to collect me. The type who smiled too much, like it could patch over the cracks. Shoulder-length chestnut-brown hair, a neatly trimmed beard, and those ridiculous gunmetal aviator glasses that made him look like a throwback to a decade he didn't understand. He tried to talk to me on the drive, but I don't remember what he said. Just the sound of the engine.

He dropped me at a children's home near the fire station. The kind of place that smelled of floor polish and old tears. Too many doors, too many rules, and no one who knew your name after lights out.

After that, it was foster homes. One after the other. Different walls, different strangers. Each time I unpacked, I left a little more behind. Until eventually, at the age of fourteen, wonder of wonders, I landed somewhere that felt less like a sentence and more like a chance. A family who didn't wince when I flinched. Who saw me, not the label pinned to my file.

The Jones family lived on a modest smallholding a few miles outside

Carmarthen, out along the winding road to Pembrokeshire where the hedgerows leaned in like they were guarding secrets. It wasn't much to look at – an old stone farmhouse with peeling paint, outbuildings sagging under the weight of time – but to me, it was almost unrecognisable as real life. Quiet. Still. No raised voices echoing down the halls. No footsteps creeping upstairs in the dead of night.

It took time. Time to lower my guard. Time to stop listening for the sound of a shoe dropping. I'd learned not to trust kindness, not to believe in comfort: it always came at a price. But the Joneses, Eva and Edward... they were different. Gentle in a way I didn't know what to do with. And they didn't ask for anything in return.

Eventually, after a few months, against every instinct screaming otherwise, I began to trust. Just a little. I liked it there. I liked them. Their calm, their consistency. They never flinched when I withdrew, never punished my silence. And the animals; wow, the animals were a lifeline. A black and white cow with mournful eyes who always stood close, like she understood. Two horses with wild spirits that mirrored my own. Pigs that grunted and snorted with a kind of joyful defiance. And chickens, scrappy, clucking things, that scattered around my feet each morning when I went to collect the eggs. It gave me purpose. Routine. Something to hold on to. My life had shifted. Not in an instant, not like in the movies. It was subtle. Uneven. Like light creeping under a locked door.

Of course, it wasn't perfect. There were rows; there always are when you've got a kid like me testing the boundaries, pushing the limits, daring them to walk away. I challenged their patience more than once, not because I wanted to, but because I needed to. I needed to know they wouldn't turn their backs. That I could be difficult and still be worth keeping.

But I don't want to linger on the bad. Not this time. Because for the first time in a long while, the good outweighed the rest. And that was everything. Overall, life was good. Eva Jones in particular took an interest in my art. She had that offbeat, free-spirited energy about her: the kind of woman who sometimes burned incense in the kitchen and believed in the healing power of lavender. A bit of a hippy, some might've said, but not in a way that grated. Not most of the time, anyway. There was something grounded in her softness, something that made the chaos inside me feel less jagged when she was around. I think my sketching spoke to something in her. Maybe she saw fragments of herself in the way I put pencil to paper: quiet, careful, searching.

It was a warm April afternoon, the kind that made you forget, for a moment, that bad things had ever happened. I was sitting cross-legged in the grass, back against the low stone wall that edged the field, sketchpad balanced on my knees. The old oak across the yard had caught my eye, its limbs gnarled and reaching, like it had seen things and kept them to itself.

That's when Eva passed by. A battered bucket of pigswill swinging from one hand, her boots falling softly on the ground. She glanced down, a casual flick of the eyes, probably expecting the usual blank stare or a half-hearted scribble.

But she stopped mid-step. Just froze there, one foot half-raised, like something had snagged her in place. She looked at the sketch, then at me. And then she smiled: slow, warm, and just a little bit sad.

There was no fanfare. No breathless praise or clumsy attempt to smother the moment with words. Just silence. The kind of silence that speaks louder than anything else ever could. Her gaze lingered a second too long, as if she saw something there on the page, in me, that others had missed or simply chosen to ignore.

It wasn't grand or dramatic. But it mattered. Wow, it mattered. Because in that quiet, sun-drenched moment, something shifted. A wire tightened. A spark caught. I didn't understand it then, not fully, but I felt it. Deep down in the part of me I'd kept hidden for so long. Recognition, maybe. Or understanding. Like she saw the storm behind the calm and didn't look away.

It was a turning point. The start of something I couldn't yet name. A subtle nudge that sent everything tilting in a new direction. The beginning of a path I didn't know I was on, one that would lead me to everything that came after. And there'd be no going back.

Eva talked about my art a few hours later. It was early evening, around five, the light slanting low through the farmhouse window, casting long amber streaks across the worn pine table. The kitchen smelled of slow-cooked meat and rosemary, the air still heavy with the comforting warmth of Eva's home-made shepherd's pie. The kind of food that filled more than just your stomach.

I sat there, fork in hand, halfway through a mouthful, when she looked across at me with that soft, knowing smile of hers. Eva had the kind of face that made you want to trust her: open, gentle, seemingly untouched by the hardness of the world. Her eyes held mine for a beat too long, as if she saw straight through the layers I'd spent years learning to hide behind.

'You have a very real artistic talent, Olivia,' she said, her voice warm, steady, and thick with sincerity. 'God given. You do know that, don't you?'

The words landed like a stone in still water. I wasn't used to hearing things like that. Not from anyone. Not without an edge of mockery or suspicion. I shifted in my seat, the wooden chair creaking, my fork pausing just above the plate. I couldn't hold her gaze, not then. Instead, I let my eyes slide to the kitchen wall, tracing the cracks in the plaster like they held the answer to what I was supposed to say. Praise like that... it didn't fit right. Not on someone like me. It made my skin itch.

But still, somewhere deep within, buried beneath the well-worn armour of mistrust and the reflex to retreat, I felt something stir. Subtle. Elusive. Hope, perhaps. Or that rare, dangerous glimmer of belief that maybe, just maybe, she meant every word.

Her eyes held mine, steady, kind, firm. And for the first time in longer than I cared to admit, I didn't look away.

'Do you really think so?' I asked, my voice quieter than intended, almost afraid to believe.

She nodded. Twice. And the certainty in that simple gesture lifted something in me.

'Absolutely,' she said, as if it was the most obvious truth in the world. 'I wouldn't have said it otherwise. I've some paints and brushes tucked away somewhere. My dad's, from years back. It was a phase, a hobby. But he never had your talent. He'd be over the moon to know they were finally being put to good use. Would you like them? There's some watercolours and oils.'

I smiled. And it wasn't forced or polite, it was genuine, full-bodied. A rare thing.

'I would,' I said, nodding. 'Yes. That would be... lovely. Thank you. I really would.'

And that was it: the spark that lit the fire. What began as distraction became something far greater. A compulsion. A salvation. Drawing had always soothed something in me, but now painting consumed me. Obsessed me. Hours would pass and I wouldn't notice. All the noise in my head, the fear, the ache, the jagged fragments of memory, would dissolve into colour and canvas. Nothing else existed. Nothing else needed to.

And to their credit, my foster parents encouraged my art from that day on. They truly did. And as the months passed, that support never faltered. They bought the supplies when mine ran out, praised my efforts, pinned my drawings and paintings to the fridge like they meant something. Like I meant something. They acted in good faith. Out of kindness. So, I hold nothing against them. Nothing. They couldn't have known what was coming. What they'd started. How could they? No one saw the gathering storm, the dark shape on the far horizon. The universe keeping its secrets, smiling quietly behind its hand.

That's life, isn't it? Just when you let yourself believe, really believe, that things might finally be turning a corner, it bares its teeth. Sinks in its claws. And it doesn't let go.

That's how it was for me. My newfound joy didn't last long. Not a tale of triumph or redemption, but one carved in shadows. A slow, merciless unravelling. I wouldn't wish it on my worst enemy, not even the ones who deserve it. Because some nightmares don't end when you open your eyes. They just settle in and wait. Quietly. Patiently. Until you're too worn down to fight them any more.

It was as if some invisible hand, some cruel, chaotic muse, had already laid out the path, brick by jagged brick. A twisted journey I was fated to walk, regardless of my choices. No detours. No escape. As if I was being led, not by ambition or instinct, but by something colder. Smarter. Darker. Malevolent, even.

And all the while he watched from the shadows, entertained. My well-being? Irrelevant. Just collateral in his little game. Art was never just art. Not for me. It was part of a trap.

In the months that followed, I poured myself into my art with an urgency I didn't fully understand: driven, possessed almost, as if the act itself might hold some kind of answer. I began by imitating the greats: Picasso's fractured brilliance, Dalí's surreal contortions, the haunted elegance of Modigliani. I studied them obsessively, dissecting their madness and genius in equal measure. But slowly, something began to shift. My hands stopped copying and started speaking in their own voice. The rigid outlines softened, the borrowed styles dissolved, and something darker, something more intimate began to emerge. A reflection of my troubled being.

My technical skill became uncanny: people, objects, entire scenes rendered with almost painful clarity, as though I'd trapped them in time. But realism, though impressive, didn't satisfy the ache in my chest. It was in the abstracts that I found true release. Bold lines, jarring colours, fragmented figures that didn't make sense to anyone but me. Looking back now, I can see it for what it was: a kind of therapy, twisted and raw. A silent scream on canvas. I reached places with a brush that talking therapy never touched, scraped at wounds too deep for words, and dragged them into the light, whether I was ready or not. There was a tension to my work, a thread of unease woven into every brushstroke. I didn't notice it at the time, too close to the canvas, too lost in the process; but looking back, it's unmistakable. The colours I gravitated towards weren't random. Deep purples, heavy blacks, visceral reds: they didn't just sit on the surface; they bled. Leached into the paper, soaked into the grain of the canvas, as if the paint itself carried something toxic that needed releasing.

Each piece pulsed with a strange kind of emotion. It wasn't beauty I was chasing, not really. It was brutal honesty. And what spilled out of me was fractured and dark, a jagged mirror held up to my own damaged soul. Even now, I struggle to recall some of those early works without feeling a familiar twist in my gut. They weren't just pictures. They were recollections. Memories I couldn't suppress.

I was sixteen by then, and my school began to see it too: the depth buried in my work, the silent screams etched between each line, the unspoken truth lurking beneath the colours. There was a weight to what I created, a gravity that pulled people in, even if they couldn't explain why. They felt it. I know they did. I had a talent I couldn't begin to explain.

On the day I turned seventeen, the world seemed to move a little slower, as if holding its breath. We spent the afternoon in the dim, dust-scented hush of a near-empty cinema in Carmarthen, just the three of us. The film was forgettable, some formulaic drama that left no lasting impression, which, in hindsight, felt deliberate. A safe choice. Background noise.

Edward sat on my left, Eva on my right. My foster parents, though I rarely called them that out loud. Their presence was steady, familiar, but that day there was something brittle at the edges. Edward kept glancing my way when he thought I wasn't looking, and Eva laughed a little too quickly at the wrong moments on screen. I felt caught between them, aware of their silences more than their words.

When the credits finally rolled and we spilled out into the early evening light, the air felt unnaturally cool against my skin. Edward turned to me with a look that didn't quite match the occasion. His smile was shaped like something he'd rehearsed, too measured, too careful, as if he were reading lines from a script he didn't fully believe in.

'I've booked us a table at the Iechyd Da Café,' he said, with a forced cheerfulness that only made me more uneasy. 'That veggie place on Jackson's Lane. Thought it might be nice.'

I nodded, grateful for the mention of somewhere familiar. That little café, cluttered, cosy, friendly, tucked away from the world, felt like a safe place. A space that belonged to us, where nothing ever seemed to go wrong. It made sense, and yet...

A thread of tension wound itself tight in my chest. I couldn't explain it then, not really, but something about the way they exchanged glances, the way Eva touched my arm and smiled just a second too late, made me feel as though the evening was already written. As though the celebration was only a prelude to something else.

Still, part of me, the foolish, hopeful part, felt a flicker of excitement. The kind that comes when you think maybe someone's planned something just for you. Something special. And it was. Something seemingly wonderful. I just didn't know where it would lead.

We sat on two black leather sofas, their surfaces worn in places, as though softened by years of whispered conversations and forgotten days.

They were pushed up close to the serving counter with a low table in between, the faint scent of cumin and roasted garlic in the warm air.

The walls – three of the four, at least – were drenched in a warm burnt orange that caught the light in strange ways, casting a soft glow that made the room feel smaller, more intimate. Cluttered across them was an eclectic collection of artwork: mismatched frames, clashing colours, wild brushstrokes and jagged abstracts that seemed to shout over one another, each piece desperate to be seen, yet none quite managing to hold the eye.

I let my gaze wander from one picture to the next, half-lost in the tangle of colour and confusion, anything to avoid looking too closely at what sat across from me. Edward and Eva were pretending to read the menu, studying it with the kind of intensity usually reserved for exam papers or bad news, as if they hadn't memorised it years ago. It was a performance, thinly veiled, their eyes skimming words they already knew, giving shape to a silence that none of us yet dared to break.

I didn't need to look at the café's offerings any more than they did. Not for a second. I never did. I always ordered the same thing: freshly made mushroom burgers with a crisp organic salad, dressed in something sharp and citrusy that lingered on the tongue. There was comfort in the ritual, a small act of certainty in a world that so often refused to offer any. God, what I wouldn't give for one of those meals now! Just one more bite, one more moment in that cocoon of safety, before the world moved and everything changed.

My foster father finally met my eyes across the small oak table after giving our order to the pretty red-haired café owner, who always remembered our names. And then he began to speak, each word measured like he was afraid of dropping something fragile. All the while, he held my gaze, steady, unwavering, in a way he rarely did. It was disarming. Intimate, almost. Like he was trying to anchor himself in my eyes, to draw courage from the steadiness he hoped to find there.

There was a tremor beneath the surface: subtle, barely there, but it laced his words with something raw and unspoken. Anticipation, yes, but not the bright, eager kind. This was the strained, desperate sort: the kind that clings to the edge of hope like a man slipping beneath the waves, clutching at driftwood that may or may not hold.

And beneath that hope, a darker current stirred. Hesitation. A flickering uncertainty that crackled at the edges of his composure. As if he was standing on a narrow ledge between confession and collapse, knowing full well that whatever came next might piece things together or crush what little remained unbroken.

Or at least that's how it all seemed to me. I could have been wrong, of course. Seeing things that weren't there. I'm told I have a knack for twisting things, for seeing shadows where there's only light, for hearing the storm when the skies are clear. My captor tells me that all the time. And maybe he's right. The master of my world. Maybe this was just another distortion, another trick of the mind, warped by too many let-downs and not enough truth.

'I've got some good news, Olivia. Or at least... I hope you'll think it's good,' Edward said, the words wrapped in forced brightness, like wrapping paper over something breakable. 'It's a fantastic opportunity; I've been looking forward to telling you all about it.'

I drew back slightly, just enough for him to notice, though I doubted he'd acknowledge it. My fingers drifted to the bracelet around my left wrist, a small silver thing worn smooth from years of absent-minded fiddling. A comfort. A shield.

The word 'opportunity' hung in the air like smoke: shapeless, unreadable. I felt my stomach tighten, an old reflex. Change had rarely brought anything worth celebrating. In my world, surprises weren't balloons and cake: they were boxes packed in silence, new foster homes with unfamiliar rules, phone calls in the dead of night. I'd learned early not to trust the promise of something new.

So I sat there, silent, bracing. Waiting for the shape of it to reveal itself, whatever it was.

And then he smiled: a real smile this time. Not the cautious, measured kind he sometimes wore, but something brighter, unguarded. It softened the lines of his face, reached his eyes, made him look younger somehow. Before life had pressed its weight on to his shoulders.

'It's about your paintings,' he said, his voice warmer now, steadier.

The tension in my chest eased, just a little. That tight, invisible fist that had become my constant companion began to unclench. The cold edge of fear ebbed away, replaced by the flicker of something far more dangerous: hope.

'My paintings?' I asked, leaning forward without realising. 'What about them?'

Now I was listening. Now I cared. Because for once, this wasn't about upheaval or endings. This was about me: something I'd made, something that mattered to me more than almost anything else.

Edward glanced at Eva, who gave the smallest of nods. She reached for her mug, fingers trembling just enough to betray her nerves. Whatever this was, they'd discussed it, rehearsed it maybe, and now it was unfolding exactly as they'd planned.

'A very good friend of ours,' Edward said, his voice careful now, as though picking his way across fragile ground, 'owns a gallery in Bath. Somerset. Located right in the centre of the city. In one of the main streets close to the theatre. It's a wonderful place. Beautiful. And Benjamin is a good man: curious, generous and influential in the art world. He saw some of your work... the pieces Eva posted online on Facebook. The Winter series. The ones you liked the best.'

My stomach gave a sharp twist, quick, instinctive: a flutter of disbelief tangled with fragile excitement. I cut a glance towards Eva, searching her face, and this time she met my eyes. A smile softened her features, small at first, then blooming as if she couldn't contain it. Her fingers traced the rim of her mug, not with unease but with the quiet energy of someone holding back words until I was ready to hear them. There was a brightness in her demeanour, an unspoken reassurance that told me more than any speech could.

I turned back to Edward, my pulse a quiet drumbeat in my ears. He was watching me closely, expectant, his hands folded neatly on the table in front of him. But I hesitated. The question hovered at the back of my throat, too delicate to voice. Because what if I'd misunderstood? What if this sudden rush of possibility was nothing more than a beautiful illusion, a trick of the light? I didn't trust hope. Not really. It had let me down before, brutally, without warning.

And so I sat there, almost too afraid to speak, in case the act of asking shattered the moment completely. I finally forced the words from my mouth.

'And he really liked my paintings?'

Edward nodded twice, a gleam in his green eyes.

'He was really impressed, Olivia. Genuinely impressed. And he wants to include some of your paintings in an exhibition. A proper one. Framed. Lit. On the wall.'

My eyes widened.

'Really?'

'Oh, yes, really.' Edward paused, his smile edging into something almost reverent. 'People will come to see your work. And they may even buy it. If you're in agreement, you can talk to Ben about prices. I'm sure he'd be more than happy to advise you. He's the expert, after all. I think you might be quite surprised by what he has to tell you.'

For a moment, I couldn't even speak. I just sat there blinking, trying to make sense of the words as they settled around me. Bath. A gallery. An exhibition. Money. Mine.

A strange, giddy warmth bloomed in my chest, catching me off guard. It had never occurred to me that what I painted alone in my room, in those quiet, ink-stained hours, might ever be seen anywhere other than online, let alone celebrated.

'You're serious?' I asked, my voice thinner than I intended.

Edward nodded again. 'Deadly serious. Ben wants to meet you. To see more of your work. If you're willing. We could travel to Bath early next Saturday morning, if it's something you'd like to do. Me, you and Eva on the train. It's only a few hours from Carmarthen. What do you think?'

'Saturday? That soon?'

'Yeah, a week today. If you're up for it.'

And just like that, the world tilted, slightly, almost imperceptibly, but enough for me to feel the shift in my bones. I felt true happiness for what I think was the first time in my life.

'Oh, yes, please, yes,' I said with evident enthusiasm as a friendly waitress delivered our tasty meals to the table. 'It all sounds wonderful. I cannot wait!'

3

The three of us caught the 07.37 from Carmarthen that Saturday morning, the platform still wet with dew, the sky smudged with the last scraps of dawn. We were heading for Bath Spa, about four hours with changes at Cardiff Central and Bristol Temple Meads, each stop a little marker of how far I'd come, and how much further I still had to go. I kept my portfolio case close, fingers brushing the faux leather like it might disappear if I let it out of my sight. Inside were several favourite paintings I'd poured everything into. I wanted the gallery owner to see them; not just glance and nod, but really see them, the way Edward and Eva swore he already did.

But hope had teeth. My enthusiasm was tempered by the inevitable anxiety that rarely left me. And the rhythmic clatter of the tracks beneath us offered no comfort. Through the window, the lush green of the Welsh countryside gave way to the soft rolling hills of England, but even the beauty felt fragile, like glass beneath a hammer. A part of me, the part too bruised to dream without caution, still believed the whole thing might unravel before we reached the end of the line. Life had taught me to expect the fall, even if I was on the rise. Especially then.

When we finally got there, we found a worn wooden bench tucked away in a quiet corner of the park by the river, the kind of place that felt like a secret, and unwrapped the picnic Eva had packed for us. And as we ate, Bath rose around us in honeyed stone and quiet grandeur, its Georgian elegance softened by the warmth of the sun. I'd never set foot in the city before, never wandered its cobbled streets or traced the curves of its sweeping crescents, but something about it stirred me. There was a quiet poetry to the place: a grace that reached into you and stayed there. I found myself unexpectedly moved, as though the beauty I'd only ever glimpsed in pictures had finally taken shape before my eyes. It was more than I'd expected. More than I thought I deserved. Almost a little piece of heaven.

Edward and Eva began gathering the remnants of our lunch twenty minutes later, folding napkins and snapping lids shut with the quiet efficiency of long familiarity. The taste of the crusty bread and ripe cheese still lingered, mingling with the scent of cut grass and sun-warmed stone. It was just before noon, the city humming softly around us, but there was a sudden shift in the air: something in Edward's expression tightening like a knot.

He glanced at Eva, then pushed up the sleeve of his cord jacket with a briskness that betrayed his usual calm, his brow furrowing as he checked the time. There was purpose in the way he stood, brushing crumbs from his lap, eyes already fixed on a point beyond the trees.

'Right,' he said, his voice lilting with that familiar Welsh cadence, 'we'd better make a move. Ben's expecting us at half past. It's only a fifteen-minute walk, but better early than late.' He paused, softening slightly. 'And it'll give us a chance to take our time... enjoy the city while we can.'

But there was something in his tone, quiet, almost buried beneath the surface; it told me this wasn't just about being on time. It was more than that. It was about making the right impression. About not wasting the opportunity. Beneath his composed exterior, I could feel the flicker of nerves, the cautious hope that everything might finally fall into place. And strangely, comfortingly, it seemed he wanted this for me almost as much as I did.

In a world that had so often taught me I was dispensable, a fleeting presence easily forgotten, that quiet urgency in Edward's voice anchored me. For a moment, I wasn't alone in the fight. For a moment, I mattered; not just to myself, but to someone else. And that, however fleeting, felt like something close to love.

A profound sense of awe settled over me as we wandered past the majestic splendour of Bath Abbey. The honeyed stone shimmered in the early summer sunlight, every weathered contour of its façade seeming to pulse with life beneath the cloudless sky. I slowed, almost involuntarily, my gaze lifting to drink in the soaring spires and intricate carvings, each detail steeped in centuries of silent witness.

The air was thick with warmth, and the rich, mournful sound of an Italian aria drifted from a nearby street performer, the notes hanging like smoke in the air, clinging to the edges of thought. I didn't understand the words, but they struck something deep within me, something raw and half-buried. My chest ached with a feeling I couldn't quite name. Joy, perhaps. Or anxiety masquerading as wonder.

The place was unlike anything I'd ever known, almost too exquisite, too achingly still, as if the world had momentarily forgotten how to suffer. A fragile perfection, untouched by the darkness I dragged behind me like a second skin. And in that suspended breath of time, the sheer beauty of it all felt almost violent in its purity: an affront to the things I'd witnessed, the things done to me, destroying my innocence. It wasn't just a contrast; it was a cruel, calculated contradiction. A silent rebuke wrapped in birdsong and golden light. A whisper of what might have been, had life dealt a gentler hand. And still, in the hushed corners of my doubt, I allowed myself the luxury of wondering: what if? What if the worst wasn't all there was? Surely, I reasoned, if hell could carve itself into the folds of this earth, then so too could heaven, however fleeting, however undeserved.

Edward and Eva had already begun to stitch together the frayed edges of something I'd long believed lost: my capacity for hope. Not in grand, sweeping gestures, but in quiet, steadfast ways that crept beneath the armour I'd worn for too long. And now this. Another flicker. Another breath of something perilously close to peace. I barely dared to name it, let alone believe in it. But still, it lingered, tentative, trembling, real. Maybe this time, whatever cruel hand had always come to tear it away would falter. Maybe, just this once, hope would be allowed to stay.

I dabbed at the corners of my eyes, catching the tear before it could trace the curve of my cheek. A quick, furtive gesture. Then I dropped my gaze to my sandalled feet, watching them move across the warm stone pavement, grounding myself in the rhythm of each step. I quickened my pace, just slightly, enough to close the gap between Edward and me. He strode ahead now with quiet determination, as if something unseen were urging him on, as though time itself had begun to slip through our fingers.

As we turned right beyond the abbey square, he pointed wordlessly, and we stepped into what looked to be one of the city's main thoroughfares. The street opened up before us: wide and bustling, alive with colour and motion. Shoppers meandered past tourists clutching guidebooks, their voices blending with the low hum of the city. Cafés spilled out onto the pavement, their tables crowded with half-finished drinks and laughter. Independent shops stood shoulder to shoulder with polished boutiques, each framed by the same soft, honeyed stone that bathed the whole street in a golden glow.

To me, it all felt like a glimpse of something sacred: an earthly echo of a place just beyond reach. A corner of the world untouched by the things that haunt the dark. And in that moment, I let myself believe, just a little, that this life, this joy, might be real. That my art, my sketches and canvases and fragile imaginings, could somehow belong there. That I might leave a mark, however small, on that beautiful, impossible place. I clung to the hope with quiet desperation, afraid that if I let it slip, the dream would dissolve into nothing. Just like everything else.

I spotted the theatre first, rising to my left as we reached Sawclose, a curious name for a place so utterly charming, as if it belonged to another time, another story altogether. The building stood like a quiet sentinel, its classical lines softened by the forgiving light.

But then Eva reached for me, suddenly, instinctively, her fingers curling around mine with a warmth that stopped my thoughts mid-stream. She smiled, that knowing smile of hers, and gently tugged me across the broad street without a word. And there it was. The gallery.

Two generously proportioned display windows flanked an open door like silent invitations, their glass surfaces alive with colour. Brightly painted canvases, abstract and unapologetically bold, called to me from behind the panes. Acrylics in sunbursts and shadows, reds and ochres and impossible blues. My heart kicked against my ribs as if it knew something my mind hadn't yet caught up with. This was it. We'd arrived.

The moment I'd dreamed of, feared, and half-convinced myself would never come. It hung in the air between us, breathless and trembling. For a second, everything else receded – the crowds, the chatter, the whisper of the summer breeze. All I could see were those paintings and the open door beckoning me in.

It felt like fate had taken my hand and placed it gently on the threshold of something extraordinary. As if, after all the false starts and quiet failures, I'd finally stumbled into life's elusive magic. Not fame. Not fortune. Just a chance. A whisper of belonging. And it overwhelmed me in the best possible way, like for once I'd somehow won life's cruel and beautiful lottery. The entire morning had been a turmoil of roller-coaster emotion. And it seemed that wasn't about to change.

Ben appeared as if conjured from some fantastical dream: tall, slim, flamboyant, and impossible to ignore. He surged towards us with the energy of a man who owned every room he entered, arms flung wide in exuberant welcome. His brown eyes sparkled with mischief, and his grin, wide and unapologetically toothy, lit up his face like stage lights catching the first mark. There was something instantly familiar about him, a surreal echo of Salvador Dalí in his eccentric charm and barely contained flair, as if he'd stepped out of a black-and-white photograph and burst into colour. He was a happy man. I felt certain of that. And so very likeable. He hadn't seen the horrors I'd seen. A man who was living his dreams.

'Eva!' he cried, his voice rich and theatrical, rolling her name like an encore. 'Darling, you're even more beautiful than I remember.'

Before she could reply, he swept her up as if she weighed nothing, spinning her in a tight, breathless arc. Her laughter tumbled out, caught between joy and disbelief.

'Put me down, you lunatic!' she gasped, though her grin gave her away.

'Not a chance,' Ben teased, before finally setting her gently back on the ground. He pressed a kiss to her forehead: soft, a vow without words.

Then he turned to Edward, clasping his hand firmly, their smiles edged with old familiarity.

'Edward, my friend,' Ben said, shaking his head in mock reproach. 'You kept her from me far too long.'

Edward laughed.

'You'd only have stolen her away.'

'You know me too well,' Ben replied, eyes gleaming. 'But I'd have returned her, eventually.'

The three of them had weathered their formative years side by side, drawn together in the faded lecture halls and smoky bars of Cardiff University. They'd shared the same cramped student digs: peeling wallpaper, communal mouldy fridge, long nights fuelled by cheap wine and half-formed dreams. And somehow, against the odds, their friendship had endured. Not just endured; persisted, like ivy clinging to stone, shaped by the passing years but never loosened. A bond forged in shared youth, tempered by time, and stubborn enough to outlive distance and the slow erosion of innocence.

I stood at the edge of the scene, a grin tugging at the corners of my mouth, though I wasn't quite sure if it belonged there. There was something surreal in the warmth of it all, something I hadn't dared expect. And then Ben turned to me, slowly, purposefully, as if he'd saved the moment for last.

His doe-brown eyes locked onto mine with unnerving precision. It was as if he could see right through me, peel back every layer, every guarded thought I'd tried to bury. I felt strangely exposed under his gaze, stripped of pretence. No words passed between us. None were needed. Not yet. He was reading me, and I knew it.

The silence stretched, just seconds in truth, but drawn out, heavy with expectation, until Ben finally spoke. His voice was deep, unmistakably masculine, but laced with a quiet warmth that curled around the edges of my anxiety, soothing without entirely banishing it.

'It's a true delight to finally meet you, Olivia,' he said, his tone almost cinematic, like a character lifted straight from that old Dickens adaptation I'd stumbled across on Netflix the week before: charming, self-assured, with a faint trace of something I couldn't quite name.

He stepped closer, a waft of musky scent, his gaze still fixed on mine. 'I was so very impressed by the artworks Eva shared with me,' he continued, each word spoken with passion. 'They have real depth. A dark energy. So much more than the usual mediocrity people pass off as talent.' He smiled again then, calm, appreciative, though I couldn't help wondering what flickered behind it. 'And I can't wait to see more.'

There was no mistaking the compliment – he'd meant it. I was sure of that. But there was something else threaded through his words, something I couldn't quite pin down. Curiosity, perhaps. Or something deeper. Calculated. Yet I was flattered all the same, disarmed by the unexpected praise. I felt the warmth flood my cheeks, unmistakable, betraying me. A slow burn that crept up my neck and flushed crimson across my skin.

I eased the paintings from my portfolio with hands that wouldn't stop trembling, each canvas a small confession laid bare between us. I spread them out on the table one by one, the colours suddenly too loud in the hushed room. Ben didn't rush. He stood over them in thoughtful silence, his gaze moving slowly, deliberately. And then he spoke. Generous with compliments. Abundent with praise.

I don't trust easily. Never have. But looking back, trying to untangle memory from instinct, I truly believe Ben meant what he said. His tone was sincere. Gentle, even. The words hadn't been rehearsed or forced. They came from somewhere real. Somewhere well-intentioned.

'Thank you so much,' I managed to force out, lowering my eyes to the nearest patch of wall, unable to hold his gaze a second longer. My voice was quieter than I'd intended, laced with self-doubt. 'Do you really think so?'

He nodded with that flourish that seemed to define him, the kind that might've seemed absurd if it hadn't landed with such perfect timing. Every movement was calculated to build me up, stroke something delicate I hadn't even realised was starving for attention. And I lapped up his words. They fed me like a mother's milk.

'Oh, I do. I do,' he said, eyes glinting with conviction. 'I wouldn't have said so otherwise. If you didn't have something rare, something honest and unflinching, you wouldn't be here. I can promise you that from the bottom of my heart.'

He lifted a manicured hand and swept it slowly through the air, the gesture precise, prolonged, like an illusionist unveiling the climax of a long-prepared trick. A master of the moment.

'Look all around you,' he said, his voice thick with pride. 'Take it all in.

Look at the quality of the work hanging on my walls. I only represent the very best of the best. It's always been that way. And I have no intention of ever changing. This is more than a business to me. It's a love affair with the creative arts.' And then a little laugh. 'And, of course, a great success. We all have to pay the bills.'

And once again, in that instant, with the soft lighting casting shadows across polished walls and the faint hum of quiet power in the air, I truly believed him. And I still do.

I never saw any trace of duplicity in Ben. No hidden motive cloaked in that easy smile or the polished charm he wore so very well. If there was an agenda, it was buried too deep for even the sharpest eye to catch. And I don't believe he had the faintest inkling of the man who would shatter everything. Not a whisper of warning, no glimpse behind the curtain. Ben was as blind to the storm as I was. He had no idea of the darkness he was about to unleash; how could he? I'd bet everything on that, stake my soul if it came to it. He couldn't have known what lay crouched in the shadows, just beyond the edge of that picture-perfect day, waiting for its moment. None of them could. Not Ben. Not my foster parents with their well-meaning ignorance. And certainly not me; least of all me.

I was wide-eyed. Blissfully unaware that something was shifting in the air. There was a storm coming, a brutal, unforgiving tempest that would tear through everything I thought I knew. And I was standing in the calm before it, smiling politely, completely blind to the darkness gathering on the horizon. We don't always hear at first when evil calls our name.

4

We spent that night in Bath, the city draped in its usual cloak of Georgian elegance and quiet, timeless beauty. Our base was a modest but inviting two-bedroom flat on Manvers Street, nothing ostentatious, just clean lines and warm lighting, found through Booking.com. It served its purpose well enough. And I'd be more than happy to stay there again were such things possible. If only! Maybe one fine day. I have to hold on to hope. What else can I do?

Ben, always the consummate host, insisted on treating us to dinner. Seven o'clock sharp. A chance, he said, to talk through the exhibition, to peel back the layers of what lay ahead. And I could barely contain myself. Excitement surged beneath my skin like static, fizzing with every step we took through the dusky streets as the time approached.

We made our way to the Oak Restaurant on North Parade Passage, a hidden gem tucked inside one of the city's oldest buildings, its history steeped in the very stone beneath our feet. A quaint, almost stage-like space I liked immediately. The scent of seasonal roasted root vegetables and fresh herbs drifted through the air as we stepped inside. It was a vegetarian place, bijou and full of charm, the sort of spot where each plate arrived like a work of art, composed with the reverence of someone who understood food as more than mere sustenance. Every detail felt deliberate. Like the night itself. And I'd never felt happier. I wish I could have frozen time. Stayed there for ever. Never faced what lay ahead.

Ben spotted us the moment we walked into the small space. He sprang up from his seat at a table tucked into the far corner of the ground-floor room, waving both arms with exaggerated cheer, his grin stretching wide and unfiltered. The gesture was bold, almost childlike in its enthusiasm, enough to draw a few curious glances from nearby diners. He beckoned us over with the easy confidence of someone who didn't care who noticed. A local celebrity.

We made our way through the scatter of tables and joined him, slipping into our seats as the warmth of the place wrapped around us: low lighting, a high ceiling, the low murmur of conversation, and the comforting clink of cutlery against crockery. The menus lay waiting, elegant, the pages offering the promise of something crafted rather than thrown together. Not just pub grub, something far better. Considered. Unfussy, but with care behind it.

We took a few quiet minutes to study them, the moment stretching just long enough to settle us. Then the waitress arrived, efficient, unhurried, a flick of her notepad in hand. She took our order with a nod, jotted it down without needing to ask twice, and disappeared down the narrow staircase to the kitchen below.

Ben waited until she was out of sight before turning to me. And that's when I saw it: the gleam in his eyes, bright and unreadable. Something stirring beneath the surface. Not just anticipation. Something heavier. Something coming. He was about to launch into a performance like an actor on a West End stage. And I was his audience.

'Right,' he declared, his voice bright with evident enthusiasm, arms sweeping wide. 'We have important things to discuss.' His eyes gleamed with a manic sort of purpose, like a man drunk on his own vision. He was revelling in the moment, feeding off our attention, drawing breath as though about to unveil some long-guarded secret. He paused for a beat. Milking the moment.

'I've been poring over my diary,' he finally continued, almost conspiratorially, 'cross-referencing dates, analysing every angle, obsessing over the smallest of details. Considering, meticulously, the very best moment to introduce your extraordinary work to the world. I want it perfect. Flawless. No errors, no second-guessing. This has to land just right. Exactly right.'

He paused again as our drinks order arrived at the table, the timing almost too perfect, letting the weight of his words settle in the room.

'So,' he said, with the air of someone delivering a verdict, 'Saturday 1 August. That's the day. Mark it in your diary. It doesn't give us much time, barely a breath between now and then. My current exhibition ends the day before, and I'm loath to let momentum slip through my fingers. The artist who was meant to be my August show needs more time to finish his works. His loss is your gain. It'll be a scramble, no doubt. But it's nothing I haven't managed before. And I've no hesitation in saying, I'm entirely confident we can pull it off.'

He met our eyes then, one by one. First my foster parents, almost expectant, like a man quietly taking measure of his audience. And then me. He lingered, holding my self-conscious stare a beat too long, his expression unreadable. It wasn't just a look; it was an excavation, as though he were probing for something buried beneath the surface, something I hadn't yet named or understood myself.

'All right,' he said at last, his voice low and measured, the silence stretching taut before him like a tightrope. 'I'm waiting. What do you all think? Are we going ahead with this?' And then, just as the tension threatened to tip into something more uncomfortable, he laughed, a sudden, jarring sound that cut through the moment like a blade. 'It's a yes from me,' he said, with a silly grin that made us all laugh too.

Edward and Eva turned in their seats almost in perfect synchrony, their expressions softening as their eyes met mine. They smiled, warm, unguarded, the kind of smile that held history and understanding beneath opportunity. And then, as if cued by some invisible hand, the three of us answered in unison.

'Yes.'

One word, spoken together, carried on a shared breath. Unrehearsed, yet perfectly timed. It had the strange, serendipitous rhythm of something fated.

Ben's face lit up, his delight unfiltered, unrestrained. He practically glowed.

'Marvellous,' he said, the word rolling off his tongue like silk. 'That's truly wonderful. I already know, know without even the faintest flicker of doubt, that the exhibition is going to be a resounding success.' He paused, his eyes gleaming with something close to triumph. 'Now then, champagne. We must order the very best this place has to offer. This is a moment worth remembering. A moment that demands to be marked.'

He leaned back with the air of a man utterly certain of the path ahead, as though he could already see the applause, the write-ups, the soft clink of glasses raised in my honour.

I was allowed a single glass of bubbly to enjoy with my food, just one, a quiet concession to my under-eighteen status. And I have to say, the food was exquisite. Small plates delivered one by one, each crafted with a care that bordered on perfection. The smoked beetroot carpaccio came first, paper-thin slices arranged like stained glass on the plate, their earthy sweetness offset by whipped goat's curd and the sharp kiss of pickled walnut. Then a bowl of wild mushroom risotto followed, rich and velvety, laced with truffle oil and crowned with shards of crisp Jerusalem artichoke. Finally, tender leeks roasted in hazelnut butter arrived, draped in a silken lemon hollandaise and scattered with toasted seeds, humble ingredients elevated to something quietly extraordinary.

Each dish felt like a small, wordless promise that the world, despite everything, still held the capacity to surprise. I'd never felt happier. Never more content as the evening passed with conversation and laughter. But there was still more to come.

'Details,' Ben declared suddenly, setting his empty wine glass down with a soft clink on the small table. His voice carried a new energy, measured but unmistakably charged, as though some internal switch had flicked into place. He leaned forward slightly, eyes alight. 'I've been thinking: seventeen works. One for each year of your life. That feels right. A little more than I originally thought, yes, but I believe it's entirely appropriate. Generous, even. There's something about that number, balanced, complete. It came to me just now, and I've learned not to question those moments. When inspiration strikes, I find it's best to grasp the metal before it cools. And my instincts, well, they rarely let me down.'

He paused for effect, fingertips tapping a slow rhythm on the tabletop:

tap… tap… tap. 'As for pricing… the larger pieces will be offered at four thousand pounds. The smaller ones? Somewhere between two and three, I think, depending on their scale and impact. We want the works accessible, but not undersold. They're not just pieces, they're statements. And people pay for certainty. For something that speaks to them, even if they don't understand why. I've already got a number of keen collectors in mind. Serious art aficionados. The kind who like to sniff out the next big thing before the rest of the world even sees it coming. And you, my love, fit that bill very nicely indeed. We can sell your backstory, your youth, your talent. And I have no doubt the desired sales will come.'

Ben eased back into his chair with the unhurried satisfaction of a man who'd already played the winning hand. A faint, smug smile curled at the corners of his mouth, and for a moment, it felt as if the very air around us shimmered with the ghostly outline of his plan, already sketched out in confident strokes, just waiting to be filled in.

I sat there, mute, my mouth hanging open like some dumbstruck child, the words caught somewhere between my racing thoughts and paralysed lips. Had I heard him right? Not hundreds. Thousands! I'd never imagined such wealth. Let alone possessed it. My brain scrambled to keep up, to rationalise, to make sense of what had just been said. Surely not? Could that really be true?

I blinked hard and leaned back, the movement slow and involuntary, as though my body were trying to recoil from the absurdity of it all. My gaze locked on Ben's face, animated now, flushed with the thrill of his own brilliance. I searched for some trace of irony, anything to suggest he was joking. Just messing with me. But there was none. Just that same gleam of confident calculation in his eyes as he spoke again as if it were the most ordinary thing in the world.

'I'll take my usual 40 per cent, naturally,' he said, smoothing a hand down the front of his jacket as if brushing off invisible lint, or doubt. 'There's a good deal of expense at my end, after all. Logistics. Promotion. The usual. And none of that comes cheap. But there'll still be a good deal of profit in it for you. You can count on that. I am, though I say so myself, rather good at what I do. You couldn't be in better hands. You, my little darling, are going to be a star. There are exciting times ahead.'

He paused, letting the silence draw out like a blade before plunging on, oblivious or indifferent to the stunned disbelief playing out across our faces.

Eva tilted her head back, raised her glass to her mouth, drank, smiled, then spoke for the three of us, saying exactly what I was thinking.

'That all sounds wonderful, Ben. Thank you so very much. It's truly appreciated. I can't thank you enough.'

Ben gave a little cough, cleared his throat.

'We'll offer a 10 per cent discount to anyone who buys more than one painting. A small gesture, but a meaningful one. Buyers like to feel they're getting something extra. Makes them feel clever. Rewarded. And they'll be congratulated on their wise choice, of course. You'd be amazed how far a little flattery goes in this game. Something I've learned over the years.'

He looked around expectantly, his expression one of almost paternal condescension, speaking to a room full of wide-eyed novices.

'So,' he continued, his tone laced with quiet certainty, the faintest trace of a smile playing at the corners of his mouth, the kind of smile that suggested the outcome had already been decided, long before I'd stepped into the room. 'Tell me, Olivia, how does all that sound to you? Shall we sign the contract?'

I didn't hesitate. I barely paused to draw breath. I leapt at the offer like a moth to the flame, blind to the heat, deaf to the crackle of warning in the air. It all felt so promising, so reassuringly straightforward. The right place, the right time, the right man saying all the right things. I smiled, nodded, gave him the answer he wanted to hear. Why wouldn't I?

But if I'd had even the faintest inkling of what lay ahead, the price that would be exacted, the shadows waiting to fall, I'd have turned on my heels and never looked back. I should have fled, screaming, before the ink touched the page. But instead, I sat there, trying to steady my racing pulse, oblivious to the quiet inevitability of my undoing. Fate had already curled its fingers around me, cold and sure, and there would be no letting go.

5

The day had arrived at last: inevitable and terrifying in equal measure. The day. The culmination of sleepless nights and frayed nerves, of doubt gnawing at the edges of my resolve like rats in the dark. My exhibition. My work. Hours upon hours of brushstrokes and torment, laid bare for the world to judge. Today, the doors would open, and the critics would descend like vultures, eyes sharp, pens sharper. I'd imagined this moment so often it had taken on a life of its own: glorious, terrible, and now horribly real. The art world was waiting. And I was about to stand naked before it.

Edward, Eva and I had arrived back in Bath at 5.32 p.m. on Friday 31 July, the city's beauty as breath-taking as ever. We didn't stay in the rental flat. This time, we were staying with Ben. His home, a vast, impeccably restored five-bedroom terraced house in the Royal Crescent, was something else entirely. All sweeping staircases, ornate cornicing and quiet, oppressive wealth. The kind of place that seemed to watch me as I moved through it. Whispering that I had no right to be there. That a girl like me didn't belong.

But I smothered the intrusive thoughts before they could fully take hold, brushing them aside with the brittle optimism of someone desperate to believe. I refused to see them as omens, not harbingers of truth, but echoes of self-doubt. The whispered tremors of an anxious mind conditioned to expect the worst.

And when we finally stepped into the gallery, everything shimmered with promise. The lighting soft, the chatter subdued and civilised: a scene carved from some fragile fantasy. It all looked perfect. Almost too perfect. The kind of perfection that dares you to trust it.

The setting. The evening. The life I'd dared to imagine, laid out before me like a curated collection of dreams, each moment framed in hope. But even then, beneath the surface gloss, something twisted low in my gut. A quiet unease. A murmur just below conscious thought. That faint but persistent truth I never quite outran: nothing good ever stays.

The exhibition, the one I'd poured myself into for what felt like forever, opened right on schedule at 7 p.m. And on the surface, it couldn't have gone any better. Guests drifted between the canvases with wine glasses in hand and carefully constructed compliments on their lips. There was praise, applause, a hum of interest that felt almost unreal. It should have been everything I wanted. And for a while, a brief, intoxicating while, it truly felt that way. As if I'd stepped into someone else's life. Someone worthy of admiration. I was no longer the forgotten girl from care, the one who slipped through the cracks unnoticed and unloved. I was someone. A name whispered with reverence, a face lit by gallery lights, not shadows.

For those few precious hours, I let myself believe it. That I'd made it. That I belonged. That the pain and the silence and the cold institutional beds were part of another life, someone else's nightmare, not mine. I smiled for the cameras, I shook hands with strangers, and for once, I didn't feel like I was faking it.

My past, the darkness, the damage, receded into the background like a half-remembered dream. Reduced to brushstrokes and colour, contained and framed on those stark white walls. Beautiful, haunting. But safely distant. As if the act of creation had exorcised the worst of it. But ghosts don't vanish just because you paint them. They wait. Patiently. Never far away. And they were waiting for me.

It was about an hour in, the gallery still buzzing with soft conversation and the clink of glasses, when I noticed Ben making his way towards me. He moved with purpose, that broad, engaging smile already fixed in place, the kind that made you feel like the centre of the universe while somehow knowing you weren't. Beside him walked a second man: older, heavier, unfamiliar, his gait uneven, marked by a subtle but unmistakable limp. There was something studied in the way he carried himself, as though he were used to being watched but rarely seen. His eyes scanned the room with the quiet calculation of someone who missed very little.

Ben reached me first, his voice lifting sharply to rise above the murmur of the crowd, the tone just a fraction too loud, too enthusiastic; the sound of someone performing rather than speaking. Something in his expression flickered as he glanced sideways at the man beside him, then back to me.

'Olivia,' he said, his tone warm, expectant. 'There's someone I'd like you to meet.'

I leaned in, just a little, my curiosity piqued despite the dull ache of fatigue humming behind my eyes. The stranger stood at Ben's side like a shadow that had only just stepped into the light: calm, composed, but with that subtle air of purpose people wore when they already knew more than they were letting on. I assumed he might be a prospective buyer, drawn in by the colours, the brushwork, maybe something deeper he couldn't quite name. But I was wrong, as I so often am.

Ben gave a half-smile, the kind that usually meant he was about to drop something of note, something with weight.

'I'd like to introduce you to a good friend of mine,' he said, his tone smooth but edged with intent. 'This is Adam Flemming. A rather influential journalist with *The Guardian*. He's got a sharp eye and a particular interest in the arts. Thought it might be worth making the introduction.'

There it was: that subtle, almost imperceptible shift in the atmosphere. Like the sudden stillness before a storm, when the air grows thick with unspoken things. The stakes had risen, quietly but unmistakably, curling around us like smoke from a slow-burning fire. I felt the heat bloom beneath my skin, a creeping flush that betrayed me before I could gather myself. My stomach coiled tight, a knot of nerves pulling hard against my composure. I was young, yes, green by most measures, but not totally naïve. I understood exactly what this meant. The weight of it. The opportunity wrapped in risk. The sharp edges hidden beneath polite conversation. This was no casual introduction. It was a moment. And moments like that don't come often.

'It's l-lovely to meet you,' I said, with a slight stutter. 'I hope you're having a nice time. Thank you so much for coming.'

'Oh, I'm glad to attend,' he replied with a barely perceptible nod of his big balding head. 'Benjamin is correct in his assessment. You have a true and individual talent. If we can make time for a formal interview on record, I'd be pleased to discuss a potential article with my editor. We have a large and engaged readership. A feature would really get you noticed.'

I was elated. It felt like another triumph, another step forward in a world I was only just beginning to understand. I accepted without hesitation, blind to the shadows that gathered quietly behind the promise. There was no warning, no prick of instinct to suggest I should pause. Just the heady rush of opportunity and the easy charm of a man who seemed to hold open doors with nothing more than a pen.

We met again just after nine that evening, tucked away in a cramped room at the rear of the gallery. It was Ben's makeshift office; cluttered, yes, but strangely inviting, a lived-in sort of chaos that smelled faintly of old paper and paint. The walls were lined with scribbled notes and half-forgotten sketches, a world away from the polished calm of the exhibition space beyond. I settled into the worn brown leather chair across from the journalist, still blissfully unaware that the real story was only just beginning, and it was one I would later wish had never been written at all.

Edward sat in on the meeting at his own suggestion, quietly, unobtrusively, like a shadow at the edge of the frame. He said little, barely more than a nod here and there, but his presence anchored me in a way I hadn't realised I needed until that moment. There was something deeply reassuring about having him there. Familiar. Solid. A steady hand in unfamiliar waters. The room felt different with him in it, less challenging, less charged. He didn't need to speak; he simply watched, eyes scanning the conversation like a man used to reading between the lines. I knew he was there for me. To make sure I was okay. And though the situation was strange, uncomfortable in that vague, indefinable way that settles somewhere just behind your ribs, his presence went some way towards quieting the nerves that had begun to gather in my chest like storm clouds. Not entirely, but enough.

The journalist was sharp: polished, practised, with the kind of quiet intensity that made it impossible to hide. He asked all the right questions, calmly and with precision, each one slicing closer to the bone. I saw the flicker of satisfaction behind his eyes every time he nudged a little deeper, as if unravelling me was some sort of professional sport. And he did it with ease.

'Do you think your childhood influences your art?' he asked, voice low, measured.

I hesitated, fingers twisting in my lap.

'Doesn't everyone's?' I muttered, though the words felt brittle.

He leaned in slightly. 'But yours... it's different, isn't it? The distortion, the muted tones, the suggestion of violence. That doesn't come from nowhere.'

And he wasn't wrong. The trauma did inform the art. It lived there: in every muted palette, every distorted form, every streak of red that wasn't quite blood. But understanding that didn't make the words come any easier. If anything, it made them stick in my throat like glass.

Tears slipped down my cheeks before I could stop them. I dabbed at my eyes with shaking fingers, desperate to pull myself together.

'It's okay,' he said softly, almost kindly. 'You don't have to say it. The paintings already do.'

And maybe that was the truth. I've always believed my art speaks louder than I ever could. Honest. Unfiltered by language.

When he finally closed his notebook, satisfied he'd mined enough from the rubble, I felt the tension in my chest ease, just slightly. A blessed reprieve. He offered me a clean tissue, crisp and untouched, plucked from the inside pocket of a well-worn jacket. A small gesture. But it felt almost too intimate. Too knowing.

Edward placed a hand on my shoulder then, brief, steady, just enough to ground me before he quietly retreated to his chair. A silent show of support. No words. None were needed. He knew. Or at least, he understood enough not to ask for more.

The journalist slipped his gold pen back into his notebook with care, the faint metallic click sounding louder than it should in the hush between us. Then he looked at me, properly this time, and something in his expression changed. Just a flicker, but unmistakable. The sharp edges dulled. The professional mask loosened at the seams. A trace of empathy crept in, uninvited but not unwelcome.

For a moment, he looked less like a man dissecting a story and more like someone who understood what it meant to bleed. His job was done, at least for now, the scalpel set aside. And in the brief few seconds' quiet that followed, I could almost believe he cared. He smiled before speaking.

'Thank you for your time, Olivia,' he said, his voice softer now. 'You've given more than most would dare. So much pain... and at such a young age.' He paused, studying me with something close to admiration, or was it pity? It was hard to tell. 'But you've risen from it all, haven't you? A phoenix clawing her way out of the wreckage. Scarred, yes, but not broken. Never broken.'

He leaned back slightly, the notebook resting in his lap, as if the weight of it anchored the moment.

'You have a story worth telling, one I believe will echo in the hearts of our readers. There's truth in what you create. Something that can't be faked.'

He offered the faintest of smiles, restrained but I think sincere. 'Your art moves me. Genuinely. Congratulations, Olivia. On surviving. On enduring. On everything you've already become.'

6

If I hadn't been placed with Edward and Eva. If they hadn't known Ben. If I hadn't picked up a brush and begun to paint.

A chain of moments, small and seemingly innocent, each one linking to the next with quiet inevitability. And somewhere along that chain, like rust beneath the surface, he appeared: the man who would unravel it all. Who brought nothing but shadows. Misery disguised as charm.

If only. But what use is that now? 'If only' is the language of fools and pointless regret. Life doesn't rewrite itself just because you wish it would. It didn't unfold any other way. The choices were made. The path walked. And there's no going back.

Only one of my paintings sold that first week: a small piece, tucked away near the back of the gallery. Modest. It wasn't what Ben had envisaged, not by a long shot. And I'd be lying if I said it wasn't a blow. Quietly humiliating. The kind of disappointment you feel in your chest, but pretend not to notice.

But things were about to shift. Ten days after my interview, the promised article appeared in *The Guardian*. A full feature: thoughtful, penetrating, the sort of piece that doesn't just fill column space but ignites something. It stirred up a ripple of interest, first local, then beyond. Not quite the media frenzy Edward had breathlessly predicted, but enough to make people pay attention.

Every Welsh paper picked it up. A journalist, warm, sharp-eyed, and refreshingly sincere, devoted a two-page spread to my work in the *Western Mail Weekend* magazine. She wrote with conviction, as if she truly understood what I was trying to say through the canvas.

Then came the interviews: Radio Wales, the local BBC evening news. My voice sounded strange to me, brittle and high-pitched, and I hated the camera's brutal honesty. It was nerve-racking. Exposing. But exhilarating too.

By then, my social media following had surged into the thousands: a tide of strangers flooding in, liking, commenting, sharing. Applauding. Reaching out as if they knew me. It was intoxicating, in its way: the rush of validation, the sudden weight of attention. The kind of recognition I'd never dared to imagine. And truthfully? I wasn't entirely sure I wanted it.

But it was happening. Fast. Relentless. A blur of momentum that left no time to stop and question whether it was all too much, too soon. And in a small but undeniable way, I began to understand what it meant to be seen. Not just as an artist, but as a person: exposed, dissected, scrutinised. I brushed, just lightly, against the brittle edges of fame. And for a time, it felt like something close to triumph.

But fame doesn't come without consequences. The praise was short-lived: a sugar rush before the crash. And then the trolls began to circle. Picking at my work. Mocking my appearance. Anonymous accounts dripping venom, each comment a quiet cut.

And worse still, far worse, I suspect that's how he found me. The man who would unravel everything. Who watched from the shadows while the world cheered or taunted. I believe, with every fibre of me, that he was already there. Lurking. Waiting. Plotting his entrance. Already forming his devil's bargain. Already playing the long game. The executioner's sword was poised above my head. I just didn't know it yet.

The call came from Ben around six in the evening, the day after my appearance on the Welsh evening news. I remember it with startling clarity: the jolt of anticipation, the sudden spike in adrenaline. I sprang from the chair as if pulled by invisible strings, heart thudding, eyes fixed on the screen as it lit up with his name. The phone was still plugged into the charger on the nearby shelf, but I snatched it up like it might vanish if I hesitated, already well on my way to addiction, hooked on the dopamine surge that came with each ping, each vibration. That tiny device had become more than just a lifeline: it was validation in plastic form. A mirror, reflecting back a version of me the world suddenly seemed to want.

And for a moment, just a moment, I let myself believe the call might bring more good news. That the tide was still turning in my favour. And it seemed it was.

'Are you sitting down, Olivia?' Ben's voice was thick with barely contained glee, that tone he adopted when he knew he was about to deliver something dramatic. 'I have some rather exciting news. Exceptional, even by the gallery's usually lofty standards.'

A chill slid over my skin, fine hairs rising along my arms and at the nape of my neck: the body's curious way of sensing a shift before the mind could catch up.

'Really?' I said, breath catching. 'What is it?'

'An anonymous client,' he said, savouring the pause like a punchline, 'has purchased all the remaining pieces. Fifteen! Every single one. No negotiation. No request for my usual 10 per cent discount. Nothing but the full asking price, and wired in advance via a representative. I feel a trumpet fanfare would be entirely appropriate at this point, if only life were so obliging.'

'Wow,' I said, just the one word.

He gave a delighted laugh. 'Wow indeed. The exhibition is now officially sold out.'

I remember the moment vividly: my feet barely touching the floor as I jumped on the spot, laughter spilling from my lips before I could stop it. Elation pulsed through me like a jolt of electricity. Every painting, sold. Every last one. It felt unreal, as if I were walking through the pages of someone else's success story. A glorious affirmation that the dream I'd nurtured for so long was finally taking flight. For a brief, shining moment, everything shimmered with possibility.

But reality, cold, calculating, and merciless, was slowly closing in. Unknown to me, the truth behind those sales carried a different weight entirely. Had I truly known who had acquired my work, had I seen the truth behind the purchases, I'd have felt the breath catch in my throat. The joy would have curdled into something sharp and sour. I'd have been wary. Watchful.

And most of all, I'd have been afraid. Not the fleeting sort of fear that passes like a shadow at dusk, but the kind that roots itself deep, that whispers in the quiet and lingers in the silence. Terrified, utterly and completely.

7

The sky was pale the day I left Eva and Edward's home: one of those indistinct Welsh mornings when the world feels like it's holding its breath. A soft, uncertain grey smudged the horizon, hovering somewhere between seasons. Neither summer nor autumn. Just a quiet in-between.

The house, my home for the past four years, had never seemed so still. The clock ticked louder. Floorboards creaked under cautious footsteps. Even the kettle, usually shrill and insistent, whistled with restraint, as if it, too, understood the weight of the moment.

My large red suitcase and three bags sat by the front door like silent witnesses. Zipped, bulging, their worn fabric stretched around the sum total of my life: sketchbooks, vintage clothes of a type I'd taken to wearing, tubes of oil paint, watercolour pallets, a favourite pottery mug with a chipped handle that Eva had slipped into my packing while I wasn't looking. And a faded toy rabbit, kept all these years without quite knowing why, peeked out from beneath a rolled hoodie. I've got no idea where it came from or from whom. But it still mattered to me.

Edward stood in the kitchen, silhouetted against the window. He was still in his navy towelling dressing gown, a cup of tea forgotten in one hand, staring out at the back garden he'd fussed over for years. The lawn was freshly mown, stripes clean and precise, but there was a tiredness to the way the plants bowed in the border. As if even they couldn't quite lift their heads today.

Eva bustled around the lounge, her energy brittle and anxious. She was fussing with a tin of shortbread biscuits, Scottish, the good kind, as though the perfect placement of a yellow ribbon might somehow delay the inevitable. She pressed the cellophane smooth for the third time, her hands trembling ever so slightly.

Neither of them said much.

'I'll be all right,' I offered, voice too bright. Too rehearsed. 'I'm only moving down the road. It's not like it's far away.'

Eva turned to me then, eyes already wet. Her lips quivered, and she stepped forward, wrapping me in a hug that squeezed the air from my lungs. She seemed so strong for such a slight woman. I think a strength born of emotion.

'You shouldn't have to be all right, Liv,' she said, voice muffled against my hair. 'You should be excited. You've got so many wonderful times ahead of you. It's going to be brilliant. I promise it is.'

'Oh, I am excited,' I whispered, and I meant it. Or at least I wanted to mean it. Because this was the plan. Art college in Carmarthen. A bedsit of my own. A clean slate, painted in bolder colours. But excitement has edges, and right now, they were cutting deep. Leaving Edward and Eva felt like peeling off skin. Necessary. Painful. Exposing.

They'd never pushed for me to think of them as Mum or Dad, never demanded that particular closeness. But over time, they had earned my affection in ways that went deeper than names. In the quiet kindnesses. The countless lifts to school. The long evenings spent helping me decipher application forms. The way Eva would leave a hot water bottle at the foot of my bed on cold nights. The way Edward always checked the locks twice before going to sleep. And their encouragement of my art, of course. I think that mattered most.

They were good people. And I'm sure they're still good people. Two of the best I ever met. Not that I see them any more. Not that I can ever contact them. If only life were that easy. If only I could.

Edward and Eva's love had not arrived in a flood. It had come in drips and droplets, quiet and consistent, until one day I realised I was no longer bracing for the flood to end.

Edward finally turned from the window, setting his cup down with more force than necessary. He cleared his throat and rubbed the back of his neck. I think the emotion of it all was getting to him too.

'You've done us proud,' he said, voice rough. 'Really proud. Of all the kids we've ever fostered, you'll always be the special one. An absolute star.'

My eyes stung. I swallowed the ache rising in my chest and forced a smile. I feared that if I started crying I might never stop. I'd just slump to the floor, drowning in my own tears.

Eva reached for my hand. Her grip was warm, soft, insistent. 'You'll call, won't you? And we'll meet up for a coffee or a bite to eat?'

'Of course we will. Every single week,' I promised. 'Try stopping me. I'll even write if you like. I know how you love a letter. Can't see the attraction myself. All that old-school stuff, you old romantic.'

Eva let out a shaky laugh. 'Don't make promises you can't keep. A call or text will be just fine.'

'I won't forget,' I said, a tear in my eye. 'There's no chance of that.'

We hugged again, the kind of hug you try to memorise, and then Edward came over and looped one arm around each of us. We stood like that for a long moment, a fragile constellation.

Then it came: the blare of the taxi horn. Sudden. Jarring. All too soon. A shrill note that sliced clean through the silence, sharp as a blade across fabric. Final. There was no mistaking it. It was time to go.

A knot tightened in my stomach. That awful, fluttering tangle of nerves, regret, and something close to excitement. A strange, shifting cocktail of emotions that made it hard to breathe.

My body moved before my heart caught up. Each step towards the door felt weighted, as though I were walking underwater. Leaving behind the warmth of familiarity, the safety of two people who had loved me without condition. Stepping into something unknown, where every joy had a shadow, and every hope carried a whisper of fear.

I wasn't sure if I wanted to cry or run or laugh. Maybe all three. But the engine was running. The future was waiting. And I couldn't stand still forever.

'I'll get your things,' Edward said, already reaching for them. 'What a day for the car to break down. Crazy. I only had the damn thing serviced last month. Talk about bad timing.'

I stepped into the morning light, cool and damp against my cheeks. Eva held the tin of biscuits out to me like an offering.

'For later,' she said. 'Or for sharing, when you find someone worth sharing with.'

I climbed into the back seat, dabbing at my eyes. The taxi smelled faintly of petrol and pine air freshener. The door shut with a dull thud that echoed louder than it should have. Almost as if it was mocking me.

Edward and Eva stood side by side by the front gate, arms folded tightly across their chests, then waving in that small, reluctant way people do when they don't want you to go but know they have to let you.

'Eat proper meals!' Eva shouted as we pulled away. 'Not just toast!'

Edward raised a hand in a quiet salute. His eyes were glassy, but he didn't wipe them. Just stood there, firm and proud, until the bend in the road took them from sight.

I watched the mirror until I couldn't see them any more. They weren't my parents by blood. But they were my family. The only one that had ever truly felt like home. And now, I was leaving them. That's what happens to foster kids. We move on.

And he was already watching. Even then. Quiet. Calculated. The man who changed everything. A brooding presence I hadn't yet recognised. But he saw me: every gesture, every glance, every careless word. Absorbing it all with unsettling patience, like a predator studying prey too naïve to run.

He told me that himself, later. The man who would bring nothing but misery. Not in apology, but as fact. As if it were inevitable. Preordained. Like the outcome had always been written, and I'd simply been too blind to read the signs.

He was studying me: measuring my weaknesses, mapping the angles of my life, weighing when best to strike. He didn't need to rush. Monsters like him rarely do.

He was biding his time. Waiting for the moment I wouldn't see coming. When the world tilted just enough for him to step in, and ruin everything.

8

The bedsit in Carmarthen's King Street was smaller than I'd remembered from first visiting with my social worker a few weeks before. But there was a window that let in good light, and the radiator worked, and it didn't smell too strongly of damp if I kept the door open. So I told myself that was all okay. That I'd lived in a lot worse in years gone by.

The wallpaper hung in curling strips from the corners, yellowed and brittle, as though the walls themselves were trying to shed their skin. Pipes groaned and clanged when the water heater kicked in: sudden, jarring bangs that echoed through the narrow space like footsteps in the dark. But I didn't mind. Not really. Because it was mine.

And that mattered more than the noise or the peeling plaster or the scent of damp that lingered just beneath the surface like an old regret.

I told myself it suited me just fine. A space in progress for a person still becoming. The kind of place a true artist might inhabit. There was a kind of romance in it, albeit imagined. The sort of poetic struggle you read about but never really feel until you're lying awake under a leaking ceiling, counting each drip like a metronome.

I could have afforded better. Cleaner. With double glazing and solid floors and a front door that didn't shudder in the wind. The exhibition had seen to that.

But that voice inside me, quiet and cruel, still whispered that I hadn't earned it. That comfort was for other people. People who hadn't clawed their way through the system. People with the right kind of past. Despite Edward and Eva's gentle protests, I chose the bedsit on King Street. Tucked just above a dusty florist's and a short walk from a gallery that had recently shown my latest work. It was good enough. Or at least, that's what I told myself.

I unpacked carefully. My sketchbooks were lined up on the windowsill. The silver framed photo of Edward and Eva went beside my bed, the glass catching the morning light. I filled the small drawers with pencils and charcoal and paints. I hung fairy lights, more for comfort than decoration. And I boiled the kettle just to hear it sing.

It was quiet. Not oppressive. Just unfamiliar. I played the radio on my mobile, left the bathroom fan on, opened the window for the sound of passing cars and footsteps. Anything to remind me I wasn't alone.

College started the following day. And that I was looking forward to immensely. I really was.

9

I adored art college. And that's no exaggeration; if anything, the words fall short. Almost from the moment I arrived, it felt like stepping into a world that had been waiting for me all along. A sanctuary. A quiet rebellion against everything I'd known. It wasn't just a place: it was a pulse, a rhythm that beat in time with my own. It exceeded every hope I'd nursed in silence, every fragile dream I'd clung to in the hush of my teenage bedroom, too afraid to voice aloud in case they shattered.

There was a kind of alchemy in being among others who saw the world not as it was, but as it might be: broken into light and shade, raw and unfinished, trembling with possibility. People who understood instinctively that art wasn't a subject, but a lifeline. We spoke in the language of line and form, in charcoal smudges and the sharp tang of turpentine, in hurried conversations over mugs of instant coffee that stretched long into the night. Laughter came easily, messy and real, echoing through cluttered studios and paint-splattered halls. And in all of it, every brushstroke, every shared moment, was a sense of belonging I'd never known before. We were dreamers, all of us, tethered to the same beautiful madness.

The lecturers, seasoned, eccentric, brilliant, held our attention like conjurers, unravelling the mysteries of form and composition, of technique and meaning. They spoke of art not as a subject, but as a lifeblood, and I drank in every word.

For the first time in my life, I felt truly awake: alive in the way that matters. A kind of joy pulsed through me then, steady and unfamiliar. It wasn't the hollow thrill of escape or distraction; it was something deeper. Real. I think – no, I *know* – it was the happiest I've ever been.

But for all that future promise, the first day of my new course didn't come without its trials. There are always trials: quiet, creeping things that press in when you least expect them.

As I hurried through the bustling streets of Carmarthen town and began the slow climb up College Road, the morning air felt close, heavy with the scent of wet stone and the earthy tang of the River Towy that wound its way through the heart of everything.

My mind was a blur of conflicting emotions: a heady cocktail of nerves and anticipation. Excitement danced at the edges of my thoughts, but it was tempered by the dull weight of uncertainty, pressing like a thumb against my chest. The buildings, familiar yet strange in the early light, loomed over me as if watching, waiting. I told myself I was ready. I wanted to believe it. But the truth? I was stepping into something new, and new things always came with shadows.

Still, I kept moving. One foot in front of the other, heart thudding, breath tight. Because sometimes that's all you can do. And beneath the nerves, beyond the fear, there was something stronger: something solid. I wanted to be there. I'd fought for this. Dreamed about it in the quiet hours when the world felt like it might swallow me whole. This was mine: a step towards the life I'd imagined, however imperfectly. And that mattered more than the fear.

I eased my pace as the college building came into view, my heart knocking a little harder than it should've been. Maybe I should've found digs closer, somewhere less of a climb, less of a daily reminder of how far I still had to go. But that thought faded as I stood before it, shoulders rising and falling with the effort, eyes fixed on the entrance that now felt larger than life.

I was there on my first day of the course. At last. A little breathless, a little uncertain, but there all the same. This was it: the threshold of something new. The next chapter. A shift in the script I'd quietly rewritten in my head a hundred times. I squared my shoulders, steadied myself, and stepped forward. Because sometimes, life doesn't wait for certainty. It just asks that you keep walking.

Carmarthen School of Art, or Coleg Sir Gâr, as it's known in the lyrical Welsh language, stretched out low and wide, a single-storey ribbon of glass and steel folded neatly into the hillside. Its architecture was sleek and understated, all clean lines and quiet confidence. The roof was its most striking feature: an expanse of angled glass that ran the full length of the building, flooding the interior with light from above. It gave the impression the whole place was open to the sky, as if the roof were holding its breath.

Inside, the corridors were bright and spacious, lined with pale walls that bore the fingerprints of creativity: pinholes, smudges, splashes of colour that hadn't quite been cleaned away. Footsteps echoed softly on polished floors. The air was filled with the crisp, unmistakable scent of oil paint, and something harder to define. The hum of concentration. The flicker of self-doubt. That sharp, electric blend of fear and potential that clung to the skin like static.

It didn't feel tired. It felt as if it was waiting. As though the building itself was holding space for what might come next.

The studio was a beautiful kind of chaos. Easels lined the walls, splattered with old paint. The wooden floor bore the scuffed legacy of generations. Light poured through the high windows like something sacred.

A lecturer asked us to introduce ourselves. Just a few words about our work, she said: casual, offhand, as if it were nothing. But for me, it was never nothing. I could feel the familiar weight tightening around my chest, that low thrum of unease I could never quite shake. You'd think I'd have been used to it by then, after the press interviews and the fuss surrounding the exhibition. But no. My throat tightened. My mouth turned to dust.

I stood there, hands clammy, heart hammering like I'd been caught out in a lie. I mumbled something about colour and memory, about painting what I felt rather than what I saw: vague phrases I'd used before, strung together like beads on a fraying thread. They rang empty even to me. Meaningless. Hollow. A clumsy attempt to sound thoughtful.

But nobody laughed. They just nodded, politely, as if I'd said something profound. As if they couldn't hear the panic clattering behind my ribs.

And then, just as I stood there, caught in that awful moment between silence and shame, silently pleading for the floor to open and drag me under, he walked in, and suddenly everything shifted. Joe.

It was as if time stilled in anticipation of his arrival. He entered the studio late, unhurried, unapologetic. No need for excuses. No nervous glance at the clock. He moved through the space like it belonged to him, like we all did. There was an ease to him, a quiet defiance in the way he held himself, as though the noise and nonsense of the world simply didn't touch him.

People turned to look, everyone, not only me, not because he demanded it, but because he didn't. There was a pull to him, something unspoken: magnetic, intangible. He didn't speak, not at first. He didn't have to. His presence said more than words ever could. And just like that, the chaos in my chest fell quiet. The room softened. And for one fragile, flickering moment, all was right in my world.

I can still see him now, as vividly as if he were standing in front of me. And sometimes, when my locked attic room is quiet and the night presses in, I close my eyes and there he is: sharp-edged and perfect, conjured from memory or madness, I'm never quite sure. Blond hair, shoulder-length and sun-kissed, framing a face carved in soft shadows. Blue-green eyes the colour of the sea before a storm: bright, searching, unreadable. A satchel slung over one shoulder with casual ease. A pencil tucked behind his ear like a signature. His expression gave nothing away, not then and not later; not warmth, not distance. Just that unsettling calm, as if nothing could touch him. As if he'd already figured out how the world worked and had quietly decided it didn't matter.

His arrival struck me like a lightning bolt: sudden, electric, and impossible to ignore. One moment I was just a girl in a paint-splattered room, half-lost in the hum of quiet conversation. The next, I was undone. Something shifted deep inside me, a jolt of recognition or fate or lust; I still don't know what to call it. But I do know it was real.

Love at first sight. People laugh at the idea, dress it up as fantasy, something reserved for romance novels and daydreams. But I lived it. It happened to me: swift and undeniable, as if the air itself had changed the moment he stepped into it. There was no build-up, no slow burn, just a single breathless instant where the world narrowed to the sound of his footsteps and the shape of his face. It felt less like falling and more like being claimed: completely, irreversibly. And I knew, in some wordless, impossible way, that everything from that moment on would be different. Whether I wanted it to be or not. I wanted to know him in every sense of the word. And right from that moment, I was determined to make it happen.

Yes, Joe was beautiful. Still is, in the quiet corners of my mind. Some people fade when they leave the room. But he never did. Not for a second.

And then, later that very same day, it happened. As though the universe had been quietly conspiring all along, shifting its weight to bring us together. A moment so perfectly timed it felt almost preordained: written in the stars, if you believe in that sort of thing. I wasn't sure I did. Not until then.

There was something in the way he looked at me: brief, searching, and then holding just a second too long. Not intrusive, not obvious. But enough. Enough to make the world blur at the edges. As if he'd felt it too, that strange, magnetic pull, like gravity had quietly realigned itself around the space between us. As if he recognised me, somehow. Not from a place, not from a time, but from something deeper. Something ancient and inexplicable.

Twin flames. That's the phrase, isn't it? Two halves of the same spark, separated by life and time and circumstance, drawn back together by some unseen thread. It sounds dramatic, even now. But in that moment, it felt true. He didn't speak, not yet, but something passed between us all the same. A charge. A certainty. And I knew, without question, that whatever this was... it had already begun.

Joe sat across from me that afternoon after lunch, his easel angled just enough so he could sneak a glance sideways. I pretended not to notice, though my brushstrokes grew clumsy under the weight of it. When class ended, he wandered over, that lazy, warm smile already in place.

'So,' he said, tilting his head, 'are you going to tell me your name, or do I have to keep calling you "mystery girl" in my head?'

I laughed, caught off guard. 'Olivia. Or Liv for short.'

'Olivia,' he said, repeating my name slowly after my reply, like he was tasting it, savouring each syllable as if it were something fragile and rare. 'I like that. It really suits you. Makes me think of an olive grove somewhere in the warm Mediterranean sunshine. Italy maybe, or Greece.'

It was a little over the top, sure, flirtation wrapped in poetry, but it landed with uncanny precision. I felt something flutter inside me, something soft and unguarded. My pulse kicked. I couldn't hold his gaze. Not for long. I dropped my eyes to the floor, a flush creeping up my neck and settling in my cheeks, burning hot and uninvited. Swooning. That's the word, isn't it? Pathetic, maybe. But I did.

For a long time, I'd carried the imprint of childhood mistrust of men, like a shadow stitched into my skin. Edward and Ben had softened that distrust, hammered away at the wall with kindness and patience. And now Joe, this stranger with a poet's tongue and a grin that knocked the air from my lungs, was quietly continuing the work. Proving, perhaps, that there were good men in the world. Not all of them hurt. Not all of them lied. Not all of them saw me as an object to use at will.

'Fancy a coffee? My treat,' he said, that white grin broadening, lighting something behind his eyes.

And I said yes, too fast, too eagerly, before I had time to think or remember who I was supposed to be. I just said yes. Because in that moment, how could I not?

We wandered hand in hand through the soft spill of late afternoon light at the end of our first college day, the heat of his palm folded around mine as though it had always belonged there. That beginning was slipping into early evening, the air cooling just enough to raise goosebumps on my arms, though I barely noticed. We made our way towards the centre of town, our footsteps falling into an easy rhythm, heading for the café tucked halfway down Jackson's Lane, the one I already knew and loved. The familiar comfort of it soothed me: the mismatched chairs, the chalkboard menus, the gentle chime of the doorbell as we stepped inside.

And I remember the strangest thing: how natural it all felt. Almost effortless. Like we'd skipped the awkward start entirely and landed in the kind of understanding people usually earn over years. We ordered our drinks first, something warm and sweet, then food, neither of us needing to say much as we claimed a small table near the door. It wasn't the sort of spot people lingered in, but I'd have happily stayed there all night.

'You're quiet,' Joe said, stirring the foam on his hot chocolate.

'So are you,' I replied, smiling.

'Yeah,' he admitted, leaning back in his chair. 'But it doesn't feel awkward, does it?'

'No,' I said softly. 'It feels... easy.'

He met my eyes then, steady and sure.

'Good. I like easy.'

I'd never felt so relaxed in anyone's company. Never. There was no performance, no second-guessing. Just him. Just me. And this strange, beautiful sense of belonging that clung to us like a shared secret. Joe made me feel seen in a way no one else ever had. Seen, valued, respected. And it just felt right.

Of course, I wasn't the only one drawn to him. I'd learn that soon enough. There were others. Girls were like moths to a flame. But that's not for now. That comes later, when the cracks began to show. For now, in that moment, there was only the warmth of his smile and the illusion that I was the only girl in the world he looked at that way. Call me naïve. And yes, maybe I was. But I can only describe it as it was.

We talked for hours, Joe and me. Tucked into a quiet corner of the café on Jackson's Lane, away from the clatter of cups and the low murmur of conversation, two smooth porcelain mugs growing cold between us. The light through the window had softened to amber, catching the dust in the air, painting everything with that faint, forgiving glow you only seem to notice when you're young and half in love.

We talked about art, mostly. About what it meant to lose yourself in it, to chase after something you couldn't quite name but knew you needed. Joe spoke of Rothko's weight, how colour alone could speak about grief. I talked about Hockney's clean lines and careful optimism, the way he made ordinary things feel intended. We touched on Giacometti and the loneliness in his figures, on Paula Rego's brutal tenderness. It wasn't a lesson. It was a kind of laying bare.

And then the talk turned, as it often does when you're not trying too hard, to home. Not in detail. Just the shape of it. The way it clung.

'Do you ever miss your foster home?' Joe asked, tracing a line on the side of his mug with his thumb.

'Sometimes,' I said. 'But not enough to go back. Not that I could anyway.'

He gave a small nod, eyes fixed on the table for a moment.

'Yeah. Same. But for different reasons.'

For both of us, there were fractures: spaces we tiptoed around. Families that didn't quite fit, pasts we couldn't rewrite. But it didn't feel heavy. Not with Joe. The things we didn't say hung between us, visible but never choking. It felt like the beginning of something fragile and rare. Something unspoken yet deeply known. The kind of connection that doesn't announce itself with grand gestures or declarations. It just settles, sure of its place.

With Joe, I was more open than I've ever been with anyone. There was no pressure, no expectation: just space. Space to unravel a little, to say the things I'd only ever rehearsed in my head. He listened without trying to fix me. Held my gaze without flinching. And in doing so, he helped in ways no therapist ever had. No tidy session notes. No quiet nods and clinical smiles. Only his presence. Solid. Constant.

Joe never pretended to have all the answers. He didn't need to. It was enough that he stayed. And now, when everything feels brittle and wrong, I find myself aching for that steadiness. That simplicity. I only wish he could help me now. But wishes are for children and fairy tales, and the world doesn't work that way. Not any more.

He didn't fill the silence with platitudes or awkward sympathy. He just listened. Really listened. Not with pity, and not with that performative concern people put on like a mask. There was no script with him. No pretence. Just a steady, open presence that made it easy to let the truth slip out. And I liked him all the more for it.

I liked the way his eyes crinkled at the corners when he laughed: properly laughed, not the polite kind, but the kind that caught you off guard and made you laugh too. I liked the way he always seemed slightly off-balance, like his mind was racing ahead, skipping over options, but hadn't quite settled on which path to follow. There was something restless in him, something bright and unfinished.

He was so easy to talk to. Easy to sit beside without feeling the need to fill the quiet. With Joe, I could simply exist. And I only wish it had stayed that way. That time could've folded in on itself and left us there, untouched. But life doesn't work like that. It never does. Everything seemed so good. Too good, in hindsight.

10

One evening, a Wednesday I think, a few days after that first wonderful café evening, Joe and I were sitting on a low wall by the river, sharing chips soaked in vinegar, when Joe reached for my hand without warning.

'You're not like anyone I've ever met,' he said, simply.

And somehow, I believed him. Not because of the words, but the way he said them: low, certain, without a trace of the usual bravado most boys his age seemed to wear like armour.

'I feel the same about you,' I said, my voice barely above a whisper. Then, without thinking, I leaned across and brushed my lips against his cheek – just a brief touch, light as breath, but it felt enormous. Monumental. It was the first time I'd kissed him. The first time I'd kissed anyone by choice. And it felt good. Not like all the men who had gone before.

'That was nice,' he said with a grin that lit up his face.

I laughed, popped the last of the chips into his mouth.

'I'm so very glad we met when we did,' I said with meaning. 'I think it's the best thing that's ever happened to me. Honestly, I really do.'

Joe smiled again, slow and quiet, like the warmth behind his eyes was working its way to the surface.

'Me too,' he said. 'It's strange, isn't it? One minute you're living your life, thinking you've got everything figured out. Then someone walks in, and suddenly nothing makes sense, but in the best possible way.'

I looked down, shy all over again, my fingers fidgeting with the paper napkin in my lap.

'I wasn't expecting any of this,' I admitted. 'Not for a second. Not... you.'

'That's the thing about moments that matter,' he said, his tone thoughtful now, the grin fading to something gentler. 'They don't wait for you to be ready. Life happens if we let it. The universe has our back.'

I doubt his words ever held a shred of truth. Not when weighed against everything that came before, and all that followed. But in that moment, I needed to believe him. Desperately. So I did. Not because it made sense, but because the alternative was too hard to face. I clung to the lie like a lifeline, knowing, deep down, that it would unravel eventually. But still, I chose the lie. I let it in.

I glanced up then and met his gaze, and for a fleeting moment, the world around us slipped into silence. The distant murmur of traffic, the cries of gulls circling overhead, even the steady rush of the river against its banks, all of it receded into the background. The town seemed to hold its breath. It was just him. Just the weight of his eyes on mine, steady and unreadable. Everything else, the people passing by, the rustle of wind in the trees, melted into nothing. The noise, the movement, the constant tug of time... gone. There was only him, and the stillness between us.

'Promise me something,' I said quietly.

'Anything.'

'Please don't disappear.'

He didn't flinch. Didn't laugh or tease. He just nodded, slowly, deliberately.

'I won't.'

And I believed that too. At the time. I wanted to. I needed to.

We started spending more time together after that. Drawing late in the studio. Wandering through antique shops. Swapping sketchbooks like secrets. He never asked for more than I could give. Not overtly, not in words. And maybe that's precisely why I ended up giving him more than I ever intended; more than I should have. It mattered to me. Far more than I can articulate, even now. Just writing this, forcing the memories onto the page, feels like picking at a wound that never quite healed. Because no matter what Joe said, no matter what kindness he showed, I've never been entirely convinced his feelings ran as deep as mine.

I don't believe he set out to hurt me. He wasn't cruel, not in the obvious sense. Not like some of the nasty bastards I encountered as a child. But intention isn't everything. Joe played his part all the same. Quietly. Unknowingly, perhaps. But the damage was done. I don't believe, even for a moment, that Joe was consciously leading me towards ruin. That wasn't his way. But he did, whether he meant to or not. And the more I lay this bare, dragging it all into the light, the more undeniable it becomes. It's there in every memory, every half-forgotten glance and careless word. As clear and unforgiving as daylight.

11

It was about three weeks later when it happened. An evening I'll never forget. The takeaway curry cartons sat half-empty on the small coffee table, two forks resting crosswise like some sort of fragile truce. Outside, the wind pushed its weight against the windowpanes, soft and persistent, as if the night itself was trying to listen in. A quiet romantic comedy flickered across the television, forgotten now, its soundtrack fading into the background hum of the street below.

We sat close on the tired old sofa that had come with my bedsit, my knees drawn up, his arm brushing mine. His thigh was warm against me, steady, present. And I remember thinking, absurdly, that I'd never really felt safe like that before. Not with anyone. Not ever. He had that effect on me. He really did.

Joe smelled faintly of cardamom and soap, a clean, simple scent that grounded me more than he could've known. He wasn't trying to be anything other than himself. That's what made it so disarming. He didn't press. Didn't push. Just sat with me in the soft glow of the lamp, his presence quiet and unassuming.

I turned to him, heart thudding in that uncomfortable, uncertain way I'd never quite made peace with. The feeling I used to associate with fear.

But it wasn't fear now, not quite. It was something else. Something unspoken and tender, with edges I didn't yet understand.

Then our eyes met. And he gave me that slight, familiar smile: the one that never reached too far, that never demanded anything in return. It just was. And that was enough.

I leaned in first. And it surprised me as much as it must've surprised him. Our lips met gently, a kiss as soft as breath, and for a moment, that was all there was: his mouth on mine, the warmth of it, the careful patience behind every movement. He didn't rush. Didn't deepen it until I did. His hands remained still on his lap, a quiet invitation, nothing more.

I felt something shift inside me then. Something old and brittle cracking open to make room for something new. Something warm. I pulled back slightly, just enough to look at him.

'Are you okay?' he asked, voice low.

I nodded. Swallowed.

'Yeah. Just...'

He waited, letting the pause bloom in the silence.

'This is... a big deal for me,' I said finally, words catching slightly on the edge of my throat.

'I know,' he said. And I believed him.

We kissed again. Slower this time. More certain. My hands found his, fingers intertwining, and he held them like they were something delicate. Something that mattered. That was the thing with Joe: he had a way of holding space for me, as if he understood the weight I carried, even if he didn't know the details.

We lay down on the narrow bed not long after, the film still playing to an empty room. He kicked off his shoes carefully, as if afraid to break the moment. I watched him, my heart thudding in my chest, not from fear but from the enormity of it all.

This wasn't just about sex. It wasn't about lust or release. It was about reclaiming something I'd long believed was lost to me.

I'd told myself for years that sex was a currency, a transaction, a means to survive or pacify or protect. But this was different. This was choosing. This was trust. And in that choice, I understood something new about myself. I wasn't damaged. I wasn't broken. I was healing. It just took the right person, the right place, and time.

Joe lay beside me, his hand finding my cheek. His thumb brushed lightly across my skin, and I closed my eyes. He didn't speak. He didn't have to. The silence between us said enough.

When his lips found mine again, it was slow. Intentional. Every kiss a question. Every touch a chance to say you can stop this at any time. And I could have. At any moment. That was what made it different. Special.

My hands trembled slightly as I ran them beneath his T-shirt, feeling the warmth of his skin. He exhaled softly, his own breath uneven, and I realised with a strange sort of clarity that he was nervous too. That meant something. He wasn't trying to be perfect. He was just being real.

Clothes came off in stages. Not torn or flung aside like in the films. Just slowly, quietly, as if each layer carried a memory we were choosing to let go of. He kissed the scars on my shoulder like they didn't matter, like they were just part of the map that led him here.

'I've never...' I whispered, my voice catching. 'Not like this.'

He paused. Looked into me, not just at me.

'We don't have to,' he said.

'I want to,' I replied. 'I just need you to know... in every way that matters, I'm still a virgin. This is my first time. The first time I've given myself to anyone with love.'

A flicker of pain crossed his face, brief, soft, then gone.

'Okay,' he said, brushing his thumb along my jaw. 'Then we take this slow. As slow as you need.'

And we did. Every touch was an offering. Every moment laced with care. He asked with his eyes before he moved. Kissed the hollow of my throat like it was sacred. When he entered me, it was with an unbearable tenderness, his forehead resting lightly against mine, our breath synchronised, our hands clasped like we might fall without each other.

It wasn't perfect. It wasn't choreographed. It was messy and emotional and real. And somewhere in the middle of it all, I began to cry; not loudly, not broken, but quietly, a few tears slipping from the corners of my eyes.

He stilled immediately. 'Liv?'

I shook my head. 'It's okay. It's... good. It's just—' I couldn't find the words.

He kissed them from my mouth.

Afterwards, we lay there tangled in each other's arms, the lamp casting a golden hue over the bed. The wind had picked up outside, rattling the loose windowpane, but inside, everything was still.

I rested my head against his chest, listening to the steady beat of his heart. It sounded strong. Reassuring.

'You okay?' he murmured.

I nodded.

'Yeah, better than okay.'

And I really was. For once, the words weren't a mask or a deflection or something I told myself to survive. They were true. Because for the first time in my life, sex hadn't been something taken from me, ripped away in silence, or bartered for safety behind closed doors. It wasn't an unwelcome transaction or a punishment or a power play.

It was something shared. Something offered freely, without fear or obligation. And more than that, it was something chosen. By me. Not coerced or expected, not endured or regretted. But willingly given. That choice mattered more than I can explain. It rewrote something inside me. Quietly. Completely.

Because in that moment, wrapped in the warmth of his arms, I stopped feeling like a survivor trying to forget and started feeling like a woman learning how to live.

I let my fingers trace lazy patterns along his skin, not to arouse, but to connect. To remind myself that this body, mine and his, could be a place of comfort. Of safety.

Joe didn't say very much at all after that. Just held me, his thumb brushing soft circles against my shoulder. That silence again, thick with meaning. With understanding.

I drifted in and out of sleep for a while, the weight of the night settling over me. And when I woke briefly, hours later, to find him still there, his arm wrapped around me, his breathing slow and even, I felt a peace I hadn't ever known before. That was love. Real love. Not fireworks or chaos.

Not drama or passion burning too fast to last. But something steadier. Kinder. Something that asked nothing of me but honesty.

And I gave it. Freely. Because in every way that mattered, I had chosen him. And he had chosen me. Or, at least, that's how I saw it at the time.

12

The term ended with more of a bang than a whimper. The final days were a blur of damp paintbrushes, sleep-deprived critiques, and last-minute portfolio adjustments. It seemed everyone had plans: trains to catch, parents to appease, Christmas to pretend to look forward to. But when the studio lights went out and I stepped back into the cold Carmarthen air, I felt oddly untethered. Like something had quietly come loose.

I hadn't expected the invitation. Joe had mentioned his aunty had a villa in Lanzarote, casually, in that way people talk about things they've always known. But then he said it plainly, while we sat cross-legged on the floor of my bedsit, picking through the remains of another vindaloo and watching some forgettable nature documentary I wouldn't have chosen for myself.

'Come with me,' he said. 'No pressure. Just... a break. You and me. All that sun, sea and sangria. My aunt isn't using the place this year. So why the hell not?'

Edward and Eva had invited me for Christmas. A kind gesture on the surface: warm, familiar. But something about it didn't sit right. They had another placement now. Two, actually. A brother and sister, younger than I'd been when I arrived on their doorstep. And though they said the invitation still stood, I couldn't shake the feeling that it came more from obligation than desire. Like I was a chapter they'd already read, revisiting out of politeness rather than longing. I might well be doing them a disservice. But that's how it felt to me.

And so, just like that, I looked Joe in the eye and said yes. Not because I didn't have doubts. I'd never been abroad before. And I always have doubts. But because something in his voice made the idea of it feel safe. And maybe, deep down, I wanted to believe I could leave the past behind, if only for a little while.

We flew out of Cardiff Airport on a grey December morning, the kind that presses down on you with a damp, unrelenting chill. The clouds swallowed the city whole as I left the UK for the first time, clutching my recently purchased passport, the hum of the engine a kind of strange comfort. I'd announced the trip on social media in far more detail than I should have. All the plans, all the details for the world to see. Where we were going. The flight we were catching. And now it was actually happening. We were on our way.

Joe reached across the narrow gap between our seats and took my hand, his fingers brushing soft lines against my skin. I leaned into him, trying not to overthink it. Telling myself the new experiences were a welcome adventure.

And that's when I noticed him for the first time. Two rows ahead, aisle seat. Early sixties, perhaps, though he carried himself with the upright confidence of someone who hadn't yet conceded to age. His hair was mostly black, streaked elegantly with grey at the temples, cut and styled with care: the sort of hair that spoke of expensive barbers and appointments booked weeks in advance. He wore a white shirt, crisp and perfectly pressed beneath a charcoal blazer that didn't crease, even after hours in a cramped cabin. Everything about him was understated. Refined. Precise.

But he didn't fit. Not there. Not on that flight. There was something off-kilter about him, something that made the hairs on the back of my neck lift almost imperceptibly. He wasn't gawking. Wasn't smiling or leering. He didn't do anything at all, really. Just sat there, composed and unreadable, leafing slowly through a glossy magazine he didn't seem to be reading.

But I felt him. Noticed the flicker of his eyes, the way they skimmed in my direction: too fast to be called a glance, too intentional to be dismissed as chance. A moment so brief it could've passed unnoticed. Except it didn't. Not by me.

Something in me stirred: an old, familiar flicker of dread that bypassed logic entirely. That low, primal warning bell. Instinct honed not by fiction but by experience. I turned away quickly, stared out at the sky beyond the wing. Swallowed. Told myself I was imagining it. That I was being oversensitive. Paranoid, even.

But the feeling didn't fade. Not initially. It clung to me, faint, unsettling, impossible to trace. And I couldn't shake the sense that something wasn't quite right. I couldn't name it. Couldn't pin it down. But it was there. I shook my head, sharp and fast, as if I could dislodge the unease building behind my eyes. Told myself to get a grip. That I was overreacting. My mind weaving shadows where there were none. Old ghosts, that's all: echoes from a past that liked to resurface when I least expected it. Trauma has a way of doing that, slipping into the present like smoke under a door.

The man was nothing. Just a stranger on a plane. I forced the thought aside, locked it behind a door in my mind that I'd nailed shut more times than I could count. I wasn't that girl any more.

Or so I told myself. And with that lie lodged deep, I pushed the man from my thoughts because I needed to. Because I had to. I was obsessing over something I couldn't yet understand. What other choice did I have?

We landed in the hush of early afternoon, the sun suspended high above a landscape that seemed carved from another world. The heat didn't smother; it lingered, dry and weightless, brushing against my skin like a whisper. Not the clinging damp of home, but something finer. The air tasted of salt and minerals, of parched stone and scorched iron, as if the island had been seared into existence and never quite cooled.

Even in winter, Lanzarote pulsed with something primal: stripped of ornament, unconcerned with softness. No lush hills or rain-slicked hedgerows, no sheltering trees. Just the stark bones of the earth laid bare beneath a sky so vast and indifferent it made you forget yourself. It was ancient, yes, but not in a way that welcomed you. It endured, that was all. And yet, I loved it. Unexpectedly. Fiercely. Something in the silence, the stillness between gusts of wind, settled me. As if the island saw straight through me and decided I didn't need to be anything more than I was. I didn't have to smile, or speak, or pretend. I could simply be. And for the first time in as long as I could remember, that was enough.

Our small French rental car whined in protest as Joe steered it north through lava fields and quiet villages. I stared out of the window, watching the black earth stretch endlessly beneath a powder-blue sky. White cubes of houses rose like bone from the rock. No soft edges. No distractions.

By the time we reached Punta Mujeres, I felt like we'd travelled to the end of something. The villa was simple, beautiful in its restraint. White walls, pale-blue shutters, and a terrace that opened straight on to the ocean. No frills. Just the sound of waves and the occasional creak of wooden beams settling into silence.

Time blurred in the best way. We swam in the natural rock pools, wandered the coastal paths, shared long breakfasts on the terrace with juice and coffee and fruit that tasted like sunlight. Sometimes we didn't speak at all. And that was okay. I didn't feel the need to fill the silence with anything false.

The nights were soft. Joe's touch was familiar now. Gentle. Reassuring. We made love beneath the ceiling fan's slow rotation, the scent of sea air slipping in through the shutters.

It was a time of wonder: unfiltered, undiluted joy that crept up on me quietly, like warmth returning to cold skin. The kind of contentment that doesn't announce itself with fanfare but settles gently into the bones. Days passed in a haze of soft light and salt air, and slowly, imperceptibly, I found myself loosening. Laughing. Living.

I was beginning to forget about the man on the plane. Or convincing myself I had. The man whose face had lingered in the back of my mind like a smudge I couldn't quite wipe clean.

Until we visited Orzola. When everything changed. And nothing would ever be the same again. We'd driven there for lunch, on a whim, as most things were by then. No map, no timetable. Just the small hire car and the road unspooling ahead of us like a promise. It clung to the coastline, winding through volcanic hills and clusters of whitewashed houses that blinked against the glare.

To our right, the Atlantic stretched vast and restless, waves biting at the jagged rocks below, flinging up sprays of salt that clung to the windscreen like ghostly prints. To the left, the land rose and fell in scorched ridges and ash-grey slopes, scattered with cactus. We passed goats dozing in the shade of crumbling walls, their bells soft and irregular, and the occasional cyclists hunched against the wind, legs pumping, faces set in grim determination.

By the time we reached our destination of choice, the road had grown narrower, quieter, like it was fading into the sea. The village was still. Almost dreamlike. Boats of various sizes bobbed lazily in the harbour, anchored in water so clear it looked like glass. Three children laughed as they scattered torn crusts for the gulls, their shrieks echoing across the quay. And an old man hunched over a battered fishing boat, hands moving with the slow precision of ritual as he mended fraying nets with a curved needle and weathered thread. There was a peace to it all. A purity. Like the place had been forgotten by the modern world and was all the better for it.

It should've felt safe. Comforting, even. The bright afternoon sun warmed my skin, and Joe's fingers were laced with mine, steady and sure. We walked in sync, our footsteps light on the sun-bleached pavement, the soft murmur of the harbour folding around us like a lullaby. But beneath the surface, just beneath, a sliver of unease twisted through the moment like a crack in glass. Thin. Cold. Impossible to ignore.

Because that was when I saw him again. The man from the plane. He was there, half-claimed by shadow near the end of the quay, as if the light itself had recoiled from him. Standing still. Watching. Not in the curious way strangers sometimes do, but with a quiet, unnatural focus. Detached. Intent. Like he belonged to some other realm entirely, one that had no place in the warmth of that day.

And just like that, the illusion fractured. The sense of ease I'd been clinging to splintered, sharp and immediate, replaced by something darker. Something that pressed cold fingers to the back of my neck and whispered that I wasn't imagining it. He was real. He was there. And he hadn't taken his eyes off me.

The man was standing near the far end of the quay, half-consumed by shadow, as though he'd emerged fully formed from the dying light. Just there. Watching. There was a strange detachment about him, a quiet intensity that seemed to leech the colour from the afternoon. The breeze tugged at his collar, lifting the fabric like a whisper, but he didn't flinch, didn't shift his weight, didn't even blink.

He might've been carved from stone: motionless, sculpted, as if time itself had paused around him. But the eyes betrayed him. Always the eyes. Strikingly blue, unnaturally so, the kind of blue that didn't soften with age but cut through you, precise and cold, like ice. They held no warmth. No curiosity. Just a relentless, unfaltering focus that made my skin crawl.

There was no doubt he was a handsome man: elegant in a restrained, noble sort of way. The years had etched lines into his face, but they hadn't diminished him. If anything, they'd added something, authority, perhaps. Gravity. And yet, beneath that cultivated exterior, there was something else.

Something I couldn't name. Something that didn't feel like peace. A face you could imagine in the background of old photographs, always waiting.

And in that breath of a moment, the fragile sense of calm I'd carried splintered. Fractured beneath a sudden strain. A creeping unease slid in around the edges, quiet and persistent, coiling itself into the folds of my thoughts. I couldn't shake it. Couldn't name it. Couldn't will it away. And it made no sense to me. No sense at all.

Joe glanced sideways, his brow furrowing slightly.

'You all right, Liv?'

I felt myself tremble slightly as the man left my sight.

'Yeah. Fine,' I said, telling myself I was being silly. That I was reacting to nothing. I pulled my smile tighter, hoped it held. 'Just got a bit over-heated all of a sudden.'

Joe didn't push. Just squeezed my hand and guided me on, towards the row of cafés spilling out onto the pavement. The sun glinted off his sunglasses. His body moved with the lazy ease of someone completely at peace.

It should've comforted me. But it didn't. I didn't glance back. Not even once, despite the temptation to look.

But still, I felt the man's eyes on my skin long after the quay had vanished behind us. Not watching in the way strangers do. Watching like he knew something. Like he knew me, despite me not knowing him.

I forced the intrusive thoughts to the back of my mind, burying them beneath the rhythm of our footsteps as we wandered on. I still felt strangely unnerved. But I was determined not to let what I saw as my over-sensitivity ruin the rest of our day.

We chose an attractive harbourside restaurant, all comfy chairs and generous sun umbrellas, its terrace gazing out across the glittering water towards the hazy outline of La Graciosa, a small island floating on the far horizon like a forgotten memory.

The menu was printed in four languages and laminated to withstand decades of salt and wind. Joe ordered the vegetarian paella. And I followed his lead. A shared meal typical of the island. And we really couldn't have made a better choice. When the aromatic dish arrived about twenty-five minutes later, it was fragrant and golden, steaming in a generously proportioned, heavy cast-iron pan. Rice crisped at the edges. Roasted peppers glistened beside artichoke hearts, slivers of tomato and garlic. Delicious.

We ate slowly, each bite grounding me, easing the tension that had coiled tight in my chest. For a while, I let myself believe it was over, that the storm inside me had passed. The sunlight danced on the sea. People laughed. And I almost felt safe again.

Then I saw him for a third time. The man who seemed so out of place. He emerged like a shadow taking shape, his steps unhurried, his gaze fixed somewhere just beyond us. He walked past our table, close enough to brush my chair, like he belonged there. Like he wanted me to see him. Like it wasn't chance.

A low hum of unease stirred beneath my skin, prickling the surface like static before a storm. I was still certain I hadn't ever seen him before catching the flight days earlier. And he hadn't actually done or even said anything to cause such a reaction in me. But now red flags flared in my mind, big, bright and relentless. My stomach clenched. Every instinct I had screamed in silence: *He's dangerous. Stay well clear. Don't even look. Don't engage.*

If only I'd listened. If only I'd trusted the warning in my bones. Seen him for what he was before it was too late. If I had, things could have worked out differently. If only.

13

Joe was already up when I rose the next morning, flipping through a dog-eared guidebook as I padded barefoot onto the cool tiles of the kitchen. He looked up, offered a half-smile, and said, 'Fancy heading down to Famara? Good surf beach. Real waves. We could rent a couple of boards. Would be a lot of fun.'

I nodded, not trusting my voice. I didn't know why I felt off, only that I did. As if something intangible had shifted in the air between us, a barely perceptible fracture. Maybe it was nothing. Maybe it was just me.

We stopped briefly in lovely old Teguise on the way, strolled the cobbled streets, browsed artisan stalls that smelled of incense, listened to an old man play flamenco guitar with eyes shut tight as if exorcising ghosts through the strings. I tried to lose myself in the colour and heat of the place, in the charm of whitewashed walls. But the heaviness clung to me like sea mist.

I tried to tell myself it was all down to the events of Orzola. The man from the plane. Unease still polluting my fragile mind. But it somehow didn't feel like that. Joe seemed less attentive than he had been. Distracted. Almost as if he was finally losing interest in an ugly duckling girl like me. Maybe the honeymoon period of our relationship was over. Perhaps, I pondered, he didn't love me nearly as much as I loved him.

'You okay, Joe?' I asked when we were back in the car, not sure if I wanted to hear the answer.

He signalled, overtaking a group of Lycra-clad cyclists.

'Yeah, course, fine. Why do you ask? What's up with you today?'

'Last night was the first time you didn't want to make love in ages. It seemed you couldn't get to sleep fast enough.'

He shrugged, fingers clenched tight around the wheel, knuckles pale beneath the strain. But he said nothing. Not a word. And it was that silence, the weight of it, that worried me most.

'You're everything to me,' I said a second later, looking for a more meaningful response. 'It's not just a physical thing. You do know that, don't you? I love you. Don't ever forget that. Love you to bits.'

I was almost certain he hesitated before responding, just for a fraction too long. Barely perceptible, but enough. A pause that stung with implication, like he was weighing the truth before deciding which version I deserved.

'Yeah, me too.'

That was all he gave me: three small words, tossed into the air. Nothing more. We drove on after that, the sun spilling across the windscreen, the road ahead glowing with late morning light. He hummed under his breath, easy, content, as if the moment meant exactly what he wanted it to mean. But doubt still needled at me, quiet and persistent, no matter how hard I tried to shove it aside. I told myself to enjoy the calm, to let the warmth of the day soften the edges. But I couldn't help wondering if being with me ever felt simple for him, or if it was only ever borrowed time.

By the time we reached Famara, the tide was high and the wind had picked up. The Atlantic roared against the shore, fierce and unapologetic. We rented a couple of surfboards as Joe had suggested. And he seemed to come alive, the leash already strapped to his ankle before I'd even finished peeling off my clothes.

The beach was wild and beautiful: volcanic cliffs standing sentry to one side, a vast open stretch of yellow sand to the other, scattered with the confident bodies of locals and tourists alike. I watched Joe jog towards the water, board tucked under his arm, muscles taut with purpose. He looked back once and grinned. I forced a smile in return, though it felt like a lie.

I settled near a windbreak for ten minutes or so and let the sun touch my skin, trying to dissolve the tension that had nested beneath my ribs. And then I saw them: three beautiful, young Spanish girls, maybe in their late teens or early twenties, sitting nearby like sun-kissed sirens. They were laughing, drinking something fizzy from a can, their bodies bronzed and unapologetically bare. Tiny thongs clung to their hips, and their breasts were unashamedly exposed to the elements. I wished I'd had their confidence. But my reality was so far from that.

I might've looked away. Should've. But then I saw Joe. He'd just come out of the surf, dripping, board under one arm. And he noticed the girls, too. Of course he had. You'd have to be blind not to. But it wasn't just a glance. It lingered, his gaze tracing each curve, each flick of windblown hair, as though he had every right.

And then he smiled. A slow, lopsided grin that I recognised only too well. The one he used on me when we first met. And worse, he waved. Not at me. At them.

The girls noticed. One leaned over and whispered something to the others. Giggles. Another coy flick of the hair. A glance over the shoulder. Flirtation, unashamed and reciprocal. And my resentment started to build.

Heat surged in my chest, sharp. Not jealousy, exactly. Something more like betrayal. A small, sharp slice of reality. I'd opened myself to this man, trusted him in a way I hadn't trusted anyone. And here he was, eye-fucking the nearest distraction like I didn't even exist. I told myself it had only ever been a matter of time. That I'd been stupid to think our love could last. That such things were not for the likes of me.

Joe returned to his beach towel as if nothing had happened, shaking saltwater from his hair like a dog.

'Waves are decent,' he said. 'You should try it. I'll be going back in soon. What are you waiting for?'

I said nothing. I didn't trust myself to speak. Held it all in until it felt like a dam was about to burst.

The row began before we even left the beach car park a few hours later. Exploded somewhere between his offhand comment about how 'everyone's more relaxed here' and my clipped reply: 'Clearly.'

'What's that supposed to mean?' he asked, keys already in the ignition.

'You know exactly what it means,' I snapped back.

He sighed as he pulled onto the road, tyres kicking up a plume of sand.

'The girls?'

'Yes, Joe, the girls. You could hardly keep your eyes in your head. I thought they might pop out at one point.'

He laughed. He actually laughed.

'It was just a bit of fun, that's all. Forget it. It was nothing.'

I wiped a tear from my cheek. 'It wasn't nothing to me.'

There was a brief silence before he replied, as if he was choosing his words with care. A second or two at most. 'You're overreacting, Liv. I looked, that's all. You're making a fuss over nothing. I didn't even speak to them. What's the problem?'

Wrong reaction. Wrong answer.

'I saw you,' I said. 'You didn't just look. You stared. You waved at them like you were looking for attention. And you were loving every second of it. Tits and bums on display.'

Joe swallowed hard, his expression tightening, changing the contours of his face.

'Shit, Liv. Such a drama queen. Drop it. Don't make this into something it's not.'

'Oh, okay, if that's how you want it. Maybe I should strip off naked and see how friendly everyone gets with me, yeah?'

His jaw tightened.

'Oh, for God's sake. Do whatever the hell you want. This is getting ridiculous.'

The rest of the drive back to Punta Mujeres was a slow descent into hostility. Accusations. Denials. Silences so sharp they felt like blades against skin. The warm, easy rhythm we'd shared since arriving had splintered, replaced by something brittle and volatile. Words we couldn't take back. Thoughts we hadn't meant to say aloud. And by the time we reached the villa, we weren't speaking at all.

The ocean still lapped at the rocks beyond the terrace, indifferent to our unravelling. I stood at the open doors, staring out into the darkening horizon, arms wrapped tight around my ribs.

It seemed the good times were over. The inevitable cracks had surfaced. And I couldn't help but wonder: what else was hiding beneath the smile I'd fallen for? Joe was just another predictable male I couldn't trust. I should've known. Should've seen through the charm and easy warmth. But I hadn't. I'd wanted to believe. And that was the real betrayal, wasn't it? Not his, but mine.

14

Joe didn't so much as glance in my direction when we stepped into the villa. Just grabbed a bath towel from the banister and disappeared upstairs, the sound of running water soon echoing through the rafters like static in my skull. I stood there, frozen, not sure what to do for the best.

On the coffee table, Joe's phone lay abandoned, screen down, as though it too had turned its back on me. Then it buzzed. Once. Then again. And I stared at it, pulse tightening, that old familiar dread curling in my gut. My fingers moved before my conscience could object. The screen came to life beneath my touch, demanding a passcode. Four digits. A puzzle I had no right to solve.

But I knew him, didn't I? First try: 0908, his birthday. No. Second: 2017, the year he started painting. Still nothing. Third: 1888, Van Gogh's *Sunflowers*. His favourite painting. He'd told me that the first night we lay tangled in the sheets, whispering secrets we hadn't known we'd regret.

The screen opened with a quiet click. And my world began to tilt. The message was from Mia Barnes. The name struck like a slap. Blonde. Confident. A walking smirk in tight denim. She was on our course, always finding excuses to touch Joe's arm during critiques, laughing too hard at his jokes. More than a little irritating. And so much prettier than me.

The latest text wasn't a one-off. That much was obvious. The thread stretched back days, message after message, each one tightening the noose. Flirty remarks. Stolen moments. Plans made in the shadows. And then the images. A gallery of deceit, laid bare in pixels. Every one of them a slap I hadn't seen coming.

The first photo crawled onto the screen, agonisingly slowly, Wi-Fi stuttering on the fringe of the Atlantic, as if even the signal hesitated to show me the truth. Dated the day before.

Mia's face appeared first, tilted in that faux-innocent way she did when she knew she was being watched. Then bare shoulders, skin catching the light. And more. Too much. Nothing left to the imagination. Naked. Legs parted wide. Mouth parted too: inviting, practised, knowing.

There was nothing accidental about it. It was posed. Performed. Intimate in a way that turned my stomach.

I recoiled as if scorched, my breath caught somewhere between a gasp and a gag. I wanted to scrub my skin raw. To claw her image out of my mind with fingernails. But it was too late. The damage was done.

She hadn't just stolen his attention; she'd stolen my peace. And he'd let her.

Below, Joe's reply. A string of emojis. And a photo taken in our villa bedroom. Him, full-frontal. Smiling. Proud. Erect. Like he'd done nothing wrong at all.

My stomach heaved. It wasn't just the betrayal; it was the intimacy of it. The easy vulgarity. The knowing way he'd looked at her at college, just as he'd once looked at me. I saw it all now, the glances, the missed calls, the way he always took his phone into the bathroom. But not this time. And now I knew.

The villa felt too small, too hot. I couldn't breathe. I dropped the phone as if it had burned me, grabbed my handbag, and stumbled outside. The sun had almost disappeared by then, bleeding orange into the sea. And I walked without thinking, barefoot on the uneven stone, each step jarring. Punta Mujeres was quiet at that hour. The sleepy fishing village oblivious to the storm unravelling inside me.

I passed shuttered windows and low walls draped in vines. Found a familiar path that led to the natural pools. Sat on a crumbling wall where the ocean met black, volcanic rock.

And then I cried. Not the soft, cinematic kind. This was ugly. Violent. Years of buried hurt pouring out in choking sobs. My chest hurt. My throat was raw. I curled forward, forehead pressed to my knees, tears dripping onto stone.

Behind closed lids I saw them: Joe and Mia. Their smiles. The photos. The lies. And myself. Foolish. Believing. Hoping. Why did I trust when I shouldn't have trusted at all?

My sobs had begun to slow, tapering into sharp, shallow breaths that rattled in my chest. I sat slumped on the wall, arms wrapped around my knees like a child, salt on my skin from tears and sea air alike. My eyes felt scraped raw.

I didn't hear him at first. Just the soft clink of cutlery from a nearby restaurant terrace, the low murmur of voices muffled by distance and grief. Then footsteps. Slow. Measured, like someone who didn't want to startle a wounded animal.

I looked up. And my heart faltered. He was there. Again. The same man I'd seen on the plane, two rows ahead, stealing glances when he thought I wouldn't notice. The same man I'd seen watching in Orzola.

It was him, wasn't it? Yes, yes, of course it was. Tall. Grey at the temples. Crisp linen shirt, sleeves rolled to the elbow, effortlessly neat. There was something about the way he moved, calm, unhurried, as if the chaos of the world couldn't touch him. So much more confident than me.

His gaze locked on to mine, eyes the colour of storm-washed slate rather than blue now, cold and disturbingly steady. He closed the space between us with measured steps, stopping just shy of the wall, close enough that I caught the faint trace of aftershave. Something earthy. A dry, woody scent that clung to him like memory. He tilted his head, just a fraction, and offered a smile: a practised thing, tight at the corners, never touching his eyes. And then he spoke. Calm. Precise. His voice carried the polish of an educated South of England accent, cultured, assured, but something in its evenness made the hairs rise at the back of my neck. Who on earth was he? And what the hell did he want?

'Are you okay?' he asked softly. Then, almost as an afterthought, 'Olivia, isn't it? I am correct, aren't I?'

My breath caught as I jerked my head back. He'd said my name like it belonged to him. There was no introduction. No apology for the intrusion. Just that quiet certainty, as if we'd met before and I'd simply forgotten. But I still couldn't place him. And I really didn't think we had.

I wiped my face with the back of my hand, smearing mascara across my cheekbones, suddenly aware of how vulnerable I must have looked: red-eyed, crumpled, broken in full view of a stranger. It felt like a shadow I hadn't noticed had been following me.

'I... Sorry, have we met?' I croaked, my voice hoarse, brittle as glass.

He smiled again, gentle, patient, like I was a child asking why the sky was blue. He didn't sit. Didn't lean. Just stood there, hands clasped loosely in front of him, as if he had all the time in the world. Watching me. Studying me. And suddenly, the sea wasn't the only thing that felt endless. It came as a relief when he finally spoke again. And then, it all became clear. How could I have known the game he was playing with such practised aplomb? How could anyone?

'Sorry, I hope that isn't weird. I'm just a bit of a fan. You see, I've long admired your art,' he began, his tone warm but measured, each word delivered with rehearsed precision. 'I caught your interview on the Welsh evening news, thought you came across exceptionally well. Then I read about you in the local press. Thoroughly impressive, if I may say so.' He offered another smile, warmer this time. 'I purchased a collection of your pieces at the Bath exhibition. Stunning. Truly. I often sit there alone at home, just taking them in. It brings a certain... pleasure.'

I won't lie; I was flattered. My ego lapped it up, hungry for approval, too eager to be seen. I leaned in, willingly captive to his voice, blind to the warning signs I should've recognised. I let him weave his Machiavellian spell around me, thread by thread. And I fell for it. Just like the fool I was.

'That's so very kind of you to say so.'

He handed me a clean tissue taken from a trouser pocket.

'There's a certain darkness in your work that speaks to something in me,' he said, voice low now, as if confessing a shared secret, almost vulnerable. 'A raw honesty beneath the surface, unflinching, unashamed. It resonates more than I can explain. And I have a feeling we're not so different, you and I, despite the years that separate us. Some things run deeper than age.'

I drew in a long, shaky breath, the air sharp in my lungs. I wasn't ready to be alone with my thoughts, not with Joe still etched behind my eyes. I needed the noise, the distraction, anything to silence the ache. And so I clung to the conversation like a lifeline, foolishly believing I was the one steering it.

'I saw you on the plane,' I said, my voice thinner than I'd intended. 'At Cardiff Airport. Do you live in Wales?'

'I do,' he said with a measured nod, his gaze steady, unreadable. Then, gently, too gently, he added, 'Now wipe away those tears. Come on. Let's sit down at the café across the way. You can tell me more about your art, and I'll share a little about myself, if you're interested, of course. Only if you've got time. The last thing I'd ever want is to be a nuisance.'

He was already reeling me in. Subtle. Assured. Skilled in the art of feigned deference. Making it feel like I held the reins, when really, I was already tangled in the strings he'd so carefully laid out.

We crossed the road in silence, the rhythm of the waves filling the spaces where words might have lived.

The café was small, tucked beneath a faded awning, its tables scattered unevenly across the pavement. He selected one near the edge, half in shadow, with a view of the ocean, not of me, and sat without hesitation, as though he already knew how this part would unfold.

I lowered myself opposite, aware of my own unease: the tension in my shoulders, the residual tremor in my fingers. A waitress approached, pad in hand, but he didn't glance at the menu.

'Two glasses of the house red, please,' he said, with effortless certainty. 'Large.'

He turned back to me with a faint smile, his voice smooth, almost self-deprecating.

'I should probably introduce myself properly, shouldn't I? Sir Charles Fairfax.' He gave a small nod, as if the weight of the title meant little. 'But please, call me Charles. Titles are for lecture halls and dust-covered corridors, not pavement cafés with beautiful young artists.'

There it was again: that subtle charm. The practised ease. He made it sound casual, harmless. As if he weren't drawing careful lines around me with every word. And I asked myself why I'd been so unnerved by him in the first place. Put it down to my past.

'I'm at art college in Carmarthen,' I said, the words spilling out before I'd thought them through.

'Of course you are,' he replied, eyes narrowing ever so slightly. 'You were born to be an artist. It shows in your work. The passion. The hunger. You're not afraid to disturb. That's rare, especially at your age.'

The wine arrived. He raised his glass but didn't clink mine. Just held it there, suspended, watching me. I took a sip, grateful for the distraction. It burned slightly on the way down.

Then he leaned in, just enough.

'Forgive me if I'm overstepping the mark,' he said, voice dipped in concern. 'But when I saw you a little earlier, sitting alone, you looked... broken. I could clearly tell something had shaken you to the core. And I can't help but wonder: what could cause someone like you to carry that kind of weight in their eyes when you should feel nothing but joy?'

He didn't blink. Didn't rush. Just sat there, composed, waiting for the fracture line to widen. And for reasons I couldn't explain, I wanted to let it. I wanted to tell him.

'Oh, it was just a stupid argument that upset me.'

Charles didn't push. He didn't need to. Instead, he sat back in his chair, swirling the wine in lazy circles, as though we were old friends slipping into familiar territory. The silence between us wasn't awkward. It was curated, crafted to give me space to fill it, to mistake it for safety.

'I've always found cafés like this strangely comforting,' he said at last, eyes on the wine, not me. 'There's something about the chaos, footsteps, traffic, plates clattering that makes people believe they're invisible. Like they can speak the things they'd never dare whisper behind closed doors.'

I nodded.

'Yes, yes, I think I know what you mean.'

He looked up then, met my gaze with what seemed quiet sincerity.

'Sometimes it's easier, isn't it? Talking to someone who doesn't quite belong to your world. Someone with no stake in your pain. No judgement. No consequences. I'm a very good listener. And I have all the time in the world. I'm at your service.'

A small, knowing smile played at the corner of his mouth. He hadn't asked again. He didn't have to. He'd opened the door and waited for me to walk through it, thinking it was my idea all along.

I took another sip of wine, longer this time, letting it bleed through my nerves, blunting the sharp edges. And then, for reasons I still can't untangle, I told him everything. Spilled it all. Why? God only knows. Even now I can't fathom why I was so reckless. So utterly stupid.

'It's Joe,' I said finally, the words brittle and thin. 'My boyfriend. Or... whatever he is now.'

I laughed, but it came out wrong: tight, humourless. My voice caught in my throat, and I blinked too fast. The wine blurred in the glass, or maybe it was the tears I didn't want to shed.

'We planned this trip together. And he was meant to love me. But something changed. He changed. And he ruined it. Ruined it just when it appeared to be real.'

Charles's eyes narrowed. 'I'm so very sorry to hear that. The boy must be an utter fool. You deserve so much better.'

I lowered my gaze, staring at my hands as they rested uselessly in my lap, fingers twitching as if betraying the weakness I'd tried so hard to hide. The shame crept in, slow and acidic, curling itself into my chest.

'Stupid, isn't it?' I muttered, my voice barely carrying across the table. 'Falling apart over someone who probably never really loved me to begin with. A dirty, cheating bastard with a smile full of promises and a conscience like smoke: here, then gone. He never intended to stay. Never intended to be loyal. I was just convenient. A phase to pass the time.'

The bitterness caught me off guard. I felt the heat behind my eyes, the sting of humiliation dressed up as anger. But Charles said nothing. He didn't interrupt. Didn't offer a comforting lie or clumsy reassurance. He just watched and nodded, the way a man might listen to a confession in the dark, without judgement but with quiet calculation.

There was something in the way he held my gaze then. Not pity. Not even curiosity. Something cooler. Sharper. As though I'd just placed a precious, damaged thing into his hands... and he intended to keep it.

And that's when I felt it: that subtle shift in the air between us. A silent transaction. I'd given him something of myself, fragile and unguarded. And he'd taken it with care. With interest. But not without intent.

Then, finally, he spoke. Softly. Calmly. Like a therapist coaxing the next line of thought.

'So tell me,' he said, swirling the wine in his glass. 'What happens now? Will you forgive him? Brush it aside and pretend the foundation's still solid? Or is this it, the end of the road?'

He tilted his head slightly, studying me.

'Not that it's my place to ask, of course. But sometimes it helps... voicing the part you've already decided in silence.'

I looked at him, properly this time. Not through tears or anger, but with the wary curiosity of someone realising they've already stepped over a line they didn't quite see.

There was something about Charles. The calm. The certainty. He didn't try to fix me or fumble for empathy. He simply held the space, gave weight to my words like they mattered. And maybe that was all it took. After Joe's silence. After the shift in his eyes. After everything I hadn't said out loud until now.

'I really don't know what happens next,' I admitted, my voice quieter, more honest. 'Part of me wants to forget Joe ever existed. But another part...' I trailed off, ashamed of the truth. 'Another part still wants to believe it meant something. That I meant something.'

I laughed again, but it wasn't laughter: it was resignation wrapped in breath.

'I sound pathetic, don't I?'

Charles leaned back slightly, his fingers still resting on the stem of his glass.

'No,' he said. 'You sound human.'

Simple. Unemotional. And yet his words landed with more weight than anything Joe had said in days.

I stared at him, studying the subtle lines at the corners of his mouth, the way his eyes gave nothing away. I wanted to know more. Needed to. Because at that moment, it felt like he understood me in a way Joe never had.

'What about you?' I asked. 'Tell me a little about yourself.'

He hesitated, just long enough to make it feel considered rather than rehearsed. Then glanced down at his wine, rotating the glass slowly between his fingers, as if the movement steadied something beneath the surface. When he spoke again, his voice was softer, more reflective, measured in a way that felt compelling.

'I was a barrister,' he began. 'A Queen's Counsel. Recently retired now, but it was a lifetime in the courts. Criminal cases, mostly. High pressure, fine margins. You learn to think fast and never show doubt, no matter what's unravelling inside you.'

He paused, letting the words settle.

'I gave it up after a stay in intensive care. One moment you're balancing the scales of justice, the next you're fighting for your life. It... changes things. Perspective, mostly. What you think you value. What you realise you truly value.'

He didn't elaborate. Didn't say what had happened or how close to the edge he'd come. Just let the space hang between us, filled only by the faint clink of glassware and the distant murmur of passing conversations.

'These days,' he went on, 'I spend my time on research. Psychological work, mostly. Exploring the extremes of human behaviour. What pushes people beyond their moral boundaries. What justifies the unacceptable in their minds. What we're all capable of, given the right conditions. I'm writing a research paper for future publication.'

'Oh, sounds interesting.'

He looked at me then, not with judgement but something sharper. Interest, perhaps. Recognition.

'Ah, yes, I thought you'd think so. It's more revealing than the law ever was. You can sew up a wound, stabilise a heart. But the mind... that's far more elusive. Far more dangerous.'

I nodded, unsure what more to say. His words were fascinating, hypnotic even, but there was something in the way he said them. Detached. Almost clinical. Like he wasn't just studying human behaviour... he understood it, intimately, perhaps even too well.

And yet, I wanted to know more.

'What exactly are you studying at the moment?' I asked, unable to mask the curiosity in my voice.

He drained the last of his wine with unhurried grace, set the glass down, and gave a small shake of the head, more amused than dismissive.

'Oh, enough of me,' he said, eyes narrowing just slightly, as if letting me in on something withheld. 'Perhaps I'll share more another time. But for now, you're far more interesting.'

The words landed softly, but with weight. Not flirtatious. Not overt. Just enough to tilt the balance. To let me feel valued without knowing exactly how or why.

Heat rushed to my cheeks before I could stop it, blooming up my neck and settling behind my ears.

'I doubt that,' I murmured, looking down at my hands again, those betraying hands, still marked by a faint tremor.

He didn't correct me. Didn't offer a compliment or attempt to reassure. He simply watched in quiet approval. And somehow, that was worse. Because looking back, I'm not sure if I was being drawn in… or dissected.

I glanced at the sky, suddenly aware of how the evening was sliding into darkness, moonlight shadows growing longer on the pavement. The heaviness in my chest returned, sharper now, edged with dread.

'I should go,' I said, reaching for my bag. 'I need to get back to the villa. Collect my things. And then…' I hesitated, the words catching in my throat. 'I'll have to find somewhere to stay tonight. I just can't face being there with Joe. Not for another second.'

Charles said nothing at first. He simply studied me, his expression unreadable, his fingertips resting lightly on the edge of the table. Then, with a soft exhale, he leaned forward.

'That doesn't sound ideal, not this late in the day,' he said gently. 'The last thing you need is to be wandering the streets on your own. Especially when you're already… carrying so much.'

I looked at him, uncertain. I was adrift in a foreign land, unmoored and bone-deep lonely, everything unfamiliar and slightly out of focus. Confused, vulnerable, so desperate for an anchor that even the faintest gesture of kindness felt like a lifeline. And in that moment, I wanted, needed, to believe his outstretched hand was offered in friendship.

'There's no need to look so alarmed,' he added, offering a small, disarming smile. 'I have a comfortable rented house in Arrieta. Just a mile or two down the road. Nothing extravagant. Just somewhere quiet while I'm on the island. There's a spare room. Separate. Comfortable. You'd be very welcome to use it, just for tonight, of course. No strings. No expectations.'

He paused, letting the offer settle before continuing, calm, measured, his voice dipped in a kind of fatherly concern.

Such a great actor.

'You remind me of my daughter, you know. She's older now, with a family of her own. But there's something in your eyes. The same stubbornness. The same sadness, too.'

He smiled again, this time with a touch of melancholy.

'I'd hate to think of her alone in a foreign place, lugging bags through the dark, trying to make sense of things. Let me help. Just for tonight. Then tomorrow, if you still want to leave, I'll drive you wherever you need to go myself. What do you think?'

Charles made it all sound so rational. So measured. So damn safe. That was the most dangerous part of all: the ease of it. The warmth in his voice. The unspoken promise that I could rest, just for a moment, without fear or consequence.

I wanted to believe him. A part of me, the wounded, exhausted part, longed to say yes. Craved comfort, sanctuary, a place to disappear from the ache of it all.

But another part of me, buried deeper, tougher, forged in the aftermath of things no one ever talks about, stirred with quiet alarm. That low, insistent thrum in the gut. The one that doesn't shout, doesn't scream, but knows. A whisper beneath the ribs that tells you when something's off, even if you can't quite name it.

I'd learned to listen to that voice over the years. Had to. It had kept me alive more than once. Because trust, for someone like me, was a luxury. A risk. A currency I could rarely afford to spend.

And yet, there I was, tired, emotionally raw, adrift in a foreign place, turning my back on instinct. Ignoring the only thing that had never lied to me.

Whether it was fatigue or that gnawing ache to feel understood, I overrode the warning. Let myself believe it was kindness. That he meant well. That I was still calling the shots.

I told myself I had nothing to fear. That he was sweet, warm and sincere. A nice dad type. That my anxieties related more to my past than the now. And so I nodded, careful not to let the hesitation show. I offered him a small, practised smile, one that didn't quite reach my eyes, and stood.

That was it. One step. One quiet betrayal of everything I'd learned. Charles had hooked me, clean through the gut, and I hadn't even felt the barb go in. Not then. Not yet. Now all he had to do was reel me in, slowly, patiently. And I was already taking the bait. Willing. Blind. Already his.

15

We drove to collect my belongings beneath a bruised sky, the last of the sun already bled out behind the hills. Darkness settled fast along the coast, swallowing the edges of the road, the sea reduced to a strip of black velvet pressed against the horizon. The headlights cut a narrow path ahead, flickering over dry scrubland and jagged volcanic rock, the world outside taking on a strange, half-formed quality: real, but only just.

Charles steered with an easy confidence, one hand resting lightly on the wheel, the other gesturing now and then as he spoke. His tone was gentle, measured, as if he'd all the time in the world to listen. The calm in his manner seeped into me by degrees, smoothing the edges of my unease. The warmth in him hadn't dimmed; if anything, it seemed more deliberate now, a steadying presence that anchored me as the road slid by.

When we reached the villa, the place looked different in the dark, stripped of all its sun-drenched charm. Just pale walls, shuttered windows, and the flickering light from the lounge casting long shadows across the path. A place that had once felt like a promise now hollowed out by disappointment.

'I won't be long,' I murmured, already reaching for the door handle.

Charles nodded, pulling the car to a slow stop outside the gate.

'Take your time,' he said. 'I'll be right here if you need me. You're doing the right thing. You have to put yourself first. Look after yourself.' And then a smile as if to lighten the mood.

The engine ticked as I stepped out of the car on shaky legs, the air still clinging to the heat of the day. I walked the path to the door with my heart hammering a dull rhythm behind my ribs.

Joe was inside, slouched on the sofa with his head in his hands. The television flickered soundlessly in the corner. He looked up when I entered, his face drawn, tired, a bottle of beer half drunk on the table beside him.

'I just came to get my things,' I said, trying to keep my voice steady. 'And don't bother trying to stop me. We're done. I saw the stuff on your phone. All of it. It told me all I need to know.'

Joe didn't speak at first. Not a word. Just watched me with the vacant sort of sadness that comes when you already know something's over.

'I didn't expect you to actually go,' he said eventually, his voice low, raw around the edges. 'The flight's not for another three days. And it's Christmas week. Mia doesn't mean anything to me. Not like you. We can get past this, can't we? It was just a sex thing, that's all. Come on, Liv. I won't do it again. Give me a break.'

I'd already decided to try to book an earlier flight. The very next day. Back to Cardiff, if possible. Or Bristol, if not. But I didn't answer. I moved past Joe, up the stairs and into the bedroom, shoving clothes into my suitcase with a kind of practised numbness. Toothbrush. Phone charger. The book I'd meant to read. It all felt strange now, like collecting the belongings of someone else entirely.

Joe stood in the doorway as I zipped the case closed.

'Where the hell will you stay?'

I hesitated. 'A place in Arrieta. Just for the night.'

He glared at me.

'What sort of place? There's no hotel in this part of the island, as far as I know. Nothing for miles. And you've got zero chance of a taxi.'

'I'm very well aware of that, thank you! Not your problem. Just back off and let me get on. The quicker I'm out of here, the happier I'll be. And that's down to you.'

Joe reached out to touch my arm but I brushed past him, unwilling to get pulled back into a conversation we'd already buried under silence and hurt. I didn't trust myself to stay rational. Or kind.

The front door clicked shut behind me, and the villa faded into the darkness like a closed chapter. Charles was still there. Still behind the wheel, engine running, one arm resting on the window ledge like he hadn't moved at all. He looked up as I approached, eyes unreadable in the dashboard light.

'All sorted?' he asked, his tone neutral.

I nodded, put my case in the back, climbed in, and shut the door. The sound of it was final.

The road widened as we left the village behind, hemmed in by dark ridges and open stretches of nothing. The island felt deserted. Just us, the road, and the mechanical rhythm of the car.

Arrieta emerged like a whisper, just a smattering of lights in the distance, a faint cluster of homes folded into the coast. It looked peaceful. Hidden. The sort of place where no one asked questions.

Charles turned down a narrow track, headlights sweeping across a low, whitewashed house with a single lamp burning outside the door.

'Here we are,' he said, cutting the engine.

I stepped out, the ground crunching beneath my feet. The air smelled of salt and dry earth. No sound but the wind moving lazily through the cacti, and the sea somewhere beyond, whispering against the rocks.

He unlocked the door and stepped aside with my case in one hand, gesturing for me to enter first.

'It's not much,' he said softly. 'But it's quiet. You'll be safe here. Stay as long as you want. You're my guest and I want you to treat the place as your own.'

I stepped across the threshold, the air inside cool and faintly scented with something herbal: rosemary, maybe, or dried eucalyptus. The door clicked shut behind me, the sound far louder than it should have been. Like something sealed.

My shoulders stiffened. I was here. Committed now, whether it felt right or not. And Charles hovered a few paces behind, calm as ever. Polite. Supportive. His voice holding the steady warmth of someone used to putting people at ease, and his words were laced with concern, not coercion. He even mentioned knowing Edward. Stressed how much he liked him. And yet...

He was still a stranger. A stranger with a title, true, a barrister from home, with the clipped vowels and quiet authority to match, but that did little to silence the whispering doubt at the back of my mind. The part of me that had learned, slowly and painfully, that charm and danger sometimes shared the same face.

Once again I tried to convince myself this was reasonable. That I wasn't being reckless. That his offer of help had been genuine, his concern authentic. But the questions still persisted, sharp as thorns pressed beneath the skin. Was this kindness? Or something far more complicated? Or perhaps both.

I glanced at him as he passed me in the hallway, heading towards the kitchen with the quiet confidence of someone moving through a space he owned. His silhouette was calm, unhurried, perfectly composed. And still... I wasn't sure. Not about him. And not about myself.

I should have rung Eva. Wished her a happy Christmas. Told her where I was, who I was with. Let her hear my voice and know I was still breathing, still trying to find my way. But kids in care learn early that life moves on without them. You become a chapter people close, even when they loved you once.

Twice I started to dial, my thumb hovering over the call button, hope flickering like a faulty bulb, only to drop the phone back into my lap, pulse unsteady. Eva and Edward had new priorities now, fresh faces to comfort and protect, small lives needing all the energy they used to spend on me. I was a memory, fond, perhaps, but distant.

So I swallowed the urge to reach out, wrapped it tight and hidden. And I kept my situation to myself, because sometimes silence feels safer than finding out you've been forgotten.

I was likely doing my foster parents a disservice, thinking the way I did, painting them as people who could set me aside as easily as closing a door. But the thought rooted itself anyway, stubborn and familiar. Maybe you'd have to grow up in care to understand how quickly doubt becomes second nature, how easily you learn to brace for the moment someone's attention shifts elsewhere. It wasn't bitterness, not really. Just the simple, worn-in truth of how life had trained me to think.

16

During that one night in Arrieta, Charles seemed, by every visible measure, the perfect gentleman. Considerate. Unobtrusive. A man who understood the unspoken rules of space, who knew precisely when to step back and when to offer quiet reassurance. Nothing in his manner gave cause for alarm. No lingering looks. No misplaced familiarity. Just quiet, practised hospitality, the kind that comes naturally to men who've spent a lifetime convincing others to trust them. He showed me to the guest room with a slight nod, offering fresh towels and pointing out the bathroom across the hall. His voice remained low, reassuring, almost clinical in its detachment. No pressure. No expectation. Nothing overt.

He offered me tea, chamomile, and I took it without thinking, needing something to do with my hands, something warm to anchor me in a house that didn't yet feel real. We sat at the kitchen table beneath a softly humming light, the windows cracked open to let in the night air. A distant sea breeze stirred the curtains.

He didn't pry. Didn't speak unless spoken to. Just sat with me in companionable silence, sipping his tea with the unhurried calm of someone who had nowhere else to be.

And slowly, despite myself, I began to unwind. The tension in my spine softened. My breathing steadied. The barbed wire in my thoughts loosened, coil by coil. I told myself I was safe. That this was what kindness looked like. That not all men had motives concealed beneath polite smiles and generous gestures. And by the time I crawled beneath the freshly made sheets at a little after ten that night, the air cool against my skin, I was no longer certain why I'd been so nervous of him in the first place.

I slept, deep and undisturbed. Too deeply, perhaps. When I woke, the room was still and softly lit, the sea wind whispering through the shutters. For a moment, I didn't know where I was. And then it came back in pieces: Joe, the villa, the café, the wine. Charles's voice. The quiet offer. The door that had closed behind me.

I found a note in the kitchen, written in beautiful flowing, looping script. Almost a work of art in itself:

Gone for a walk along the beach. Help yourself to whatever you want.
Charles

He returned mid-morning, salt in his hair, sand dusted in the hem of his trousers, looking like a man entirely at peace with himself. Like he'd walked straight out of a postcard.

'I've booked a flight,' I said. 'Cardiff. Tomorrow afternoon.'

He frowned. 'Last minute?'

'Yeah. There were quite a few available seats. Lucky, really. Must be the time of year. Seems the plane's half empty.'

He listened without interruption, his eyes fixed on me with that look that always felt like more than attention. Then he smiled, a thought hidden behind curved lips.

'As it happens,' he said, 'I've booked the same flight. Something unexpected I have to get home for.'

It sounded harmless. A coincidence wrapped in charm. And I accepted it at face value, too tired, or too trusting, to dig deeper. I hadn't planned on staying another night. That had never been the intention. But I told myself it was practicality, nothing more. A simple decision based on comfort and timing. And when I mentioned it over coffee that afternoon, Charles simply nodded, as if he'd expected it all along.

'You're most welcome,' he said, his voice low and measured. 'There's no rush. As I told you before, treat this place as though it were your own.'

And so I stayed. The second evening passed much like the first. Calm. Uncomplicated. He cooked, pasta with fresh herbs and just the right amount of garlic, and we ate on the small terrace at the back of the house, the stone still warm beneath our feet from the day's heat.

A faint breeze whispered in from the sea, and the lights from the village blinked faintly in the distance, softened by the dark. And we talked. About books. About art. About places he'd visited and places we still hoped to see. Nothing personal. Nothing probing. Just easy, meandering conversation that filled the space between us without asking for anything more.

He poured me a glass of local wine, then retreated to his own corner of the terrace, never sitting too close. Never looking too long. A man who knew how to make a girl feel at ease without crossing invisible lines.

He seemed thoughtful in a way that felt deliberate, a spare towel left folded on my bed, a small lamp switched on in the hallway so I wouldn't have to navigate the dark alone. Subtle gestures that didn't draw attention to themselves.

And once again, there was nothing that gave me cause for concern. No suggestion of menace. Not then. No shift in tone. Just quiet company in a quiet house, almost comforting now.

Still, as I lay in bed that night, the ceiling fan humming softly above, I couldn't quite ignore the faint unease at the back of my mind. Not fear, exactly. Not distrust. Something less defined. A thread I didn't want to pull. I closed my eyes and told myself, again, that everything was fine. Because it was. Wasn't it? Of course it was. I just had to learn to trust.

17

By early afternoon the following day, the sky had dulled to a hard slate grey. We hefted our bags into the boot of Charles's hire car, the muted thud of luggage against metal carried on the warm, desiccated wind. Dust spiralled along the narrow track, whispering through gaps in the low stone walls, stirring the brittle scrub, laced with the tang of salt and the acrid trace of something scorched. Charles said nothing. He settled behind the wheel with practised ease, slipped the car into gear, and guided us onto the serpentine coastal road that wound towards César Manrique Airport.

The island felt different somehow: emptier, as though it had drawn a long breath and was holding it now, watching us go. I'd arrived here with Joe, full of hope and anticipation, naively convinced the sun-drenched days ahead would strengthen what we had. But now I was leaving with Charles. A very different man, in very different circumstances. One calm and self-contained. The other reckless, selfish, already fading in the rear-view mirror of my thoughts. And change, I'd learned, often came without warning – uninvited, unwelcome. But it was a language I'd long since learned to speak.

Thoughts of Joe's betrayal, blatant and cowardly, had stripped away the last of my uncertainty. The decision to leave him no longer felt dramatic or impulsive; it felt necessary. I could trace the moment our relationship broke, like a thread pulled too tight, finally snapping under the weight of everything.

Some things, I told myself, you couldn't mend, however tempting it might be to try. Some wounds refused stitching. And forgiveness wasn't always the noble choice; sometimes it was simply a surrender I couldn't afford.

And so I turned my face to the window, let the blurred landscape pass in silence, and told myself, for once with conviction, that I was doing the right thing.

There was something reassuring about the sound of the engine ticking over, the soft purr of tyres against tarmac as we wound our way inland. The road to the airport was long and largely quiet, flanked by low stone walls and half-sleeping villages where shuttered windows watched from the shade. Charles kept one hand on the wheel, the other resting loosely on the gearstick, his posture relaxed, as if ferrying me through this last stretch of the island was just another part of the plan.

We didn't speak much during the half-hour drive, and yet the silence between us felt easy now. Strangely familiar. I stared out of the window, letting the landscape blur into tones of grey and gold, trying not to think about Joe or the half-formed regrets I'd packed into my luggage. I felt ready to return to Wales.

Inside, the airport was a hum of announcements and restless travellers. The flight, it seemed, was running late. A one-hour delay, according to the departures board. Charles didn't flinch. He bought us coffee from a tired-looking kiosk near the gate, handed mine over without ceremony, and led us to a pair of empty seats facing the runway. And we talked.

Charles took a slow sip of his drink, then glanced at me, his tone as casual as the question itself.

'So tell me, what drew you to art in the first place?'

I hesitated, thrown slightly by the directness. But his gaze held no judgement, just a quiet curiosity. The kind that made you feel safe enough to answer.

'I don't know,' I said eventually. 'It was the only thing that ever made sense to me. The only thing I could lose myself in without feeling like I was trying too hard to be someone else.'

He nodded, thoughtful.

'Do you have a favourite style since college? A particular school you lean towards?'

I smiled faintly. 'Not really. I like what most people find uncomfortable: expressionism, abstraction, raw texture. The stuff that doesn't tie itself up neatly. I can't stand the overly polished or sentimental. It feels dishonest.'

Charles didn't respond right away. He let the words settle, comfortable and unhurried, before asking, 'And your tutors? Any that stand out?'

'Um, one or two,' I said. 'The rest just talk about the process like it's something sacred, like the pain behind it shouldn't show. But I think it should. If it doesn't hurt a little, what's the point?'

He gave the slightest smile at that. Not amusement. Something closer to agreement. Then his tone shifted, so gently I almost didn't notice.

'I couldn't agree with you more.'

I nodded, thinking he really did understand. That he had a depth to him I hadn't encountered before. Not in anyone.

'What about before Carmarthen?' he asked next. 'Before all this. Where did you grow up?'

I froze for a beat, the words catching in my throat. No one usually asked me that. Not really. Not unless they were trying to categorise me. File me away under 'damaged' or 'difficult'.

But his eyes didn't shift. Didn't flicker with pity or assumption.

And somehow, before I'd even decided to speak, the words began to spill. Not polished or curated, just raw. Disjointed. The truth, or something close to it.

'I was in care,' I heard myself say. 'A children's home. And foster homes. One after another. Some worse than others. Art was the only thing that didn't ask anything from me. Didn't judge. It took me as I was.'

He didn't interrupt. Didn't offer hollow sympathy or lean into the moment like it was something to be fixed.

He just listened. Like I was the only person in the room that mattered. And, for once, I was glad to be heard.

Later, somewhere high above the Bay of Biscay, as the clouds stretched in endless rolling folds beneath the plane, he turned to me again, that same composed ease in his voice.

'I have a large house in the country,' he said. 'Georgian. Detached. Just a few miles outside Carmarthen. Quiet. Private.'

His eyes remained on the window as he spoke, as though the words weren't intended to impress.

'I've converted one of the larger rooms into a gallery. My private collection. Paintings, sculptures... including a number of your pieces, of course. As I mentioned before. Yours have pride of place.'

That surprised me. I turned to face him fully, unsure if I'd heard him right.

'Mine? Pride of place?'

He nodded, still calm, still composed.

'I've displayed them properly: framed, lit, given room to breathe. They carry even more weight in my house than they seemed to in the gallery. It's strange, isn't it, how art changes depending on where it lives.'

Then he looked at me directly, voice soft. 'You should come and see them sometime. I think you'd be pleased. And I'd love to know your thoughts. Who better to comment than you?'

There was no obvious suggestion in his tone. No apparent pressure. Just quiet admiration, offered like a gift. There was nothing in his tone that felt out of place. No glint of ulterior motive. Just admiration, gentle, measured, sincere, spoken with the quiet pride of a man who truly believed what he was saying. And in that moment, it made me feel like I mattered in a way I hadn't dared to hope for.

Yes, Charles played his part flawlessly. I didn't see the man behind the illusion he created, not then. Not in that soft glow of overhead lights and filtered sky. He was composed, articulate, entirely self-contained. The very picture of an older, cultivated gentleman extending a hand of quiet generosity to a younger woman adrift.

He wore the mask well. So well that I didn't think to look beneath it. But that would come later. When it was already far too late.

18

By the time we touched down at Cardiff Airport, the sky had surrendered to a blanket of grey, low and heavy, pressing down on the terminal roof like a warning I didn't heed. Outside, the rain came in sheets: fine, relentless, and the runway shimmered under it, slick and silvered, reflecting the ghostly glow of the landing lights.

Charles didn't seem fazed. Not in the slightest. He moved with his usual quiet purpose, steering us through arrivals without fuss or fanfare, as though he'd rehearsed it all in advance. We didn't queue for taxis. We didn't look for trains. He led me directly to his car: a black Mercedes parked neatly in the long-stay, polished to a mirror shine despite the rain. The kind of car you didn't own unless you lived a very particular kind of life.

He unlocked the doors, the soft glow of the interior lighting spilling out across the wet tarmac like an invitation. And I got in. Just like that. A moth to the flame. We were both travelling to Carmarthen. So, why wouldn't I get in?

The leather inside was soft and cold to the touch, the air scented faintly with cedar and something more clinical beneath, maybe polish, maybe something he used to keep things just so. Chemical. A smell I couldn't place.

The cabin felt sealed off from the world, insulated, designed for comfort. He didn't speak as he started the powerful engine, didn't ask if I was warm enough or if I wanted music. He simply eased the car out of the space with that same composed assurance I'd come to recognise: every movement unhurried, in control.

The M4 unfurled in front of us, slick with rain, the tyres sounding softly beneath us. The world outside the windows blurred into shadows and fog. I stared out, watching Wales slip past in silence, my thoughts scattered like leaves in the wind.

My relationship with Joe was gone. Our villa and the love I'd thought we shared already felt like a memory someone else had lived. And there I was, being driven home by a man who, only days earlier, had been a complete stranger to me. A man who made me feel, somehow, listened to. So much had changed in such a short time. And, as unlikely as it seemed, I really did think I'd made a new friend.

The silhouette of Port Talbot's steelworks loomed into view around the midpoint of our journey to Carmarthen: a sprawl of shadow and smoke, its skeletal towers lit by the orange flicker of industrial flame. The air thickened with the scent of something acrid, clinging to the back of the throat. For a while, we said nothing, just listened to the low hum of the engine.

Then, without turning his head, Charles spoke. His voice cut through the stillness: calm, as controlled as ever, playing his next card.

'I truly meant what I said earlier,' he said, eyes fixed on the road ahead. 'You really should see your paintings. They live differently in the house. More fully, I think. Like they finally belong somewhere. Truly wonderful.'

I turned to him, his face faintly lit by the dash. Serene. Still.

'Um, yes, I'd like that.'

He beamed. 'You'll come?'

I said I'd love to. And I meant every word, not giving it nearly as much thought as I should have. Already caught in his spider's web. Blind to the danger.

'Ah, that is excellent news, Olivia. Come on Saturday. I'll drive over to collect you at about seven. Save you the potential hassle of finding a taxi at that time of the evening. The least I can do. I'll see if my daughter can make it too, I think you'd get on.'

I hesitated, but only briefly. I had no other plans.

'Yes, great,' I said. 'I'll look forward to it. Should I bring anything?'

He gave a little laugh. 'Just yourself. That will suffice very nicely. We'll have a bite to eat and a glass or two of vino before the big reveal.'

And just like that, it was agreed. The rest of the journey passed quickly, the car a cocoon of air-conditioned warmth and soft seating, the outside world kept at a polite distance.

By the time we reached Carmarthen, the town lay shrouded in mist: a low, clinging veil that softened the edges of buildings. The rain had eased to a fine drizzle, enough to make the roads and pavements glisten, slick and dark like spilt ink. The narrow streets were mostly quiet, save for the parked cars and the occasional passer-by.

The old market town didn't have the bright, effortless charm of Lanzarote: the sun-washed villas, the dry heat clinging to your skin, the illusion of escape. No palm trees or sea breeze. Just damp stone, cold air, and a kind of quiet familiarity that settled in the bones. But for all that, I was glad to be back.

It wasn't paradise. It wasn't even particularly beautiful. Not in winter. But it was mine. Familiar in its imperfections. Steady in a way the island never could be. And in that moment, beneath the soft flicker of the street-lamps and the weight of the night, it felt like home. Not because it welcomed me with open arms. But because it expected nothing at all.

Charles turned into King Street with unhurried precision, guiding the Mercedes through the familiar road as though he'd driven it a hundred times before. He passed the old town library without hesitation, its darkened windows and impressive façade barely warranting a glance. And moments later, the car rolled to a smooth stop outside my bedsit, the engine purring into silence as if on command.

'Here we are,' he said softly. 'Back safe and sound. You've had a difficult few days. Get some rest. And I'll see you again on Saturday, as planned. I hope you're looking forward to it as much as I am.'

There was no pressure in his voice. No suggestion. Just that same calm warmth. That same careful tone.

'Thank you,' I said, barely above a whisper.

I stepped out into the cold, pulling my coat tighter around me, my boots splashing gently through shallow puddles. The car door closed behind me. I asked for his mobile number as he retrieved my bag from the back, but he gave a little laugh.

'I don't have one. Technology unsettles me. I haven't yet fully embraced the modern world. But that won't stop me keeping in touch. You can be sure of that.'

I thought his response unusual. Strange even. I briefly wondered how he'd booked his flight. But I pushed it from my mind. And then he was gone, the tail-lights of the Mercedes disappearing slowly down the street.

Inside, the bedsit was exactly as I'd left it. Still. Dim. Slightly stale, like a room that had forgotten how to be lived in. I dropped my case in the small hallway and stood for a long moment, listening to the silence press in from the walls.

I should've felt safe. The walls were familiar. The furniture untouched. Every chipped skirting board and faded light switch exactly as I'd left it. I should've felt like I was home. But I didn't.

Instead, I felt adrift, displaced. As if some part of me had been shed on that island, left behind in the sun-scorched dust and volcanic peaks. Or worse: dragged something back with me. Something I couldn't quite name. A weight. A whisper. A shadow that hadn't been there before.

Life had shifted again: another strange, unexpected turn in a long line of them. A pattern I knew far too well. Change that came without warning. Consequence without explanation.

And not for the first time, I found myself grasping at the edges of my own emotions, trying to shape them into something I could understand. But they slipped through my fingers, just out of reach. Joe was the past. I had a new future now. And I had no idea of what that held.

Later that night, long after I'd returned to the flat and the lights were dimmed, I scrolled absently through the news on my phone, chasing distraction more than information. And that was when I saw it. A nineteen-year-old sex worker had been murdered in Arrecife while I'd been on the island. While I'd been sipping wine under the Canarian sun. Torn apart in what the article described as a frenzied knife attack. No motive. No suspect. Just blood in the alleyway behind a bar and a photograph blurred at the edges, her name withheld pending family notification.

I stared at the screen far too long, the glow of it burning into my eyes. A shiver crawled up my spine.

Whatever grief I'd been nursing, whatever heartbreak or betrayal I'd thought I was entitled to, it all felt grotesquely small in that moment. Petty. Self-indulgent. She was just nineteen. Brutalised. Erased.

And I had been there. Breathing the same air. Existing parallel to her final moments without even knowing it.

I shut the phone off and placed it face down on the bedside table. My hands were trembling.

No more late-night headlines, I told myself. No more looking for pain in places I had no power to change. What good did it do? What comfort did it bring? Better to focus on the good. The beautiful. The safe.

Or at the very least, pretend it was still possible to believe in such things in a world so wracked with woe.

19

Charles arrived precisely on time the following Saturday evening. Not a minute early. Not a second late. The Mercedes was parked outside my bedsit like something alive, the headlights slicing through the dimming evening light, catching on the wet pavement. I watched from the bedsit window for a moment longer than I meant to, the keys clenched in my palm, breath held. And then I stepped outside.

Charles greeted me with a polite smile and a manicured hand. Always immaculate. Always in control. He opened the front passenger door and waited for me to settle before closing it with a gentle click, like sealing something into place.

The drive was quiet. The sort of silence that isn't accidental. The sort that carries weight. The sort that doesn't invite conversation.

He took a turning I didn't recognise, the road narrowing as we moved further into the countryside. Fields pressed close on either side, the hedgerows tall and wild, the sky above bruised with the light of the moon. Then, without warning, he indicated left and turned between a pair of high iron gates, which opened at the slow crawl of a motorised system, creaking apart as though reluctant to allow anyone in.

We followed a long gravel driveway, winding behind a dense row of trees, until the house finally revealed itself, tall, Georgian, commanding.

The windows stared out like empty eyes. The gravel crunched under the tyres as we moved to the back of the property, past what looked like acres of grounds. A conservatory jutted from one side of the house, choked with ivy, its glass streaked with grime.

He parked behind the building, near a side entrance.

'Less formal,' he said, smiling. 'And warmer. The front of the house tends to be a little draughty. Whatever the time of year. My daughter couldn't make it, I'm afraid. She has other commitments. Another time.'

I didn't suspect for a single second that she didn't exist. Not then.

'Oh, that's a shame.'

Inside, the air hit me like a slap, thick and sour, clinging to the back of my throat. It smelled like decay, masked badly by something chemical. Disinfectant, maybe. Bleach. Too much of it. Or not enough.

Charles paused in the hallway and turned, his expression apologetic but composed.

'I must apologise,' he said. 'There's a problem with the drains. It all happened while we were away. Awful timing. I've had someone out to look, but, well, you know how these old houses are. It's going to be a few more days before it's sorted out.'

I nodded, though my stomach had begun to turn. He led me through to a high-ceilinged dining room where the lights were dimmed low. The table was laid. Two settings. Polished cutlery, the finest white porcelain plates, and two tall silver candlesticks. A bottle of red wine already breathing. I recall thinking there was something strangely dramatic about it all. As if the meal were part of a performance I hadn't agreed to join.

We ate in near silence, seated opposite one another at a long dark mahogany table polished to a dull sheen. Candlelight flickered between us, casting distorted shadows on the walls, the flames guttering in the draught that moved through the old house like a breath held too long.

Or rather, he ate. I pushed food around my plate, my appetite swallowed by uncertainty. The meat was dark, dense, unfamiliar. Its surface glossed with a thick red sauce that bled into the potatoes like congealed blood. The smell was rich, sweet, wrong somehow. I took a bite, then set my fork down and reached for my empty glass instead, thinking alcohol might help me relax and oil the conversational wheels.

Charles poured the wine with loving care, the bottle held steady in his hands. The ruby liquid coiled into the glass like blood drawn in silk, graceful, controlled. He filled my glass first, then his own, eyes never once leaving my face. There was an intensity in his stare now that hadn't been there before. Something sharpened. Focused.

His gaze was no longer the quiet curiosity of an admirer. It was fixed. Unblinking. Possessive. Like I was no longer a guest, but something more.

A flicker of doubt crept into my chest, cold and unwelcome. A quiet voice urging me to be cautious, to leave, to make an excuse and go. He seemed different somehow, more watchful, more calculating than when I'd first met him. The easy charm had thinned, replaced by something harder beneath the surface. Something I couldn't quite name. And I asked myself if I'd made a mistake in being there at all.

The silence pressed in, tight, until he broke it, his voice softening.

'Art isn't only about technique,' he said, leaning back as though lecturing some invisible class. 'It's about truth. About letting the canvas hold what words can't. Composition, brushstroke, colour, they're nothing without honesty.'

I nodded, though my chest still felt tight.

'When I look at your work,' he went on, blue eyes bright now, 'I see emotion stripped bare. Pain. Beauty. Fragility. That's what I respond to, not perfection. You've given something real, Olivia. Something primal.'

And for a moment, the unease loosened its grip. I let myself believe him. Told myself I was imagining things. Overreacting. That I was simply tired, unsettled by everything that had happened in recent days.

I took a sip of the wine, warm and unfamiliar on my tongue. And told myself that maybe, just maybe, I was worrying about nothing. Charles spoke only occasionally, soft sentences threaded through the silence like brushstrokes on a canvas. He talked about my art as he had before, describing my work with a kind of respect that felt almost religious, like he was reciting scripture rather than offering opinion.

'There's something rare in what you do,' he said, his voice barely more than a whisper, as if speaking the words too loudly might break the spell. 'As if you paint straight from the wound, without filter, without fear, without shame.'

He leaned back again, the candlelight catching the sharp lines of his face, dancing in his eyes.

'I admire that,' he continued. 'Truly. Most people spend their lives hiding from themselves. But you... you put it all out there. Every fracture. Every shadow. It's wonderful, Olivia. So very special.'

He paused and the room seemed to contract around us.

'I can relate to that kind of brutal honesty. More than you know. And that's why' – he tilted his head, his tone now edged with something darker – 'that's why I believe you're the one person who'll be able to properly appreciate what I've done here. I am an artist like you. Although, I work with a very different medium.'

His words hung in the room. And somewhere deep inside me, something began to twist. I offered a faint smile. Or tried to. The wine burned slightly at the back of my throat as my head began to ache. And looking around the room, really looking, I noticed the details I'd missed at first: the closed shutters, the absence of any visible clocks. Just us. Just him. And the old house, listening. Something shifted inside me then. A tightening. But I kept smiling. And sipped the wine again.

Looking back, I don't think Charles touched his drink. Not even once. He raised his crystal glass to his mouth a few times but didn't even sip. But I drank to soften the unease. And soon my limbs began to feel heavier, as if the world had slowed by half a step. The wine had a strange taste. Sharp at the back of the tongue. I told myself it was the vintage. My lack of sleep. Nothing more. But I really couldn't have been more wrong.

Charles rose slowly from his chair after we'd been seated for about twenty minutes or so, eyes dark and fixed. There was an intensity in his stare that made my skin prickle. It wasn't just that he was looking at me. It was as if he was searching me. Reaching past my expression and peeling back the layers beneath. As if he could read every thought I hadn't spoken aloud.

His voice, when it came, was respectful, almost hushed, as though he were sharing a sacred truth.

'There's something rather wonderful I have to show you,' he said. 'The real reason I brought you here. The paintings, your paintings. You deserve to see how they breathe in this space. How I've paired them... with my own creation. It's a series I've been working on for some time now. Waiting for the right person to share my vision. And I believe that person is you.'

He moved in closer, too quickly, closing the space between us before I had a chance to move. His presence pressed against me like a wall, suffocating. I could see it now, the shift in his expression. The mask slipping. There was a wildness in his eyes that hadn't been there before. Something unhinged. Like the dam inside him had cracked and the truth was beginning to seep through.

And he kept talking. Faster now. His voice rising with a manic energy that made my skin crawl.

'I feel sure you're going to love my creation as much as I do,' he said, the words tumbling out in a breathless rush. 'You will love it. You're not like the others. You're the one person I can trust. I knew it the very first time I saw you, your eyes, your work, the way you see things. I knew. I really did.'

He stroked my face, his fingers lingering, his mouth close to my ear now. I froze, trembling as he continued.

'And soon, very soon, you'll understand. We're kindred spirits, you and I. Destined to meet. Destined to explore the limits of human behaviour... together. Without guilt. Without shame. Without restraint.'

He paused, just long enough for the silence to thicken, then smiled, a slow, joyless thing. 'You'll see. Soon you'll know it too.'

And in that moment, I knew with chilling certainty... he believed every word.

My mouth was dry. I nodded, slowly, unsure why. My limbs felt even heavier now, disconnected, as though I were moving through water. My legs trembled, struggling to bear the weight of my body when I stood. I couldn't make sense of it. None of it felt real. Not the room. Not the flickering light. Not the man standing inches from me with that terrible, searching smile. It was like being trapped in a dream. One of those dreams that starts in soft focus... and ends in a scream.

Charles took my arm, his grip firm beneath the courtesy as the room began to blur, going in and out of focus as I fought to stay awake.

He led me through a wide corridor lined with framed sketches and photographs I didn't look at too closely. My legs felt like they weren't fully mine, one step lagging behind the other, as if my body were beginning to betray me.

Then he opened a door and guided me into the room. His art room. It was bigger than I expected, more gallery than studio. High walls, track lighting, polished wooden floors. My paintings hung in calculated positions, perfectly lit, perfectly spaced. They looked different here. Bleak. Bitter. As though the house itself had changed their tone.

'Beautiful, aren't they?' he said quietly, his voice behind me now. 'There's such depth in your work. Something that reminds me of death.'

I turned to him, but again my vision swam slightly. The floor seemed to tip, just for a second, before righting itself. He paused, resting a hand lightly on my shoulder.

'I've waited a very long time to share my work,' he whispered, his breath brushing the side of my face like something cold and intimate. 'Not with just anyone. That would be pointless. No, I needed someone... exceptional. Someone unburdened by the chains of conventional morality. Someone not shackled to society's tired, hypocritical codes.'

He paused, his look fixed, unblinking. The air between us felt thick, stagnant.

'And you, my dear....' he murmured, his voice low and reverent, almost trembling with conviction. 'You are that special person. The one I've been waiting for so very long. I saw it in your work long before you ever saw it in yourself. It spoke to me, as if you were already reaching out without even knowing it.'

Charles took a step closer, his eyes never leaving mine.

'I've been watching you, Olivia. For quite some time. Since before Lanzarote, of course. Waiting. Studying. I needed to be sure. Needed to know you'd grown into what I always sensed you would become. And now... now the time is finally right.'

He smiled then, manic, calculated, the kind of smile that was colder than the grave.

'Think of me as your mentor. Your guide. Your master. Your God. I will show you beauty as it's meant to be seen, stripped of lies, unspoiled by the dull conventions of the world outside. You'll see what others can't. What they refuse to see.' His voice dropped to a whisper, his tone almost tender. 'And I know, Olivia... I know you'll understand.'

There wasn't a single flicker of doubt in his voice. Just calm conviction. That quiet, terrifying certainty that only the truly deranged possess. And it hit me then: he was mad. Not eccentric or unorthodox, but utterly detached from reality. Delusional. Dangerous. And that, more than anything, made my blood run cold.

The smell worsened as he led me further into the room, a rancid, putrid stench. Rot layered with chemicals. Death trying to wear a mask.

It rolled over me in waves, and I gagged, once, then again, harder, my stomach turning itself inside out. But he didn't so much as flinch. Didn't acknowledge the smell or my reaction to it. As if it were nothing. As if it were normal.

His grip tightened on my arm, fingers digging into my skin with unnatural strength. Not angry. Not rushed. Just purposeful.

I stumbled, my legs sluggish and uncooperative, but he held me upright. Steered me forward. One relentless step at a time. Like a man guiding his prized guest to witness something sacred. Something final.

'The time has finally come,' he said with a grin. 'The centrepiece. My big reveal, if you like. The culmination of all that has gone before. I cannot wait a second longer before sharing my creation with you.'

He guided me towards the far corner of the room, where a red velvet curtain hung from a curved rail, concealing a recessed alcove. It looked like something out of a theatre. Out of a dream. Or a nightmare.

Then, suddenly, he drew back the curtain. And the breath caught in my throat. At first, my mind recoiled, refusing to make sense of what my eyes were seeing. The scene before me fractured into fragments, disjointed, surreal, like something half-remembered from a fevered dream. A grotesque tableau, frozen in time.

The young woman was seated against the far wall, legs splayed unnaturally, her spine bowed like a marionette abandoned mid-performance. Her head lolled to one side, chin sunk to her collarbone, as if it no longer had the strength, or the will, to stay upright. Blonde hair, once brushed and cared for, now hung in matted clumps around her shoulders, darkened by time and rot. It clung to the greying hollows of her face.

Her skin was collapsing in on itself, papery, puckered, stretched too tightly over bone. The colour had long since drained away, leaving behind a mottled, waxy pallor that spoke of death not hours ago, but longer. Her mouth was parted slightly, lips cracked and shrivelled, as though she had died mid-sentence. Or mid-scream.

Her eyes were the worst. Fixed, glassy. Staring out into the middle distance, lifeless, unseeing, and yet full of something far more terrible than pain.

A silk dress clung to her frame, its once-delicate fabric now stiff with decay. Stains bloomed across the bodice and hem, rust coloured, black at the edges, like the ghost of a wound too deep to heal.

Flies circled in slow, lazy orbits. Some rested on her cheeks, others on the folds of her dress. Unbothered. As if they, too, belonged there.

And in that moment, every part of me screamed to run. To get out of there. To escape. To summon help before it was too late. But my body wouldn't move. I stumbled back, hand clamped to my mouth, bile rising thick and bitter at the back of my throat. My legs buckled under me, useless and trembling, and I crumpled to the cold wooden floor. The impact barely registered. Shock numbed everything. My chest heaved, a dry, shuddering sob forcing its way up from somewhere deep inside.

But Charles didn't move. Didn't flinch. Didn't so much as blink. He simply stood there, watching me with quiet detachment, head tilted slightly, eyes filled not with alarm or remorse, but curiosity. As though he were studying the results of an experiment. Gauging my reaction. Assessing how the subject responded to the reveal.

His voice followed a moment later. Chilling in its restraint. The same tone he'd used to describe brushwork and canvas technique. As if the decaying body in the alcove was no more shocking than a still life. No more offensive than a poorly framed print.

'She was a prostitute from Birmingham,' he said, his voice low and disturbingly calm, almost reflective, as though recalling an old painting or a half-finished composition. 'A tart. A whore. Not as beautiful as you, of course. No... she lacked your nuance, your complexity. But still, there was something about her. A kind of bruised fragility. A rawness she couldn't hide, no matter how hard she tried.'

He took a step closer, his eyes gleaming in the low light, his tone darkening as he reached down to touch the corpse, stroking her blood-matted hair.

'There was a truth in her... a terrible, broken veracity that most people would turn away from. But I saw it. I see those things. That's the difference. And I know you see it, too.'

He paused. Just long enough for the words to settle like poison in the air. Then he gestured towards the rotting figure slumped against the wall.

'Look at her, Olivia,' he murmured, almost tenderly. 'Really look. And think on what I've achieved.'

His voice was calm, respectful, like a man describing a masterpiece, his masterpiece.

'She was nothing. A cast-off. A hollow shell barely clinging to the margins of a city that never gave a damn whether she lived or died. One of society's lost ones, used, dismissed, erased.'

He tilted his head, studying the corpse with a kind of fondness that made my stomach twist, as he reached down again, touching her.

'But in death... through me... she became something more. Something fixed. Eternal. A moment caught in time, beyond shame, beyond noise. She was worthless in life. A ghost. But now, now she's whole. Finally made complete in death.'

His eyes flicked back to mine. Steady. Pleased. As if what he'd done wasn't horrifying, but holy. As if what he'd just said was beautiful. As if it was art.

My heart pounded like a war drum, thundering against my ribs, but my limbs lagged behind, numb, leaden, as though my body no longer belonged to me. The air thickened, pressing down on my chest like water, each breath shallow, laboured. The edges of the room blurred again, colours bleeding into one another, shapes dissolving as the walls seemed to lean in.

I opened my mouth as if to speak, anything, scream, but no sound came. My throat was tight. Frozen. My mind yelled run, but my body betrayed me, locked beneath the weight of fear and whatever drug had been laced in the wine.

Charles didn't move. Just watched. That faint, terrible smile curling at the edges of his mouth, like an artist stepping back to admire his finished work.

As if that moment, my terror, my paralysis, was part of the exhibition. Part of the performance he'd so carefully staged. Then everything fractured. Sound receded. And the darkness rushed in, cold, absolute, as the world blinked out and I slipped into unconsciousness.

20

I surfaced slowly, dragged from insensibility like something hauled from deep water, gasping, disoriented, every inch of me aching.

My head throbbed with a low, sickening pulse, the pain blooming behind my eyes and crawling down the back of my neck. A metallic taste coated my tongue. My limbs were heavy. Wrong. And the air was thick with that stench so vile it curled my stomach, a rancid blend of decay and damp, seeping into my skin, into my hair, into every breath I drew.

For a moment, I told myself it was a dream. A nightmare conjured from too much wine, too little sleep, and far too much trust in the wrong man. That was the only thing that made sense. Because no reality – no reality – could possibly be like this.

But then I opened my eyes. And the truth came crashing down. I was lying on a cold wooden floor, the grain splintered beneath my skin, sticky in places I didn't dare investigate. The light was dim and yellowed, casting shadows that moved when I did. The room was the same one he'd shown me before, the so-called gallery. The shrine. Only now it felt different. Bigger. Rotting from the inside.

And she was still there. The girl. The corpse. Still seated in the corner, just feet away, her head tilted at that same unnatural angle, her mouth slightly open in eternal terror. A fly crawled across her cheek and disappeared into the mess of her hair.

I recoiled with a strangled sound, half gasp, half sob, and instinctively reached for my phone, my pockets, anything. But there was nothing. Because there were no clothes. No protection. No dignity.

Just my naked body, sprawled on the floor, exposed and cold.

My arms moved awkwardly, pulled by a resistance I hadn't noticed at first. I tried to sit up but found I couldn't straighten fully. My wrists burned. And so did my ankles.

I looked down. Thick steel restraints fastened tight around each limb, raw skin bulging against the edges. Shackles. One at each wrist. One at each ankle. Anchored to heavy chains, bolted into the wall like something medieval. Something obscene.

Panic rose hard and fast, tearing through my throat. My breath came in ragged gasps. My heart slammed against my ribs. This wasn't a nightmare. It was real.

And I was trapped.

Terror hit me like a wave, cold and suffocating, crashing down before I had the breath to brace for it. I twisted hard against the restraints, muscles straining, wrists screaming, ankles scraping against the iron rings that held me in place. The chains clinked with a sickening finality. Solid. Unmoving. Unforgiving. No slack. No give. No hope.

A sob broke from my throat, raw, jagged.

And then another. I wasn't just restrained. I was displayed. Positioned. Laid out like an exhibit in some monstrous installation, forced to share space with the corpse Charles had so proudly unveiled, as though her presence might keep me company. As if this was where I belonged.

My pulse roared in my ears, drowning out everything but the sound of my own fear. I glanced again towards the far corner, towards her, and bile surged hot in my throat. The rot had deepened since before. Or maybe now, in this helpless state, I was simply unable to ignore it. The smell was thick, clinging, inescapable. It filled my nose. Settled in my chest like damp cotton.

I turned my face away, eyes stinging. But even in the dim light with shutters closed, the image stayed burned behind my lids. Her skin. Her eyes. The silence that wrapped around her. And I knew, truly knew, that if I didn't find a way out, I'd end up like her. A trophy. A statement. A thing.

The panic came again in waves, each one harder than the last, ripping through me with jagged edges. I pulled until my shoulders burned, until skin tore, until I cried out without caring if he heard.

Let him hear. Because this wasn't art. It was a prison. And I was already starting to disappear inside it.

21

I don't know how much time passed before he returned. The sound came first, soft footfalls across aged timber, slow and regular. I froze, every muscle pulled taut, my breath caught in my throat. The door creaked open with exaggerated care, and there he was, backlit by the low hallway light, framed like the final stroke in a grim oil painting.

Charles. Calm. Composed. Immaculate. Dressed in a stylish navy-blue suit. As if nothing at all had changed. As if I weren't naked and shackled beside a rotting corpse.

He stepped into the room with a measured grace, closing the door behind him with a soft click, as though we were about to resume a private conversation rather than continue a living hell.

'I regret your distress, Olivia,' he said smoothly, setting down a metal bucket and a plastic bottle of water beside me, as though performing an act of kindness. 'Truly I do. But the restraints are necessary. At least until I'm certain. If I didn't believe, truly believe, that you might well be my soulmate... you'd have been dead long before now. No hesitation. And no remorse.'

He crouched beside me then, close enough for me to smell his cologne: woody, dry, like old books and faded privilege. The scent made my stomach turn.

'You may have gathered from our conversation last night,' he said, his tone soft, almost tender, like a father offering comfort before delivering a punishment, 'that I need more than words. I need certainty. Absolute certainty. Nothing less is acceptable.'

He placed his face only inches from mine.

'You see, it's not enough to simply claim understanding. Anyone can parrot ideas about truth and beauty. About seeing the world as it really is. But most people... they lie. To themselves, most of all.'

He paused, the corners of his mouth twitching into something resembling a smile.

'That's why all this is necessary. Think of it as... an evaluation. A trial period. A sort of probationary partnership. You're not a prisoner, Olivia. Not really. You're a candidate. And this' – he gestured to the restraints, the bucket, the rotting girl in the corner – 'this is your examination.' His eyes narrowed, voice dipping to a near whisper. 'And you need to pass.'

He pointed towards the body again with the calm precision of a man unveiling a painting in a gallery, proud, composed, utterly without shame.

'You don't want to end up like her,' he said quietly. 'She disappointed me. Deeply. Such a limited creature. Couldn't appreciate my genius at all.'

A pause. His eyes lingered on the lifeless form, as though still expecting something from it.

'And so she had to suffer. Terribly, I'm afraid. Because that's what failure brings. Consequence. Correction. She earned her pain. Invited it. Every moment of it was hers to own. Her fault. All her fault.'

He turned back to me slowly, the faintest trace of a frown changing the contours of his face.

'I'm sure you can appreciate that... Yes?'

I flinched. Then nodded, thinking I had to.

And he smirked before continuing, 'So until I'm sure, until you prove yourself worthy, you'll remain here. Safe. Observed. Prepared.'

He picked up the bucket and set it down with a metallic thud just inches from my feet. 'This is for when nature calls,' he said, almost cheerfully. 'And the water, of course, to keep you hydrated. I take your wellbeing seriously. Believe that. I'm not a monster. I simply require... honesty. Alignment. You'll see that, given time.'

I stared at him, bile thick in my throat, trembling so hard my teeth chattered.

'Please,' I whispered, voice cracking. 'Please, let me go. I won't tell anyone. I won't say a word. Just let me go...'

Something in his face shifted, only slightly, but enough to chill the blood in my veins. The smile faded. His eyes narrowed. And then, still crouched, his voice dropped to a whisper, low and menacing.

'Ask me that again,' he said, 'and the consequences will be final. Do you understand me? Final. I won't tolerate weakness. Not now. Not after all we've shared. Not when we've come this far. This is your home now. The place you truly belong.'

I recoiled instinctively, pressing myself against the floorboards, the restraints digging cruelly into raw skin.

'Can I... can I please have my clothes?' I asked, barely daring to breathe.

He tilted his head. Considered me.

'Clothes are a barrier,' he said softly. 'They're gone. Used for a better purpose.'

I screwed up my face. Confused. But fearful of asking more.

Then he rose, brushing invisible dust from the crease of his trousers with meticulous care. His gaze settled on me, cold and appraising, like a sculptor studying a block of stone he'd only half carved, calculating where to cut next, what to chip away, what to destroy to reach the shape he desired.

'Think carefully, Olivia,' he said, his voice smooth, almost kind. 'Think deeply. I know what you are. But I need you to know it too. I'll give you a month to prove yourself. Any reasonable person would consider that generous. And I don't want you wasting your energy hoping someone's coming for you. No one ever is.'

He laughed then, gleeful, brimming with self-satisfaction.

'I left your coat, your trainers, and your mobile on the Pembrokeshire coastal path,' he said quietly, with obvious pride. 'Somewhere between Marloes Sands and St Ann's Head. Early hours while you slept. No one around. Just the wind, the dark... and the sea.'

He gave a small, satisfied nod, a man pleased with a job well executed.

'It took me an hour or so to get there. A drive west. Then a short hike through the heather and rock. But it was well worth it. Every step. It's a dramatic spot, windswept, desolate. Cliffs that drop clean into the churn of the water below. Rugged. Beautiful.'

A pause.

'The kind of place where it's easy to believe someone might have lost their footing. Or their will to live.'

He laughed again, head back, throat bobbing.

'I also left a printed note wrapped in plastic. No fingerprints, of course, that wouldn't do at all. It says the split with Joe was too much for you. That the future looked bleak. That you couldn't carry on. It was very moving in its own way. Very believable. Even included a few artistic references. Touching, when you think about it. The story tells itself, Olivia. And it's a convincing one. I have no doubt the moronic, interfering authorities will believe you are lost to the waves.'

He rose to his full height again, smoothing the sleeve of his jacket, as though discussing the weather.

'Genius doesn't ask for permission, Olivia,' he said, his voice low and measured. 'It doesn't apologise. It doesn't explain. It simply is. Uncompromising. Absolute. I'm nothing if not meticulous. Every action I take is methodical. Every moment, calculated. I've planned this, all of it, with military precision. Every step mapped out. Every variable accounted for.'

He waited, watching me as if daring me to contradict him. But I didn't utter a sound.

'I've made mistakes before,' he said, his tone almost contemplative, as if sifting through old memories best left undisturbed. 'I'll admit to that much. Painful errors. Lessons etched in blood and silence. But I learned. I watched. I evolved.'

He paused again, eyes gleaming with quiet conviction.

'That's what men of exceptional quality do. We adapt. We refine. We perfect. Superior individuals, those rare few perched at the very top of the evolutionary ladder, we don't stagnate. We overcome. And in doing so, we rise above the rest.'

He smiled then. Cold. Certain. Unshakeable. The widest yet. And his eyes glistened with a fanatic's certainty.

'That's what sets me apart,' he said, as though confiding a sacred truth. 'I'm not like those I kill. I'm better. Smarter. Their lives, what little they are, exist only in relation to mine. Their purpose begins and ends with what they can give me. My needs matter more. My vision, my work, it outweighs their right to existence a hundred times over. They breathe, they suffer, they die, for me. And in doing so, they become something they never could have been on their own – useful.'

His voice hardened then as I avoided his stare.

'So, no more mistakes. Not now. Not ever again.' His voice tightened, as if the words were carved from something harder than resolve. 'The world doesn't understand people like us. It never has.'

He paused, his eyes drifting to some distant memory only he could see. 'Alexander Aitken told me that before he fled the country. A good friend. A murderous inspiration. A man I admired more than I ever admitted. He saw the truth long before the rest of us, saw how unforgiving reality can be.'

He glanced around the room then, a slow, reverent sweep of his gaze. 'I bought this house from him before he left the country. This place steeped in history and in death. A place he understood, and now I do too.

'Ten years,' he said, almost wistfully, as if recalling a long-forgotten exile. 'That's how long they kept him caged, buried behind locked doors and reinforced glass. A secure hospital, they called it. But it was a prison in all but name. Filled with slack-jawed orderlies and muttering lunatics who pissed themselves in corridors. And the doctors... pathetic.'

Charles shook his head slowly, a smirk tugging at the corners of his mouth.

'Grey-faced men and women with clipboards and degrees they thought made them superior. Thought they could understand him. Thought they could fix what they couldn't even comprehend with their limited minds. But they didn't. Not one of them. They didn't even come close.'

Charles stepped closer, his voice dropping to a conspiratorial whisper, as though sharing a joke only he found funny.

'He gave the gullible fools what they needed. Told them he was sorry. That he understood. That he'd seen the error of his ways. He recited their psychobabble back at them like scripture, until they nodded and smiled and scribbled their little notes in the margins of his file. And he convinced them. One session at a time. Made them believe their ridiculous treatment plan had reformed him. That he was rehabilitated. Rewired. No longer a danger to society.'

He giggled then. Quietly.

'And they bought it. The fools. Every single word. They set him free.'

He grinned. Wide. Empty.

'But he never changed. He just got better at pretending. That's his brilliance. His triumph.'

He took a long breath, measured, slow.

'And when he got out... when he was free... he taught me all I need to know. Avoiding the mistakes he made. I have no intention of ever getting caught. Do you understand me, Olivia? Ever. There is so much more left for me to achieve.'

He stalled, just for a second, his expression clouded with something close to reflection. And when he spoke again, his voice was calm. Each word delivered with clinical precision, sharpened like a scalpel designed to cut straight through the bone.

'I always hunt far from home. The cities of the North of England. The backstreets of the Midlands. Red light districts. Places where no one looks too closely. Where lives slip through the cracks without notice.'

He was more animated now, his eyes alive with a feverish light.

'Never local. Never Wales. Too predictable. Too risky. And that's how I stay ahead. That's how I endure. Something of an inconvenience given the distances involved. But well worth the additional effort. Being caught was never a part of the plan. You are the one exception to that rule. Because you're special. I hope you can fully appreciate that.'

And then, without warning, Charles danced. A crazy little jig, brief, erratic, twirling in places like a child in the grip of some private, manic delight. His shoes scuffed against the floorboards, arms loosely outstretched, fingers twitching with barely contained energy. It was absurd. Horrifying. A moment torn straight from a nightmare dressed up in theatre.

When he stopped, breathless, his chest rose and fell with shallow pants. He turned his head towards me, face flushed, eyes gleaming with something wild.

And when he spoke next, his voice sounded almost intimate, tinged with exertion and a sickening sense of joy.

'And soon, you'll join me. In the pursuit. In the work. Together, we'll seek them out, the weak, the broken, the unwanted. Victims, ripe for dissection. To study. To break. To bleed.'

His breath was warm against my skin as he kissed my cheek, but the words were ice.

'And from their suffering, we'll craft something greater than death. Masterpieces, Olivia. Composed in pain. Shaped in blood. And signed in flesh. Art... in its truest form.'

He stood statue-like, and for a heartbeat, there was nothing but the soft rattle of the chain at my wrist as I instinctively shrank back.

'So don't ever ask to leave again,' he said, voice hardening around the edges. 'Don't plead. And don't you ever beg. For now, your survival depends on obedience. So keep your mouth shut until you learn to adapt. Until you prove you're worthy of the trust I've extended.'

He looked me in the eye, levelling his gaze with mine, his tone softening into something almost fatherly. 'You're not a victim, Olivia. Not some pathetic creature waiting for the knife. That's not who you are, not yet. Not if you're The One. But if you fail to meet my expectations... if you let me down...'

A pause. Long. Heavy.

'It wouldn't end well for you. I can promise you that much. Think of compliance as a commandment. Carve it in tablets of stone.'

He turned away then, walking slowly to the door, pausing with his hand on the frame.

'Make the right impression,' he said, 'or you'll vanish. Quietly. Cleanly. Without a trace. Just like the others.'

A pause. His gaze lingered, full of quiet calculation.

'But if you perform, if you meet my expectations, rise to the occasion, we have a future. A glorious one. Side by side. As partners. As pioneers. Think on that, won't you? Let it settle while the hours pass. Let it bloom.'

He ran a hand through his hair like a man preparing for a dinner party, then glanced towards the far corner of the room again, towards her.

'After a bit of lunch,' he added casually, 'I'll have a task for you. Your first practical test. Something simple... but necessary.'

His expression stretched. Cold. Perverse.

'Disposal of my guest's corpse. She's a little overripe now, even for me.'

He turned the door handle, his voice lilting, as if making a joke between friends.

'Dismemberment is always a somewhat demanding task. I'm invariably exhausted by its end. It's over to you now. And we'll have a bit of fun along the way.'

22

Charles returned after what I can only guess was a couple of hours, though truthfully, it could've been more. Or less. There was day, and there was night, but beyond that, time had unravelled. It no longer ticked in minutes or hours, but in the slow drip of dread and the rhythm of my own uneven breath. I existed in limbo, trapped between moments, suspended in a silence that stretched and snapped like wire pulled too tight.

When the door creaked open and his shadow spilled across the floor once more, I couldn't tell if it had been hours... or a lifetime.

Charles entered the room with a typical flourish, a jaunty skip in his step, as though arriving at a garden party rather than stepping into a room steeped in rot and ruin. He beamed, broadly, unnervingly, the kind of smile a man wears when delivering good news, or a eulogy he's been looking forward to. There was a lightness to his movements, a cheerfulness that jarred against the stench of decay and the weight of the chains at my wrists.

He looked almost... euphoric. As if he'd never been more content, more alive, than in that moment, surrounded by chains, stench, and pain. His eyes gleamed with a boyish joy that made my stomach turn. It was the expression of a man utterly at peace in hell... because he'd built it himself.

I watched through tear-stung eyes as he crossed the room, carrying a silver tray with the poise of a waiter in a five-star hotel. His footsteps were light, careful, controlled.

'Lunch,' he announced brightly, with the breezy enthusiasm of a man presenting a summer spread beneath parasols in a country garden. He held the tray aloft with almost ceremonial flair, his smile wide, eyes glinting with a twisted sense of purpose.

'A toothsome offering to keep up my strength. And yours, of course,' he added, as though we were sharing an afternoon meal between friends, not locked in the quiet horror of captivity.

He set the tray down with the utmost care, then turned to me, his expression softening into something dangerously close to affection. His tone was steady. Gentle. The voice of a man totally convinced by his words.

'I have your very best interests at heart, Olivia,' he said softly, as though confiding something precious. 'Truly, I do. You must remember that, cling to it, when things become... difficult. Especially then.'

He reached out slowly, with a tenderness that made my skin crawl, and brushed a tear from my cheek with the pad of his thumb. His touch was gentle, almost adoring, but his gaze never shifted, never softened. It held mine, fixed, possessive, like a predator reassuring its prey that the end would be quick.

'There are challenges ahead. Of course there are. Transformation is rarely painless. It takes time to unlearn the rules, to quiet the noise they've pumped into you since birth. Time to truly embrace one's darker nature. The part most people deny even exists.'

He smiled then. Serene.

'But not you,' he murmured, his voice almost tender, though the intensity in his eyes never wavered. They remained locked on mine, searching for something beneath the surface, something he believed only he could see.

'You're different. I knew it from the very beginning, before a single word passed between us. It was there in the way you held yourself, in the quiet behind your eyes. You feel things more deeply than others. You carry pain like an old friend. Just as I do.'

He leaned in slightly, his tone slipping into something almost conspiratorial.

'You understand what most people refuse to even look at. The cracks. The ugliness. The truth. That kind of clarity isn't taught, it's born. Darkness doesn't frighten you, Olivia. Not really. If it did, you wouldn't paint the way you do. You wouldn't pour your soul onto canvas with such unapologetic force.'

He smiled faintly, as though pleased with his own diagnosis.

'You're capable of killing, Olivia,' he said, the words falling with quiet conviction, as though stating a scientific fact rather than voicing an accusation. 'Of taking life as easily as drawing breath. Of turning death into art, pure, visceral, eternal.'

He tilted his head, eyes narrowing as he studied me.

'It's written all over you. In your eyes. As unmistakable to me as the brushstrokes in your work. You don't just see the darkness. You understand it. You shape it. And now, the only question that matters is this.'

He moved closer, his knees pressed against mine, lowering his voice to a murmur, intimate and chilling.

'Will you keep hiding behind the lie? Or will you finally stop denying who you are? Will you welcome it, as I have? Will you rise to your true potential… or rot in the shallow comfort of delusion?'

He nodded softly as I listened, resisting the impulse to vomit.

'You were born for more than mediocrity. You're far more like me than you realise. And that, that's something to celebrate. Not fear. It means you're ready for greatness. Or you will be, soon. Very soon. The time has come.'

A faint smile curled at the corners of his mouth, calm, composed, the quiet certainty of a man who believed utterly in his own madness. He watched me as if studying the finer details of a painting only he could fully appreciate.

And I broke. The fear tore through me in waves, unstoppable, primal. Warmth spilled between my legs, sudden and shaming, my bladder giving way as my body betrayed me completely. Yellow urine pooled on the cold wooden floor, spreading, soaking into the grain.

But Charles didn't flinch. His gaze never shifted. He simply stayed there, his expression unchanging, calm, almost tranquil. As though this moment, this pitiful collapse, confirmed something he'd known all along.

And the worst part? That smile still lingered. Soft. Satisfied. Triumphant.

'It's a case of adapt or die,' he said. 'And I have no intention of standing by and watching you fail. Not without doing everything in my power to facilitate your success.'

He picked up the tray from where he'd placed it on the floor to his left, setting it down between us with ceremony, revealing the contents like a magician unveiling a trick.

Veined blue cheese, sweating. Three thick slices of wholemeal bread, arranged with care. A small jar of sweet pickle. Two crystal wine glasses, their stems catching the dim light like blades. A bottle of sparkling spring water, chilled, droplets clinging to the glass. And finally, folded white paper napkins, each creased into precise triangles as though laid for royalty.

There was something obscenely civilised about it all. A grotesque mimicry of normality. A picnic for two, served in a room that stank of death and madness. Charles's idea of intimacy. His version of romance.

And all I could do was stare. Frozen. Hollowed out. Trying not to breathe.

Without ceremony, he sat beside me on the floor, cross-legged like a child at story time, rubbing his chin before pointing at the tray between us. His proximity made my skin crawl.

'We must eat, Olivia,' he said, selecting a slice of bread and tearing it in half. 'Even genius requires fuel. We are human, after all. Better than most. But still human.'

I didn't speak. Couldn't. My mouth was dry, my limbs trembling. The air was thick with rot and mildew, the smell of the girl's decaying body crawling into every breath I took. It hung around us like a living thing, present. Watching.

But Charles seemed entirely unaffected. He ate with quiet pleasure, smearing pickle with the tip of a knife, humming softly through his nose. Occasionally, he glanced towards the corner, towards her, and offered a contented nod, like the dead woman was a dinner guest observing from a respectful distance.

When he passed me a piece of bread, I took it with numb fingers, my chains rattling as I moved. I held it in my lap. But I couldn't bring myself to eat. The very idea of swallowing made my throat tighten, my stomach churn.

Charles watched me for a moment, his smile fading like mist burned away by sun.

'Eat,' he said quietly.

I shook my head, barely, an involuntary flicker of defiance that barely registered as resistance. But it was enough.

His eyes darkened. He reached forward and gripped my jaw with one hand, fingers digging into my cheeks, forcing my face upward.

'I said eat, Olivia.'

The words were soft, but the menace beneath them coiled like wire pulled tight. He held the bread in his free hand, pressing it to my lips like communion turned cruel.

'Refuse again, and I'll assume you're no longer invested in your survival. That would be such a shame after all we've shared. And believe me when I say this: hunger is nothing compared to what I'll do to you if you continue to disobey.'

His thumb brushed over my lips, not tenderly, but with calculated pressure, then released slowly, as if reeling in slack on a line.

'I won't repeat myself again.'

And I knew he wouldn't.

With a trembling hand, I brought the bread to my mouth. My fingers barely worked. My skin felt too tight, my breath too shallow. The crust scratched at my lips as I bit down, the stale dough sticking to the roof of my mouth. I chewed mechanically, the taste sour and sickly, the texture like ash in my throat.

My stomach lurched. I gagged, once, twice, my body trying to reject what my mind knew I had no choice but to endure. The bile rose, burned, settled. I swallowed hard. Then again. Each mouthful forced down like punishment.

And Charles chortled at the spectacle. Not cruelly. Not with the loud, gloating bark of a bully. But quietly, low and breathy, as though savouring the moment in the back of his throat. There was a twisted satisfaction in the sound, a cold, private delight, like a scientist watching a lab animal respond exactly as predicted.

To him, this wasn't suffering. It was progress. Proof that I was pliable. That the breaking-in process was working.

His eyes lingered on me, not with pity, not even with triumph, but with the calm appraisal of a man who had seen enough obedience to know when control had truly taken root.

'Good girl,' he murmured with approval. 'See? That wasn't so hard now, was it?' He leaned back on his haunches, smiling with genuine pleasure, as if I were a dog learning to heel. 'You'll adapt. I knew you would. There's hope for you yet. Real potential. Obedience is the first step. Once that's in place, everything else follows.'

He poured himself a glass of water, raised it in mock salute. 'To small victories,' he said. 'And to those clever enough to survive.'

And I sat there, shaking, forcing down the last dry mouthful as tears slid down my cheeks.

Something inside me had died just then. Not with a scream, but with a whisper. Quiet. Final. A small part of my soul, extinguished under the weight of what he'd done… and what I'd be forced to do.

I couldn't think of anything beyond the instinct to survive. Not justice. Not rescue. Just escape. Some way out of that twisted place. Out of the house that had become a tomb dressed in antique furniture and false civility.

But there were no answers. No unlocked doors. No open windows. The walls were thick, the chains strong.

I needed a plan, any plan. Even a threadbare fantasy would do. Something, anything, to keep me from falling too far, too fast. Because once you give up hope, the rest follows. And he would see that. He would feed on it like the predator he was.

Despite everything, the chains, the stink of death, the suffocating weight of his madness, I wasn't ready to give up. Not yet. Some stubborn part of me still smouldered, refusing to be snuffed out. I just had to endure. Keep breathing. Keep thinking. Wait for the cracks to show. For his guard to drop. For anything that might shift the balance, even by a fraction.

Hope was a fragile thing in that room, brittle, but it was all I had. And I clung to it with all the strength I had left.

Because given even the smallest window, the narrowest sliver of a chance, I'd run. I'd fight. I'd throw myself at the darkness if that's what it took. Or I'd die trying.

Either way, it would be movement. It would be change. And anything – anything – was better than being trapped in that house of horrors, waiting for the next nightmare to unfold.

23

After the meal, Charles sat back with a contented sigh, plucked a folded napkin from the tray, and wiped his hands with slow, even strokes. He dabbed at the corners of his mouth with meticulous care, like a dinner guest mindful of his manners, then rose to his feet, lifting the silver tray with an effortless grace that made me wince.

He looked down at me, still shackled, still seated on the wet, stained floor, with the kind of smug satisfaction that comes from knowing the rules no longer apply. There was something clinical about his stare. Measured. Almost proud. The sharp angles of his face caught the light, casting shadows beneath his cheekbones.

'I've been reasonably pleased with your performance so far,' he said, his tone almost tender. 'You ate. You drank. Admittedly through tears, but still... you complied with my encouragement. And that, Olivia, is a mark of success.'

He paused for a moment, allowing the praise to hang in the air before flashing a smile that made me shudder.

'And I'm sure you'll be delighted to hear that I have a little reward in mind. A well-earned treat for all your hard work.'

He took a step back, eyes bright with anticipation.

'A short film I'd like to share with you. Just a clip. Something I recorded earlier on the Welsh news.'

He chuckled softly, under his breath.

'It's always important to keep up with current events, don't you think?'

My mind lurched into overdrive, thoughts tumbling over one another in a tangle of panic and dread. A film? The news? What the hell was he talking about? My stomach turned cold. Had he killed again and recorded the report of the death for his own perverse pleasure? Was that what this was? Some awful trophy parade he expected me to applaud? Or was it something else entirely?

The not knowing was a torment all of its own. My breath came shallow, my pulse deafening in my ears. A big part of me didn't want to see. Didn't want to know. But that luxury, like every other, had been stripped from me the moment I stepped through his door. My life was no longer my own. I braced myself, knowing full well there was no mercy to be found there. Only the next horror. And the one after that.

Charles left the room without another word, his footsteps fading into the hush of the house like a whisper swallowed by stone. I didn't move. Couldn't. The silence he left behind felt loaded, like the pause between lightning and thunder.

When he returned minutes later, he was cradling a red laptop in both hands, the colour oddly bright, almost cheerful, like something meant for a child. That made it worse somehow.

He crossed the floor with practised ease and lowered himself onto the boards just a few short feet from where I sat chained. He placed the laptop down with reverence, as if unveiling some precious artefact, then flicked it open. The screen flared to life, casting his face in a cold, flickering glow. His fingers moved fast over the keys, fluid, purposeful, like someone who'd done this many times before.

He didn't speak. Not yet. Didn't even look at me. Just worked in silence, as though setting the stage for a performance only he could fully appreciate. And as his face broke into a slow, triumphant smile, tight and unnatural, I knew. He was ready. Whatever was coming, whatever he was about to show me, he'd planned it down to the last second. And I would be made to watch every twisted frame.

Charles tilted the screen towards me, angling it just so. Then he looked up, finally, and met my eyes with a steely glare.

'Now, Olivia,' he said softly, almost coaxing. 'You need to watch very carefully. Eyes forward. No looking away. No blinking until it's over. Do you understand me?'

I didn't answer. I couldn't. My mouth was too dry to form words, my throat too tight to swallow. But I nodded, once, because I knew the command wasn't a request. It was a test. Another line in the sand I couldn't afford to cross. I had to survive.

He pressed play. And the screen shifted to the branding of a familiar local news channel. A presenter appeared, mid-thirties, polished, detached, seated behind a curved desk. Her voice was calm, controlled, at odds with the content of the report that followed.

'We begin tonight with breaking news from the Pembrokeshire coast, where a search operation is underway following the discovery of a suspected suicide site near St Ann's Head.'

I felt the blood drain from my face. Footage played, grainy shots of police tape whipping in the wind, a cluster of officers in high-vis jackets scouring the cliff edge, dogs straining at their leads. Then close-ups: a pair of trainers placed neatly beside a grassy verge. A mobile phone. Folded clothing. A blurred-out note tucked into a clear evidence bag, its edges flapping in the sea breeze.

'The items are believed to belong to Olivia Ashford, a gifted young art student from Carmarthen who achieved a great deal of early success. The suicide note, found at the scene, suggests the recent breakdown of a relationship may have played a significant role in the tragic turn of events.'

I stared at the screen, numb, my image now filling the frame, my student headshot, the one I'd submitted with my college application. A smiling girl with bright eyes and soft curls. A stranger to the version of me now shackled to the wall, naked and broken, in a house steeped in the stench of death.

'Police and coastguard teams have been searching the coastline for several hours but, as of yet, without success.'

Then, as I sat there weeping, silent, broken, the truth pressing down like a vice, the screen shifted once more. And that's when the interview began.

The final nail in the coffin of my identity. The cruel confirmation of what had been taken from me, and what the world now believed.

The report cut to the familiar face of one of my lecturers, Mike Lee, standing outside the college's stone façade, hands stuffed into his coat pockets, eyes heavy with disbelief.

'I just... I can't believe it,' he said, voice brittle. 'Olivia was bright. Talented. Sensitive, yes, but in a beautiful way. Her work was emotional... real. None of us saw this coming. Absolutely none of us.' His voice cracked. 'She was one of our most promising students. It's just... devastating.'

Charles paused the recording and silence descended like a curtain falling at the end of a performance. Then he stared at me with something resembling awe, his expression alight with a terrible pride.

'It's perfect, isn't it?' he said, his voice soft with triumph. 'They've written your ending exactly as I intended. Tragic. Artistic. Complete. You're no longer a missing person, Olivia. You're a ghost. A myth. A beautifully tragic figure, lost to the sea.'

His smile widened, slow, serpentine, stretching across his face like something unearned, unnatural. His eyes gleamed with a fanatic's certainty, and when he spoke, his voice dropped to a hush, thick with possession.

'And no one, not one single soul, is coming to save you. I told you that before. And I'll tell you again until it sinks into your bones. I own you now. Every thought. Every tear. Every inch of your trembling flesh. You're mine, to shape, to twist, to remake as I see fit. That's the reality. Your only reality.'

He tilted his head slightly, as if admiring a fragile sculpture.

'So it's time. Time to stop resisting. Time to fully embrace your new life. To adapt. To grow. Because the sooner you accept the truth of who you are now, the easier it will be.'

Charles's smile held firm, fixed, unnatural, but his eyes had changed. They were flat now. Lifeless. Void of empathy or doubt. Like glass marbles set into the skull of something wearing human skin. There was no flicker of reason behind them. No conscience. No brake on the madness. Just the cold certainty of a man who saw himself as God. The lord of all he surveyed.

And it was in that moment, with his shadow stretching long across the floor and the stench of death thick in my nostrils, that I understood something with absolute, bone-deep clarity: if I wanted to live, if I was ever to get out of that house and feel daylight on my skin again, I had to become what he expected. Or at least convince him I had. I had to lie. Flawlessly.

He'd told me how his deranged friend had fooled the doctors, those dull-eyed professionals in white coats, fed them the script they needed to hear until they signed his release papers with shaking hands. Aitken had played their game and walked out the front door.

Maybe, I told myself, that was my way out too. A lesson wrapped in horror. I just had to smile through the fear. Speak my captor's language. Numb myself to the rot and blood and lunacy long enough to become the version of me he wanted to see. His prodigy. His puppet. His mirror.

And if I could manage that, if I could sell the lie with enough conviction, mirror his madness with just the right tilt of the head, the right tremor of awe in my voice, then maybe, just maybe, I'd have a chance. A sliver. A breath.

It was the only card left in my bloodied hand. The final, desperate act in a play I never auditioned for. There was nothing left to lose. No pride. No dignity. Just survival. Raw and absolute. So I would try. God help me, I had to try.

24

Charles told me it was morning when he next appeared, though time had long since blurred into something shapeless and cruel. He arrived with a spring in his step, humming to himself as he crossed the threshold like a man welcoming the day. Cheerful. Upbeat. Like we were lovers waking late on a Sunday, not captor and captive in a house of death and madness.

He moved to the windows, their shutters closed tight since my arrival, and unlatched them with a flourish, flooding the room with cold, grey light. Dust motes spiralled through the air like ash. The sudden brightness stung my eyes.

'A new day,' he said lightly, as though that meant something good. 'And I thought you'd earned a little treat, given your progress.'

He handed me a white porcelain cup filled with thick black coffee, steam curling upward like smoke from a fire, followed by a small plate bearing a slice of toast, slick with honey. The sweetness turned my stomach, but I forced a grateful nod.

Then he sat, arms folded, watching me. Studying me. Like a scientist observing a subject he wasn't quite done with.

And I ate. Bit by slow bit, I chewed and swallowed, the taste cloying, the bitterness of the coffee catching at the back of my throat. I forced it down, not because I wanted it, but because I needed it. Strength was vital now. I couldn't afford to grow weak. And I needed to please him. All part of the performance. Part of the lie. The tapestry I was attempting to weave.

I smiled faintly, murmured thanks, met his gaze without flinching. Let him believe it. Let him think I was adapting, folding neatly into the shape he wanted me to become. Because if I was to live, I had to play his game even better than he did. Because he was mad, not a fool. And I had to play to win.

'Time for your first assignment, Olivia,' he said brightly, plucking the empty cup and plate from my trembling hands as if clearing away the remains of a civilised breakfast. His tone was almost sing-song, cheerful in that sickly, off-kilter way that always left my nerves frayed. Too cheerful.

He turned towards the door, but not before glancing back, his smile firmly in place, eyes glittering with expectation.

He always used my name. Always. Like a label. A subtle, constant reminder of who I was, who he thought I was, as if stripping me of any chance to forget. Or escape.

It came more often than normal conversation would dictate. More than was natural. A repeated beat. A tether. Olivia. Said like ownership. Spoken like command.

I didn't understand what he meant. Not at first. But when he returned, my heart seemed to stop entirely.

He carried tools. Surgical saws. Bone cutters. Gloves. He dropped them beside me with a dull metallic clatter. As if it were normal.

'You're going to help me now, Olivia,' he said, voice low and almost reverential, as though he were bestowing a sanctified duty. 'This is the next crucial step on your journey, your evolution into something more. Something greater than the ordinary, than the weak and deluded moronic masses who cling to so-called decency like it means something.'

He crouched beside me, fingertips brushing the chain that bound my ankle, his eyes burning with conviction.

'It's not art. What you're about to do. And it's not creation, not in the purest sense. But it is necessary. Vital, in fact. Practical work. The kind of thing no one likes to talk about. The dirty truth beneath every masterpiece.'

He smiled softly, almost fondly.

'A task that has to be done. And it's time you proved you're capable of doing it.'

He unfastened one of the wrist restraints, replacing it with a longer length of chain attached to a bolt embedded deep in the floor. I could move now, but only within a tight, controlled radius.

His smile returned, steady, unhurried, and disturbingly composed, as he lifted a hand and pointed towards the rotting corpse slumped in the corner. There was a quiet pride in the gesture, like a curator drawing attention to a prized exhibit.

The young woman's remains lay twisted and sunken, flesh greying, hair matted to her scalp, the stench thick in the air like something alive. Charles's look lingered on her with something close to adoration.

'She served her purpose well enough, for a time,' he murmured, his voice almost fond, like he was reminiscing about an old lover rather than a lifeless body slumped against the wall. 'Oh, she begged. She wailed. Screamed until her throat gave out. Quite the symphony, really. But everything ends, doesn't it?'

He turned to me then, eyes gleaming with a manic sort of clarity. 'Now it's time to move on,' he said, his voice lilting, almost musical in its rhythm. 'Time for the next one. There's always a next one, Olivia. Always another delight waiting in the shadows, another blank canvas, another living lesson.'

He paused, turning his gaze back to the decomposing corpse with something resembling disappointment, or perhaps boredom. Such a sudden change. No longer devotion.

'That time has come. Her usefulness has run its course. There's only so long any captive holds its value, only so long they can show us what we need to see before the decay sets in, literally and otherwise. Once the screaming stops, the silence tells you everything. It's when the body dulls that the mind grows sharper.'

He smiled again, serene and self-satisfied.

'And now... it's your turn to help usher in what comes next.'

He leaned in, his smile stretching, slow and knowing.

'Wouldn't you agree, Olivia?'

I wiped away a tear. Nodded once. What else could I do?

'She's to be buried in the garden,' he said matter-of-factly, his voice almost casual, as though discussing weekend chores. He gestured lazily towards the contorted remains, his fingers slicing the air like a conductor cueing an orchestra.

'With the others, of course. There's a system to these things. Order matters.'

He stepped closer, eyes drifting across the corpse with detached appraisal, like a butcher eyeing a carcass.

'But first... she must be reduced. Broken down to something more manageable. Clean work, if you can manage it. Try not to splinter the bone unnecessarily, I like to keep the structure as intact as possible. A clean separation of parts. The head. The arms. The legs.'

He turned to me then, smiling with twisted civility.

'It makes transport easier, you see. Stackable. Neat. You won't need to dig such a large hole that way. I'm thinking of you, Olivia. Always trying to minimise the effort required. It's efficiency, really. Method. Science in motion.'

His tone never wavered. Calm. Controlled. Insane. And I shook my head slowly. Tears streamed down my face. My body refused to move. I'd known this was coming, had resolved to play along. I was falling at the first hurdle.

'No,' I whispered. 'Please... I can't.'

Charles's expression didn't change. He simply stepped back, folding his arms. But I could see his rage bubbling under the surface.

'You will do it, Olivia,' he said, each word sharpened like a blade. 'And you'll do it well. Because if you ever hope to leave this room with breath still in your lungs, you won't give me reason to doubt you.'

He reached down with calm precision, fingers closing around the thick handle of a cleaver resting beside the tools like it belonged there, like he belonged there. Then he straightened, the blade catching a sliver of dull light as he began to walk towards me.

His eyes locked on mine, narrowing with a terrifying stillness. Not anger. Not even menace. Something colder. More absolute. The certainty of a man who knew he wouldn't be stopped. Who'd already decided how the next chapter of my life, or death, would unfold.

'I've placed my trust in you. And that's no small thing. Not for a man like me. And it wouldn't be wise to let me down. Not now. Not after everything I've done for you.'

He smiled then, a thin, joyless stretch of the lips, more a grimace of intent than anything resembling warmth. Slowly, he reached into the inside pocket of his jacket and drew out a scalpel. Its blade caught the light, gleaming like something freshly honed for a singular purpose. He held it between thumb and forefinger, as if it were an extension of himself.

'Disappointment,' he murmured, his voice soft but edged with steel, 'has consequences.'

My hands shook so violently I could barely control them, fingers twitching like live wires as I forced myself upright. My legs felt like glass, brittle, unreliable, but I stood. Somehow. And time had lost all meaning. First, I looked at her, what was left of her, slumped in grotesque stillness, a stranger in life, now a terrible companion in death.

Then I looked at him. Charles Fairfax. The man who'd smiled at me on a sunlit terrace. The man I'd once believed was kind. A monster, revealed in full. And I wished, more than anything, I'd never crossed his path, never heard his name, never answered his voice.

It was one of the lowest, most degrading moments of my life. I felt hollowed out. Reduced to skin and instinct. But Charles? He was euphoric. The very picture of deranged joy. He let out a sharp, high yelp, almost childlike in its glee, his face lit with the unfiltered delight of a man watching his darkest fantasies begin to take shape.

'Yes!' he cried, eyes gleaming, a manic light dancing behind them as his lips stretched into a grin far too wide to be sane. He looked almost triumphant, like a director unveiling the climax of a twisted play only he could truly appreciate.

'Yes, Olivia. That's it. We're making real progress now.'

His voice dropped to a coaxing murmur, each word soaked in a perverse kind of pride. 'Good girl. Do this. Follow my instructions to the letter, no improvisation, no mistakes.' He massaged the back of his neck, watching me like a teacher assessing a favoured pupil. 'And when it's done, when you've proven yourself again, you can enjoy a few hours of well-earned rest. Recuperation, even. Before we bury the creature's remains under cover of darkness. Piece by piece. Quietly. Efficiently.'

He chuckled softly then, as if the very idea soothed him. Like it was all part of a well-rehearsed ritual. 'Progress, Olivia. That's what this is. And you're doing ever so well. I don't think I'm going to need the scalpel after all.'

I forced a reluctant nod, every muscle in my neck stiff with resistance. Charles didn't blink. He just stared, unwavering, his gaze crawling over me like something invasive. Studying me. Dissecting me. Watching the twitch of a brow, the flicker of a nerve in my jaw, the slight hitch in my breath. He was parsing it all, expressions, posture, silence, as if decoding some secret language only he understood. Like a human lie detector wired to madness.

And I could feel it, his scrutiny, pressing against my skin, peeling back layers I hadn't given him permission to see.

'My grounds are entirely private,' he said, tone calm and assured, as if delivering a property tour rather than plotting concealment. 'Shielded on the left by a dense, towering wall of leylandii, planted years ago for their height and speed. They form a living barricade, a thick green curtain between me and the nearest neighbour, who minds her own business and sees nothing through the trees.'

He paused, gaze sharpening.

'But caution, Olivia... caution is essential. Because discovery, exposure, is unthinkable. My friend learned that the hard way. He paid in years, behind locked doors and padded walls.'

His expression darkened.

'Getting caught isn't an option,' he said, his voice hardening to granite. 'It's not even a footnote in the margins of the plan. Everything must be executed with absolute precision. No flaws. No oversights. Perfection, Olivia. That's the standard.'

He stepped closer, his breath calm, steady, as if discussing something as mundane as exam results.

'So, if you're to be my student, and I your mentor, I expect a level of discipline and commitment that borders on the divine. I require excellence. Unquestioning. Resolute. I need you to excel... to transcend the weak, sentimental thing you used to be.'

He grinned again, soulless. 'Because anything less, any further signs of failure, doubt, or defiance, and I will kill you. Without hesitation. Without regret. You understand that, don't you?' His voice softened to something perversely close to tenderness, almost gentle, almost affectionate, as though he were offering comfort rather than delivering a threat. 'It's simply the price of ambition,' he murmured, eyes locked on mine with disarming calm. 'If you want to live long enough to hold a brush again, to feel the weight of paint beneath your fingers, the pull of colour across canvas, then you'll have to please me. It really is as simple as that.

'Not in a sexual way,' he added, almost thoughtfully as he touched his genitals through the cloth of his tailored trousers. 'Not yet. That part comes later. Once our bond deepens. Once trust is fully established. When our relationship has matured into something... meaningful. But in every other way that counts, you'll give me what I need. Your loyalty. Your obedience. Your understanding. That's how this begins. That's how you earn the right to create again.' He paused, letting the words settle like dust in stale air, the silence between us stretching, tightening. 'Then,' he said with a faint smile, 'and only then... I'll consider a reward. Something small. Something earned. But first... you'll prove your worth. Have I made myself clear?'

I nodded as he stepped towards me, erect now, a bulge in his trousers, his eyes never leaving mine.

'Yes is the word you're looking for. Say it. I need to hear you say it loud and clear. No more half-hearted nods. You're an intelligent girl. Use your words.'

'Y-yes,' I stuttered through my tears.

And Charles laughed, clapping like a performing seal. 'Louder!'

'Yes!'

'Good, good, now you're getting it. One more time. That's the enthusiasm I'm looking for.'

I screamed now, pouring out my angst, spittle spraying from my mouth, tears flowing freely. 'Yes, yes, y-yes!'

And then, without warning, his easy mask of pleasure slipped, replaced by something even colder, more calculating. His jaw tightened. A stillness took hold of him, cold and unnatural, like a cobra poised to strike.

He lifted a single finger, pointing, his voice low and unyielding. 'That's enough. No more words. Show me what you are. Drag her, now. To the centre of the floor.'

And so I obeyed. Like a puppet on fraying strings, I played along, his game, his rules, because defiance was never an option. Not then. Not yet. Not in that room. I dragged her as he'd ordered, my breath coming in ragged gasps, each one catching in my throat like broken glass. I panted. I wept. Silent tears at first, then loud, gut-wrenching sobs that echoed off the walls, swallowed whole by the horror pressing in from every side.

I wanted the ground to split beneath me, to disappear into the void and never come back. Anything to escape that place. That moment. Him.

Had I been able, I'd have killed him without hesitation. I'd have ended Charles. Not just for the girl lying limp in my arms, stripped of dignity and breath, but for me. For the part of me he'd already murdered. A small act of justice in a world where justice had long since stopped making sense.

A sickening weight settled in my gut as my hand moved, almost against my will, towards the saw. Cold metal. Cold intent. My vision swam, the edges of the room smearing into shadow, as if the world itself recoiled from what was about to happen. The floor felt unsteady, as though the very earth had shifted, rejecting the savagery unfolding on its surface.

I forced myself to look, to really look, at what was left of the girl. Not a person now, just a broken thing. A ruin of innocence. Flesh robbed of meaning. And in that moment, a splintering deep within my chest left me feeling less than human.

I turned to the side and vomited violently, the sound loud and ugly.

And Charles clapped his hands again.

'Oh, the initiation!' he cried out, laughing. 'It always gets them the first time. A baptism of sorts. You'll be stronger for it, I promise. Well done, remove the head first. That's the way.'

I stayed there, on all fours, retching until there was nothing left to give. He fetched a bucket of water, sloshed it over the mess, then spun in a circle like a drunk on a festival lawn, dancing, singing an old nursery rhyme with eerie cheer.

'Ring-a-ring o' roses... a pocket full of posies... they all fall down.'

The sound ricocheted off the walls, sharp, unrelenting, filling every corner of the room with its cruel rhythm. It merged with the rising pressure in my throat, the scream clawing its way upward, desperate for release. But I held it in. Swallowed it down like poison.

Not yet. That wasn't the moment. I had to stay composed. Let him see what he wanted to see – obedience, fear, submission. Play the part until the curtain dropped. Because one thing was certain: there would be a moment. A flicker of weakness. A lapse in control. And when it came, I'd be ready. I'd take it. Run like hell. As fast as my feet could carry me.

Or stand my ground, if it came to that. Use whatever strength remained, however broken or bruised. I wasn't ready to die in that godforsaken place, not on his terms. Not without a fight.

25

The door creaked open, pulling me from the thin, fractured edge of sleep into brutal clarity. My heart punched hard against my ribs, the shock of it stealing my breath before I could drag it back under control. Sleep, when it came, was shallow and splintered, but it was the only place I could hide. Consciousness was the real prison. My waking hours were the nightmare, every second another turn of the screw.

Charles stood in the doorway, a tall, unmoving shadow, his outline carved by the thin spill of light from the wide corridor behind him. The glow caught the edge of his face, just enough to show the pale glint of his eyes, watching, assessing. He moved with the confidence of a man who never needed to rush, a man who understood, with absolute conviction, that I couldn't run. The bite of cold steel around my wrists and ankles held me exactly where he wanted me, each link and clasp a reminder of my captivity. That truth pressed down on me like a weight I could never lift, striking again and again, until it was all I could feel.

'Midnight,' he said, the word rolling off his tongue with the ease of small talk, though there was nothing casual in the way his eyes held mine. 'I trust you're well rested... after your earlier efforts.' His mouth curled faintly, the ghost of a smile that carried no warmth. He let the silence stretch, as if savouring my tension. 'But enough of indulgence.' His voice dipped, a shade colder, every syllable clear. 'You're here for a purpose, Olivia.' He paused again, his gaze never shifting. 'Time to get back to work.'

I was curled on my side on the wooden floor, knees to my chest, arms clamped across my breasts. The boards were cold against my skin, the grain rough beneath my hip and shoulder. I kept my gaze fixed on the floorboards, refusing even the briefest glance at what lay beside me. I didn't need to look. The image was etched into my mind with cruel precision: pale, severed limbs splayed at ghastly angles, joints twisted in ways that spoke of violence, not life. The clean, decisive lines where flesh had been severed, the stark contrast of skin against the dark wood, the obscene, unnatural stillness of something that had once drawn breath. The knowledge of it pressed down on me, heavy and suffocating, until it felt as though the air itself had thickened around me. And as I lay there I feared there was worse to come. That there was no end to his depravity.

Charles's black leather boots creaked against the boards, each step measured, one, then another, the sound growing louder, closer, until it seemed to fill the room. He crouched in front of me with unhurried precision, as though time itself bent to his will. Cold metal grazed my skin as he unlocked the shackles at my ankles, the bite of steel lifting from my flesh, then the weight falling away from my wrists. The release felt wrong, unsettling; not freedom, but the opening of another door I had no wish to pass through. And yet, beneath the dread, something else stirred, unbidden and dangerous. Hope. Fragile, foolish, and utterly out of place.

'Up,' he snapped, the word cracking through the air like a whip. 'Now. On your feet.' His eyes held mine, cold and piercing, the faint curl of his lip daring me to hesitate. 'Show some enthusiasm, girl.'

The way he said it made me flinch: not a request, not even an order, but another test. One I already knew I couldn't afford to fail.

And then, as I forced myself upright on unsteady legs, my muscles trembling, my mind fixed on the act of obedience, hoping to please him, playing along with his rules while my thoughts scraped for any path to escape, he moved. His right arm swung back, a blur in the half-light, and his fist slammed into my gut with a sickening, solid thud.

The world snapped white. The breath was driven from my lungs in a wheezing gasp, my mouth opening soundlessly, the air refusing to come. Pain radiated outwards, hot and sharp, folding me double. The taste of bile surged up my throat, acrid and burning, flooding my mouth. My ears roared with the sound of my own ragged breath as I fought to pull air back in.

Before I could straighten, his hand fisted in my hair, yanking me upright with savage force. Fire lanced across my scalp, a tearing sensation so fierce it made my eyes water. I felt the sickening give as a clump tore free, warm against my skin for a heartbeat before it fell away. My vision swam, black edges creeping in, my pulse hammering against my ribs. His face loomed close, eyes flat and fixed on mine, as if weighing exactly how much more he could take from me before I broke completely.

Every instinct screamed at me to fight, to claw at his face, to kick, to make him bleed. The fury burned hot and sudden, igniting in the pit of my stomach where his fist had landed, pulsing outwards with every ragged breath. But the fear was there too, colder, heavier, sinking into my bones, whispering the truth I already knew: fight now and I'd lose. Lose, and it was over. I had to wait.

I forced myself still, teeth clamped against the metallic tang of vomit on my tongue. My heart hammered, every beat too loud in my ears, but I kept my eyes steady on his, swallowing back the tremor that wanted to take hold of me. I couldn't give him the satisfaction of seeing me crumble. Not there. Not then. So I played my part. Small. Beaten. Compliant. Let him believe I was broken enough to control.

But all the while, I counted each breath, each shift of his weight, every sound in the room, filing it away. Every second I stayed alive was another second closer to the moment I could take back control, and when it came, I'd make sure he never saw it coming. But now wasn't that time. Not yet.

His grip on my hair slackened, though several strands remained tangled between his fingers, and then he shoved me, a single, powerful thrust that sent me stumbling back into the wall. The impact jarred through my spine. My chest rose and fell in shallow, wheezing gasps, the echo of the blow still burning in my gut.

He stepped in close now, the smell of sweat and cold air clinging to him, and fastened a collar around my neck. The metal was icy against my skin, biting into the delicate hollow of my throat. A long, thin chain hung from it, swaying between us, the faint rattle the sound of ownership. Like a dog on a lead.

Without a glance at me, he turned, the chain shifting in his fist as he pointed to the wheelbarrow he'd brought with him. His movements were calm, practised, devoid of urgency, as if nothing significant had happened, as if moments ago he hadn't driven the air from my lungs or ripped hair from my scalp. To him, it was nothing more than a casual adjustment, the way another man might straighten a picture on the wall.

'Put the creature in the barrow. Come on, all of her, one piece at a time. Get it done, girl. I need my beauty sleep. No time for delay.' He jerked the chain once when I didn't move, a small, sharp movement, and nodded towards the remains. 'Load it.' His voice cut like wire. 'Now. Disobey, and I'll make you regret it. I gave you an order; you'll obey.'

And his words landed like stones this time. I moved because I had no choice. Fearing another blow or something worse. My knees bent slowly, the cold biting through my skin as I crouched beside the heap.

The pale limbs lay in obscene disarray, the severed edges almost clinical, like a butcher's work. My fingers trembled as I reached for the first piece of her. It was heavier than I remembered, its weight wrong in my hands, the flesh clammy. I placed it in the wheelbarrow, the metal tub clanging under the load.

One by one, I followed his orders. An arm. A leg. The head that I dared not look at too closely. The dull sound of each body part meeting the metal rang in my ears, and with each deposit, my heart sank.

When the last fragment was in place, Charles stepped closer. 'Out,' he ordered. 'Quickly now. Come on. Let's go.'

The wheelbarrow handles were cool in my grip, the rough metal biting into my palms. I pushed, the barrow's weight forcing my bare feet to press hard into the boards. Behind me, I heard the faint scrape of his boots, steady and unhurried. The chain between us shifted with each step, tugging against my throat, a constant reminder of exactly who held control.

The door to the rear garden yawned open ahead of me, spilling a welcome breath of night air into the house. Frost glistened on the grass beyond, catching the moonlight in tiny shards. The single wheel crunched over the gravel path, the sound loud in the hush, and behind me his footsteps matched my pace exactly.

The chain was light, almost delicate, in his grip as he quickened his pace, moving ahead of me. But each sharp tug against my throat was a reminder that it bound me as completely as any shackle. He walked me forward with quiet authority now, steering me across the wide expanse of lawn towards the midpoint, perhaps fifty metres from the building.

The night opened up around me, vast and silent. To my left, a dark wall of trees loomed as he'd described, their close-knit branches interlacing like skeletal fingers against the sky. Ahead and to my right, the land fell away into open Welsh countryside, rolling hills sleeping under a shroud of frost, hedgerows silvered by the moon. And beyond them, the slow glint of the River Towy cut through the darkness, its surface catching the faintest shimmer of light as it wound away into the far distance.

And still the chain moved in his hand, small, precise tugs guiding me forward, each step taking me further from the house… and deeper into his world.

I glanced around me, my eyes flicking from shadow to shadow in quick, desperate bursts, scanning for any sign of life, any glimmer of hope. Should I shout? Scream until my throat tore, call for help and keep calling until someone came? The thought burned hot for a heartbeat, but it died just as quickly. The nearest property I could see was far off, no more than a smudge of roofline on the crest of a distant hill, half a mile away, or maybe more. Between us lay nothing but frost-hardened fields and hedgerows under the mute gaze of the moon. I knew with a sick certainty that I'd suffer, horribly, or die long before my voice ever reached another human ear.

Charles suddenly stopped, standing directly in front of me. No more than six feet away.

'Don't ever make the mistake of underestimating me, Olivia. You're wondering,' he said, his voice low but certain, the faintest curl of amusement in it, 'if you should scream. If you should run.' The chain gave a small tug, pulling me towards him. 'I know exactly what you're thinking.

And I can tell you, you wouldn't be the first to be killed right where you're standing.'

My stomach knotted tight, a cold, hard twist that seemed to draw the air from my lungs. I kept my gaze on the river, a thin ribbon of steel under the winter light, winking on its slow, reluctant current. Anything but him. I didn't want to see his eyes when he said it, didn't want to read the truth or the lie in the shape of his mouth.

Should I respond? Speak, and risk what might follow? Stay silent, and risk worse? The questions circled, tightening like a noose. 'I wasn't thinking anything.' The words came out thin, brittle. It was the best I had, and even that felt like a mistake the moment it left my lips.

I braced for his reaction, the winter grass biting into my bare feet, each blade stiff. The cold seeped up through my legs, mingling with the dread that already had me shaking. My breath smoked in the air between us, thin and ragged, but I didn't dare move.

Then... nothing. His eyes slid away, interest gone, as if I'd been erased. He turned his attention elsewhere, and the shift left me more unsettled than any blow could have. The man was entirely unpredictable.

'There used to be a bunker under this lawn when Alexander owned the property,' he said, conversational, almost nostalgic. 'Remnants of the Cold War. Solid concrete. A steel hatch. Soundproof. And a wonderful state-of-the-art surveillance system linked wirelessly to the house.'

He paused, and I felt the weight of his gaze on the side of my face.

'Perfect, really. An ideal place to keep his... victims. For study. For... enjoyment. And he made the most of it for as long as he could.'

The words seemed to sink into the icy air, hanging there between us as I stared at the frozen ground.

'The interfering authorities destroyed it after his arrest,' Charles said, a hint of irritation creeping into his tone. 'No planning permission, they told him. Bureaucratic nonsense.'

Another pause, then, softly, almost to himself: 'A pity. I regret that. It was perfect. His happy place. I could have made good use of it as he did. But I like to think of my burial ground as a nod to all he achieved here.'

The chain rattled again, a reminder that whatever pit had once been under this lawn, I was standing in the open now, and that he didn't need a bunker to make me disappear.

'Enough small talk,' he said at last, his tone sharpening, all pretence of casualness gone. He nodded towards the spade lying a few feet away on the frost-hardened ground, its wooden handle pale in the moonlight, the metal blade glinting cold and hard.

'You see the shovel I left for you earlier, for your convenience.' The faintest smile ghosted across his lips, gone as quickly as it appeared. 'Time's getting on. Tick tock.' He tilted his head, eyes fixed on mine, letting the silence stretch until it scraped. 'I suggest you start digging.'

The first thrust of the spade jarred through my arms, the metal edge skidding off the hard crust of earth. Beneath the frost, the ground was stubborn, each inch fought for like a small war. The winter air gnawed at me, every nerve raw. And somehow, despite my youth and fragile state, something primal took over. Fear sharpened my senses, flooding my veins with a surge of adrenaline that burned away hesitation and pushed me forward, carrying me long after reason said I should have collapsed.

The frost bit deeper into my bare feet with each shift of weight, slicing through skin already torn by the grit and stones hidden under the thin white layer. My blood darkened the grass where I stood, seeping into the frozen blades. My hands, numbed by the cold, were a mess, skin split and raw, blisters swelling under my grip. I struggled on, weeping, trembling, desperate for reprieve.

But Charles didn't move. He just stood there, still as a statue, his eyes unreadable. The spade felt heavier with every strike, my shoulders screaming, but his voice cut through the silence, low and merciless.

'Keep going.'

I wanted to stop. God, I wanted to stop. But there was no choice. The metal bit the ground again, scraping, clanging against buried stone. I stole a glance at him, hoping for something, pity, a sign he might relent.

But there was nothing in him, no flicker of sympathy, no shadow of empathy. Those emotions weren't just absent, they'd been stripped away, excised like a useless organ. To him, they were weaknesses, chinks in the armour of lesser people. He'd studied them in others the way a hunter studies prey, not to understand, but to learn how best to use them.

Compassion, pity, love, tools to lure, to control, to break. In their place was something bleaker. A mind built for the hunt. And so I continued digging, slow as death, the hours bleeding together into one endless, frozen moment.

Each thrust of the spade jarred through my arms, rattling my bones, the shock biting into my blistered hands. My body shook from cold and something deeper, the weight of what I was doing. The ground gave grudgingly, inch by inch, as if it knew what was coming and meant to resist.

Dawn's first light crept over the horizon, a thin smear of grey that caught on the frost and glinted along the jagged edges of the shallow grave. My arms hung heavy, the spade handle slick with sweat and blood from my torn palms. My legs quivered, muscles burning, each step a battle I was losing. And when they gave out completely, I dropped to my knees on the still frozen ground, the shock of it jarring up through my spine. My head sagged forward, chin sinking to my bare chest, the world narrowing to the hard bite of cold against my skin and the hollow thud of my heartbeat in my ears.

Charles stepped closer. He looked down at the grave, then at me, a small smile playing at his mouth: not warmth, not kindness, but the satisfaction of a man who'd got what he wanted.

'Well done,' he said. The words didn't fit, wrong in the bitter morning air, congratulations spoken over a broken corpse.

His gaze shifted to the barrow. Limbs lay heaped inside, pale in the half-light, stiff and twisted like branches after a storm.

'I can see you're tired,' he said with feigned concern, calm, almost bored. 'And I'm glad of my thermals. I know it's cold. But that's no excuse for a job half done. Up you get. Come on, on your feet. Put the creature in the ground. Then cover the bitch up. I've got a warm bed waiting for me. Tick tock. Time's getting on.'

The ground seemed to shift under me, a slow, sickening tilt that sent the world off. My fingers locked around the spade handle, knuckles white, the wood biting into my blistered skin. The shallow grave yawned at my feet. Waiting. And so did he.

I tried to rise, but my legs buckled again, pitching me onto the frozen ground. His shadow fell over me, and then the kick came, a hard, precise blow to the ribs that left me sprawled and gasping soundlessly.

Through the haze, I saw him take the barrow handles, tilting it forward. Body parts slid into the grave, hitting the bottom with dull, final thuds. He worked the spade with practised ease, the semi-frozen soil pattering down over pale flesh until nothing showed but the dark, churned earth.

Then he came for me. I was lifted without effort, my head lolling, my arms hanging loose, and dropped into the rust-flecked belly of the barrow. And a moment later it jolted forward, wheels crunching over the frost as he pushed me back towards the house.

26

I woke to the sharp crackle of fire, the sound splintering the silence like breaking bone. For a moment, the heat wrapped itself around me with the intimacy of a half-forgotten embrace, coaxing me back from the shadowed edge where consciousness faltered. The coarse weight of a thick woollen blanket pinned me to the hard boards beneath, its scratch against my skin a small, grounding pain. The air trembled in the furnace glow, each flicker of flame clawing at the blackened grate, twisting and writhing as resin spat and hissed into the flue. It was a jarring, almost indecent contrast to the bitter void of the night garden, the raw, bone-deep cold that had gnawed at me until thought itself had slowed, threatening to leave me empty and still.

I shifted, and the illusion of safety shattered. Metal bit into the tender skin of my ankle, a cold, unyielding presence that yanked me sharply into the present. The sound came next, the dry clink of chain against chain, so small, so final. My pulse lurched. I followed the line of iron to its anchor, embedded in the wall like a promise I would never leave.

Lifting my head, I let my eyes drift beyond the firelight. The paintings were there, as they had been before, hung in precise rows along the walls. My work, every line, every smear of colour mine, yet not mine at all. I knew the faces, the shapes, the jagged edges of my own hand in every frame, but they seemed altered now, as if the room had stripped them bare and shown me what I hadn't wanted to see. There was a darkness in me, as there was in Charles. Not the same as his, not that cold, evident malice that seemed to flow through his veins like poison, but a shadow nonetheless. His was calculated, sharpened to a fine point, wielded without mercy. Mine was different, quieter, coiled deep inside where I rarely dared to look. But perhaps, in ways I didn't want to admit, we shared more than I cared to acknowledge. That thought lodged itself in me like a splinter, impossible to ignore, whispering that the line between us might be thinner than I wanted to believe.

My artworks stared back in silence, their eyes catching the fire's reflection, shadows stretched long and restless against the walls. The reds felt redder. The darks darker. The air was thicker there, heavy with what had been done and said within those walls, so much so that I could almost hear it still, woven into the grain of the floorboards, seeping into the paint itself.

I'd seen them here before. But now, together like this, framed by the knowledge of what had happened in that room, they seemed different.

I tried to flex my feet and winced. They burned and throbbed in equal measure, my toes mottled with an ugly bloom of red and blue, as frostbite had crept under my skin during the night. The ache in my muscles was deep and total, my shoulders, my back, my jaw. Even breathing hurt.

Fragments of the night before flickered and faded in my mind like the last embers of a dying fire. The cold had been absolute, a living thing that wrapped itself around me, pressing into my bones until each breath felt stolen, wrenched from somewhere deep inside. Time had lost all shape as I dug, hour after hour, the metallic tang of sweat and soil thick on my tongue. His voice had been there, always at my back, low, precise, directing, correcting, controlling, the rhythm of my labour chained to the cadence of his words. Each command scraped against something deep inside me, fuelling a quiet defiance that I held on to like a secret.

But beneath it, shame festered, growing heavier with every spadeful, every moment I obeyed. My muscles had burned, then numbed, until they no longer felt like mine. And then I'd folded in on myself, the strength gone from my body, the edges of the world collapsing inward until there was nothing left but black.

I drew the blanket tighter around me, though it did nothing against the memory. And then Charles. The latch turned. My breath caught. And he stepped inside the room, a tray balanced with care in both hands. The smell of fresh coffee reached me first, strong, dark, promising.

'Morning,' he said, the word delivered with the ease of a man greeting a friend across a breakfast table, as if this were some cosy domestic scene instead of what it was. His voice was soft, but the softness was an artifice, calculated, practised, every note placed exactly where he intended.

He set the tray on a small table that wasn't there before, just beyond the reach of my chain, arranging it with meticulous care. Every movement was intentional, slow enough to appear casual, precise enough to remind me that nothing he did was without purpose. His hands never trembled. His posture never faltered.

'Refreshments,' he continued, his gaze flicking briefly to mine, the faintest curl at the corner of his mouth.

'A reward for all your progress. Bacon, eggs, and fresh Colombian coffee. My favourite blend.'

The rich, oily aroma curled through the air, stirring an unwelcome hunger that knotted with my unease. He straightened, adjusting the angle of the tray as if it mattered. His eyes roamed the room, pausing on the fire, the paintings, before returning to me.

'I hope you appreciate the warmth of the room. A little stifling for me. But I thought you needed it.' A brief pause. 'I know how to keep a guest alive... when I want to.'

He leaned back slightly, hands clasped loosely in front of him, a stance that might have seemed relaxed if not for the undercurrent of ownership in it. He was close enough that I could see the faint twitch at the edge of his jaw, the subtle narrowing of his eyes when he studied me: tiny tells, but loaded. He held my look longer than necessary, as though waiting for me to blink first, asserting without words who was in control.

The words, the movements, the pauses, every detail was another thread in the same web, and I knew he was watching to see how tightly it was binding.

And despite everything, everything he'd said, everything he'd done, I found myself fastening on to a single word. Progress. It clung to me, bright and sharp against the darker weight of all else he had spoken. It seemed my plan – fragile, reckless, balanced on a knife's edge – might be working, at least for now. And with every carefully chosen word, every feigned glance of submission, I felt I was winning. I was gaining his trust, dangerous, precarious, but real.

The words settled in me like a barbed hook. I didn't move. Didn't speak. I kept my breathing even, forcing a reluctant smile that I hoped looked natural. Every muscle in my face felt tight, as if it might betray me. I chose my words with care, weighing each syllable before I let it go.

'Thank you for the blanket and the fire,' I said, my voice steady. 'And for breakfast too. It smells wonderful. Very much appreciated.'

The taste of the words was bitter, but I uttered them all the same.

He took a step towards me. 'You're very welcome, Olivia,' he said, his tone almost warm – almost. But there was a glint in his eyes that stripped the words of any comfort they might have carried. 'But please don't mistake my actions for kindness. Abandon any thought of such weaknesses. It's a matter of practicalities. No more and no less. It really is as simple as that.'

Should I ask? I wasn't sure. The words formed and dissolved in my mind, each one feeling heavier than it should. Still, I forced them out, keeping my tone even, careful. 'Could I please have some painkillers? Anything to help. My hands and feet... they're in a bad state after the cold.'

Charles's smile was faint. He tilted his head, studying me as though weighing whether the request amused him or annoyed him. 'Oh, I don't think so,' he said at last, his voice hushed, almost tender, as if delivering some small kindness. 'Best not try to take advantage of my generosity.' His gaze dropped briefly to my feet before returning to my face. 'I might decide on amputation, if you do.' Then a moment's silence, letting the words settle like ice water down my spine. 'So, put up with it... and stop complaining. That's my advice.'

His smile lingered, fixed and shallow, before it drained away altogether. The air felt tighter, heavier, as if the room itself were listening. He let the quiet stretch, just long enough for the threat in his words to root itself in me.

'But enough of all that,' he said, with a sudden brightness that rang false. 'On to the positives.' His shift in tone was almost theatrical, as though we were participants in some grotesque award ceremony. 'I'm glad to say you've passed the first two tests of your apprenticeship.' He lingered on the word apprenticeship, savouring it, shaping it as though it were a privilege to be earned rather than a sentence to be endured.

'The creature's dissection,' he went on, 'was performed to an acceptable standard for an untrained beginner. And you showed some grit and determination when digging the grave.'

His eyes fixed on mine as though searching through my expression for signs of pride, fear, defiance... anything I might try to hide.

'You should be reasonably pleased with yourself,' he said at last, the words delivered like a verdict.

'Thank you.' That's all I could think to say. Just the two words.

Charles dragged the table and two chairs closer. He positioned them with precision, adjusting angles, aligning edges, as if setting a stage. Then he began to lay the table, each plate, each piece of cutlery placed with an almost ceremonial care.

'Stand. On your feet,' he said, the command clipped, leaving no room for hesitation. 'I've gone to the trouble of preparing breakfast. The least you can do is eat it.' His gaze held mine for a beat before drifting to the chain at my ankle. 'You'll have realised by now,' he went on, 'that I removed the restraints from your hands while you slept.' His tone softened, but only slightly, a mockery of generosity. 'Another small reward... for your rapid evolution.'

The word 'evolution' hung in the air, as though he were marking my progress the way one might measure a sample in a laboratory.

And in that moment, I knew. Progress. Evolution. My plan really was working. I no longer had any doubt. I was drawing him in, inch by inch, the threads of trust weaving tighter around us. It was a small victory, fragile, precarious, but a victory all the same.

I forced myself upright, the movement dragging pain through me in sharp, punishing waves. My legs trembled under my weight, every muscle protesting, my feet screaming with each shift. But beyond the ache, beyond the throbbing in my bones, there was something else: an image, bright and dangerous, of freedom.

It sat at the forefront of my mind, stubborn and determined, a lifeline I refused to let slip. And because I had that, because I could see it, feel it, I could endure whatever came next. I clung to the thought with every cell of my being, holding it close, feeding on it like oxygen in a room starved of air.

'Sit, girl, sit. And enough of your pathetic whimpering. The sound of it irritates me. Never a good idea.'

The words slithered across the space between us, quiet but edged with something sharp. And I'd never hated a man more.

I lowered myself into the chair as instructed, relieved to take the pressure off my feet, the throbbing in them pulsing in time with my heartbeat.

'I'm... s-sorry. I'll keep quiet.' The apology tasted sour, like something spoiled, but I forced it out.

And Charles ignored me, as if I hadn't uttered a word. He poured the coffee with ease, the dark liquid swirling into the cup, the aroma rich and heavy in the warm air. Without looking at me, he reached for the small jug of cream and held it out, a parody of courtesy.

'As I said earlier, you've done rather well, all things considered,' he murmured, his voice dropping lower, softer, more intimate, almost confiding. But there was no warmth in it, only calculation. 'But that doesn't mean there's any room for complacency. There are far more demanding tasks ahead.'

He set the jug down with care, the faint clink of porcelain punctuating his words.

'We'll talk about that a little later, once you're fed and watered. So eat up. Enjoy.'

Eating was an effort, every bite turning heavy in my mouth. But I forced it down because I had to, because strength meant survival. Each mouthful felt like swallowing stones, the taste dulled by the knot in my stomach. I kept my eyes on the plate, never lifting them to meet his, conscious of his presence in every breath I took. I spoke only when spoken to, my voice measured, my words pared to the minimum, knowing that anything more could be dangerous.

But Charles, in contrast, seemed to savour every moment. His tone shifted, light, conversational, almost affable, as though we were two acquaintances passing the time over coffee. The words rolled out easily, unhurried, the cadence warm enough to pass for friendly if you ignored the iron at my ankles. It was the kind of voice you might hear in a garden on a summer afternoon, not in a room where a young artist sat chained to the wall. Yet to him, the setting seemed irrelevant. As if this was entirely normal.

And that was terrifying. The absence of overt threat. The lack of raised voice or clenched fists. His calm, steady rhythm crawled under my skin, making my stomach clench and my pulse stutter. I could feel the wrongness of it in the tightness at the back of my neck, in the cold coil settling low in my gut. Somehow, his casualness felt more threatening than any shouted order or sudden blow, because it told me he was completely at ease with what he was doing.

He lifted his cup to his mouth, drained it before placing it back on its matching saucer. 'Am I correct in thinking that ridiculous ex-boyfriend of yours is back from Lanzarote? I'm sure you mentioned something when we were on the island.'

The mention of Joe sent my thoughts spinning. The memory of him felt close enough to touch, yet impossibly distant, like a photograph fading in the sun. The life we'd shared belonged to another time, another person entirely.

'What day is it?' My voice sounded flat in my own ears.

Charles laughed, head tilted back, Adam's apple rising and falling in a slow motion. The sound was warm enough to pass for genuine amusement, but it carried something else beneath it. 'Tuesday 4 January.'

Why was he asking about Joe? I had no idea, but the question sat between us like a weight.

'Um... In that case, yes. That was his original plan, anyway.'

'And he has a flatshare near the college?'

I nodded, swallowing a strip of bacon that tasted far saltier than it should have, the grease coating my tongue. 'On the small estate behind the old hospital.'

'Ah, okay, good to know.'

Charles stalled then, his gaze sliding past me for a moment, unfocused, as though following some private thread of thought. His fingertips tapped once against the table, barely audible, like the faint ticking of a clock. He sat very still after that, his shoulders loose but his posture rigid.

I tried to read him, to find some hint in the set of his jaw or the narrowing of his eyes, but he gave me nothing. He was a mask. Perfectly silent, perfectly still. The kind of stillness that didn't mean calm, it meant calculation.

Whatever he was thinking, I knew it wasn't idle conversation. But it seemed he was ready to talk of other things.

'I'm going to move you to my attic room today,' he said, his voice almost warm, as if this were some act of kindness. 'Up three flights of stairs. It's spacious. Comfortable. A token of my admiration for your... effort.'

He let the word hang there, just long enough to remind me what it had cost to earn.

'It will be firmly bolted shut, of course.'

His eyes didn't waver. The matter was settled before I'd even drawn breath.

'But there'll be no need for the shackles while you're in the room,' he went on, as though granting a privilege I should be grateful for. 'And you'll have access to paints, pens, paper, canvas, everything you need to continue your... artistic development. I want you to produce something darker. Something reflecting your new self. Show me who you really are.'

A strange mix of emotions coiled inside me. The thought of no shackles, of space to move and paint, sent a flicker of relief through me, but it was poisoned almost instantly by the knowledge that it was still a cell, just a room to pace. Like a lion in a cage.

He leaned in, elbows rested on the table, close enough that I could feel the weight of his attention.

'What do you say? I would think thanks are in order.' His head tilted, a predator's angle. 'Come on... I'm waiting.'

I kept my face still, my voice steady, careful to hide the twist of revulsion beneath the thin veneer of compliance.

'Thank you,' I said, the words forced from my mouth.

The thought of 'freedom' in that attic room felt like a trick, a longer leash, nothing more. But if it kept him convinced, if it bought me time, I would take it.

He continued talking after ordering me to stand, freeing me from my chain and pushing me in the direction of the hall.

His hand pressed into the small of my back, firm enough to move me but not quite shoving. Each step groaned under my weight as he steered me up the narrow staircase, the close walls swallowing what little light there was.

'I'll give you time to rest and recuperate, once you're settled in,' he said behind me, his breath brushing the back of my neck. The tone was almost indulgent, as though he were offering me a holiday rather than granting me a reprieve. 'Let those blue feet of yours calm down a bit.' His gaze – I could feel it even without turning – lingered there for a heartbeat too long.

'And then... we're off to hunt.' The words slid into the air, planned, savoured. 'Your next test.'

The staircase turned sharply, his presence shadowing mine, close enough that I could smell the faint trace of soap on his skin beneath the stronger scent of coffee.

'Off to the backstreets of Bristol,' he went on, his voice dropping lower as if confiding a secret. 'Where the lost sell themselves to feed their ghastly habit. Easy pickings.' He said it as though we were about to choose fruit from a market stall.

A harder push between my shoulder blades forced me up the final steps.

'We'll capture our guest and bring her home.' His hand didn't leave me. 'And then... we'll see exactly what you're capable of.'

The pause was almost palpable. 'And then I'll know if you're the one... or not. Either you'll slit her throat, or I'll kill you both. That really does depend on you.'

27

The final step creaked under my weight as Charles guided me forward, his firm hand now resting between my shoulders, a constant reminder of control. A heavy bolt scraped back, the sound loud in the hush of the narrow landing.

And he pushed the door open. Light flooded the space ahead, unexpected, almost blinding after the dim climb. The attic room stretched wider than I'd imagined, the ceiling sloping into thick beams, the air warmer and drier than the killing room below. A single barred dormer window cut the far wall, throwing a pale rectangle of daylight across bare boards that looked recently scrubbed.

There was a single bed in the corner, low, narrow, neatly made. A small table with two chairs. Against the opposite wall, a workbench had been laid out with precision: jars of brushes, pens, pencils, paper, tubes of paint, stacked canvases, each one waiting for whatever he wanted from me next.

It should have felt like a reprieve. No shackles, no human remains. But the bolt on the outside of the door glinted in the light, a reminder that freedom here was no more than an illusion.

'Your new home,' he said, stepping in beside me. His voice was calm, satisfied. 'I'd make yourself comfortable if I were you. You'll need to fully recuperate before the hunt.'

The bolt slid home with a hard, final scrape, the sound reverberating in the stillness long after his footsteps faded. I stayed where I was for a moment, listening, making sure I was alone, before my eyes began to sweep the room.

I searched for anything: a crack in the wall, a loose board, a tool left carelessly within reach that might offer a way out. My gaze moved over the low bed, the small table, the workbench along the wall. It was painfully clear Charles had planned every detail, thought through every angle, sealing off possibilities I hadn't yet considered. My arrival here wasn't chance, it was preparation. Anticipated.

He'd covered every base long before I even knew I was playing his game.

My eyes lingered, wooden handles, metal ferrules, glass jars, mentally weighing their worth as weapons. But they were flimsy, brittle things, built for making marks on paper, not breaking flesh or bones. The very order of them seemed to mock me, a reminder that everything here had been chosen, placed, and permitted by him. Nothing was done by chance.

And there was no way out. Nothing that could truly help me fight. Just the paints, the pens, the paper – his tools for shaping me into whatever he wanted me to become. And that knowledge pressed down on me like a dead weight.

I reached for a brush very soon after Charles closed the attic door behind him. New. Untouched. The pale wood unscarred, the bristles sharp and springing back against my grip. No history, no residue of another's hand. Its weight was unfamiliar, yet it grounded me. Something solid to cling to in the wake of his departure.

I dipped the bristles into the thick, glistening oil paint, watching them drink in the colour until they were slick and heavy. Then I pressed them to the canvas, the first stroke cutting across the blank surface like a wound opening. And I saw the beauty in it. My creation.

It felt almost dangerous, the relief it brought to let my anger, my unease, my caged and restless thoughts seep out through the bristles. To watch them take form in shape and shadow, each line carrying something I couldn't risk speaking aloud. Every mark on the canvas was a small defiance, a whisper of rebellion dressed in colour and light, daring him to read it without ever knowing the truth beneath.

And I hate to admit, even to myself, that Charles had been correct about one thing. My work had changed. Without realising it at first, I'd let the colours darken, the lines twist and knot, as though my hand was mapping places I'd never willingly go. The shapes that emerged were not planned, not controlled, but they felt like true images dragged from the blackest corners of my mind, places I'd rather keep locked away.

It struck me then he would see this. He would study every stroke, every shadow, every twisted contour, convinced they were an unfiltered reflection of me. A window into my mind. He would believe he could read me through the canvas as easily as turning the pages of a large-print book.

And if that's what he believed, then perhaps I could write something there for him to find. Not the whole truth, never that, but an exaggerated fiction tailored to his appetites.

If escape wasn't immediately possible, then I would have to wait. Watch. Show patience. That part of the plan hadn't changed; it couldn't. It was all I had.

The brushes, the paints, the clean white canvas... they couldn't smash a lock or prise open a bolt, but they could be used for something else, something quieter. Subtler. A painting could become a mask. A mask could hide intent. And intent, buried deep and kept close, could be sharpened into a weapon he would never see coming. I would give him exactly what he wanted to see, until the moment came to show him something else entirely.

The brush felt different in my hand now; not just a tool for painting, but a weapon I could wield in plain sight. I set the first canvas aside, letting the dark shapes stare back at me, raw and unguarded. That one was for me alone. The next would be for him.

I pulled a fresh canvas from the stack and fixed it to the easel, the blank white expanse staring at me like a challenge. My palette changed too, colours chosen with care, not for truth, but for effect. The shadows I would paint here would be the ones he wanted. Controlled darkness. A performance of menace and cruelty that looked authentic enough to convince him he was succeeding in shaping me.

I slowed my movements, considering each line, each smear of colour, picturing the satisfaction in his eyes when he saw it. The trick was to give him enough of the truth to make it believable, but never so much that he saw anything real.

The deception steadied me. Every stroke felt like a small victory, another step towards the moment when his confidence in me would be the very thing that undid him.

I was full of new hope, riding it like a wave, certain I was simply playing him as I had to, in order to survive. Every movement, every word, every flick of the brush part of the act.

But as I worked, my hand moving almost of its own accord, a thought began to take shape. Slow. Uncomfortable. Persistent. It settled in the back of my mind like a shadow that refused to shift, no matter how hard I tried to push it away.

Was this painting just another calculated move in the game, a lure to please him, to draw him in, to buy myself the smallest chance of survival... of escape? Or was there something else seeping into the strokes? Something unplanned. A violent thread winding through the work, not because I willed it there, but because some part of me, some part I didn't recognise, wanted it there.

I shuddered, a tremor running through me that had nothing to do with the cold. The thought lodged deep, chilling me from the inside out, the possibility that some part of me, however unwilling, might be edging towards his deviant world. Drawn to it. Lured by the extremes, the sharp edge of danger, the unflinching darkness that seemed to hum beneath everything he touched.

No. It was his voice in my head, that was all. Another of his manipulations burrowing under my skin, twisting my perception until I could no longer trust what was mine and what was his. He wanted me to doubt myself, to wonder if I was cut from the same cloth, to blur the line between us until it no longer existed.

I forced the thought down, locking it away with the others I couldn't afford to examine too closely. I would not give him that ground. Not then. Not ever.

I didn't want to think it, but the question rooted itself in my mind and refused to loosen. Was I more like Charles than I'd ever dared to believe? Just as he'd said. Had he been watching me for a reason? Seen something in me, in my work, that I'd been blind to until now?

The thought was jagged, sharp enough to hurt. It burrowed deep, sending a slow trickle of ice through my veins. I told myself it was nonsense, that it was simply another of his manipulations worming its way into my head. But a sliver of doubt remained, and it terrified me.

I forced my breathing steady and pushed the thought aside again, shoving it into the same locked place I kept every other fear. My grip on the brush tightened. I would not falter, not in front of him, not in the work he'd see.

My movements slowed, precise, as I built the layers, shadows creeping into light, light swallowed back into shadow. I painted as if nothing had shifted inside me, as if my thoughts were untouched, my purpose unchanged.

But under the surface, something coiled. Whether it was fear, defiance, or something darker, I couldn't yet tell. All I knew was that I would finish the piece. And when he saw it, he would believe. See what I now feared might already be there.

When the painting was done, I stepped back, studying the canvas as though it belonged to someone else. The shapes and shadows stared back at me, offering no answers, only more questions I didn't want to face. I pushed the painting aside, turning it so I wouldn't have to see it.

Enough. My mind was playing tricks on me, that was all. That's what I told myself, forcing the words into a loop, repeating them over and over until they became a dull, rhythmic beat in my head. A mantra. A lifeline. If I kept saying it, maybe I could make it true.

The strain. The fear. The unbroken tension that clung to me like a second skin. They had twisted my thoughts out of shape, blurred the edges between who I was and who he was moulding me to be. I told myself it was nothing more than fallout, the aftershocks of everything I'd endured. Nothing real. Nothing dangerous. And yet the words didn't land the way they should. They felt light. Fragile. As though the truth might slip through the cracks at any moment.

I stood and crossed the room, the floorboards cool beneath my aching feet, and lowered myself into the chair at the small table. My fingers closed around the pen, the plastic warm from the sunlight slanting through the barred window. I pulled a sheet of paper towards me, its whiteness almost glaring in the muted light.

The first words came slowly, hesitant, as though testing the air. Then they began to pour fast, jagged, unfiltered, spilling across the page in black strokes my hand could barely keep up with, each line dragged from the chaos in my head before it could twist into something worse.

Fragments of memory. Snatches of conversation. The rotting corpse. The bite of the cold sinking through my skin to the bone. The scrape of the shovel tearing into frozen earth. And always his voice, inescapable, seeping through every moment like black ink dropped into water, spreading until it touched everything.

I wrote it all down, the words tumbling out in a rush, the pen clawing at the paper. I didn't care how crooked the lines were or how the ink bled. I needed to see it outside of me, laid bare in black and white before it could fester any deeper.

Maybe then I could make sense of it all. Perhaps I could find the outline of myself again, trace the edges before he smudged them into nothing, before the shape of me became something I no longer recognised. If I hid it well. If Charles never saw it. Never read a word.

28

I lost an entire week to the attic after that, though I marked the passing days on the inside of the wardrobe door, a prisoner's tally scratched into paint. Each stroke felt faintly absurd, like counting heartbeats in the dark. The light shifted in its narrow cycle, cold dawn leaking in through the barred window, thinning to a pale, grudging noon, then draining away until the room held only shadow. Time became a dull, repeating shape, blurred at the edges.

I measured it not in hours, but in his visits. Charles came once, sometimes twice a day, the creak of the stairs or quiet click of the lock my first warning. His presence entered the room before he did, as if he displaced the air on the stairwell. He always carried food, sandwiches wrapped in waxed paper, a flask of soup, offerings that felt almost ceremonial. I forced myself to eat, not from hunger but from the knowledge that refusing would lead to questions, and I had no answers I wanted to give. The taste hardly registered; the act of swallowing was enough.

And every time, without fail, his eyes turned to my paintings. I worked in a kind of fever, brush to canvas until my fingers cramped, paint drying in ridges beneath my nails. It wasn't inspiration that drove me but compulsion, a restless itch in the back of my skull that only the act of creating seemed to soothe.

He'd stand behind me, silent at first, then study each piece as though he could step through the surface and into the world I'd made.

'You've captured despair here,' he said once, fingertip hovering an inch from the canvas. 'Not sadness. Despair. Do you see the difference?'

I swallowed, unsure if it was a question or a verdict.

'Another brushstroke and you'd have lost it,' he added, smiling. 'But you didn't. That's instinct. That's rare.'

His praise landed with an unsettling precision, never too much, never too little, calculated to cut as much as it soothed.

Another time, he tilted his head. 'Why the muted tones? Afraid of colour? Or afraid of what colour might reveal?'

I gripped my brush tighter, heat rising in my chest. 'No,' I managed. 'I just... like it that way.'

'Like it,' he echoed, soft with amusement, as though repeating a child's answer. 'Interesting.'

His insights, if that's what they were, came in measured fragments, truths disguised as riddles, questions wrapped in compliments. And always, always, I was left wondering if he saw more in the paintings than I ever intended.

It became a pattern before I ever realised it, a rhythm I fell into without thought. And there, in the repetition, something shifted. The edges of my fear softened into something dangerously like trust. I told myself it was just the comfort of predictability, the way a shipwreck survivor might grow used to the sound of the waves that almost killed them.

But I hate to admit even to myself that there were moments, brief, treacherous moments, when I felt something like affection for him. A phantom warmth that didn't belong, that had no right to exist yet seeped in all the same. When I could almost forget the long, fractured shadow of murder, as if those events belonged to another life, another girl. The mind is a traitor in such moments; it tells you the bars are just lines in the wallpaper, the lock on the door is for your protection, and you were never a victim at all.

And then, on the grey morning of day eight, everything changed. The light itself felt different flat, colourless, the kind that makes the world seem drained of warmth. It was the sort of morning where the air tasted faintly of sweat, where the silence pressed in, heavy and expectant.

What came was no accident of mood or imagination, but a graphic, unflinching reminder of exactly who and what he was. The mask of civility he'd worn so easily in recent days slipped, and beneath it was the thing I'd always known was there: not a mentor, not a friend, but something colder, hungrier. A monster with human skin.

And in that instant, I was reminded of myself, too, stripped of the illusions I'd been building like fragile scaffolding. Not a working artist, not an independent soul at the height of some creative fever, but a helpless creature thrashing in the sticky threads of his web. A fly that had mistaken the stillness for safety, only to feel the tremor of the spider drawing near.

The Georgian staircase gave its warning, one long, aching creak, then another, the sound carrying up through the bones of the house. That old, familiar prelude. My pulse found its own rhythm against it, quickening without permission. I knew it meant only one thing: Charles was coming.

My chest tightened in that involuntary way it always did before he opened the door, as if my body remembered something my mind tried not to. A private reflex I'd never managed to unlearn.

Then the sound of metal turning against metal, unhurried, a lock surrendering. The click was small, almost delicate, yet it struck me as something intimate, intrusive. Like the faint pressure of a fingertip pressing into the hollow at the base of my throat.

And when the door opened and he stepped inside, the atmosphere seemed to thin. I stared at him, my gaze locked on his face, static, as if a moment's distraction might cause him to dissolve. For a heartbeat, no more, I thought I'd conjured a stranger out of the dim air. A beard, thick and coarse, sat unnaturally, heavy along his jaw, the bristles catching the light like wire. Long hair, too dark, too abundant, spilled to his shoulders, a curtain framing a face that was his and not his.

Tinted glasses dulled his sky-blue eyes to flat amber coins, robbing them of their depth, making them unreadable, like the varnish on an old portrait that hides more than it preserves. He seemed taller, but it was the kind of height achieved by intention, the subtle lift of posture, the quiet declaration of presence. Broader too, though I could see it was the coat doing the work, its cut engineered to give him a shape that commanded space.

Familiar and unfamiliar all at once, he stood there like a photograph left too long in the sun, the outlines still visible, the details blurred, distorted. My heart missed a beat, then lurched to catch up, a stumble that left me faintly winded. The room seemed to tilt around us, as though the whole building had shifted on its foundations in the night.

A dozen thoughts collided in the narrow space of my mind: suspicion, curiosity, and a sharp prickle of unease that made my fingertips tingle. I wanted to ask why, but the question caught in my throat, snagged on the absurdity of the disguise. Part of me wanted to laugh, to break the tension before it took root. Another part wanted to retreat to the furthest corner of the room and watch him from behind the shield of my easel.

Instead, I stood frozen, caught between the urge to move closer and the instinct to pull away. He was still Charles, the voice, the posture, the invisible gravity of him, and yet something in me reacted to the man in front of me as if he were a stranger. That uncertainty slid through me like cold water, and I realised I was holding my breath.

Then he laughed, low and soft, chuckling as if my shock pleased him.

'Not what you were expecting,' he said. Not a question. A statement of fact. Like he read my every thought.

'You look…' The word didn't come at first. Then I heard my own voice and hated how thin it sounded. 'Different.'

'Very true, my lovely girl. And that's exactly the point.'

He closed the door behind him with an unhurried care that made me think of hands smoothing down a shroud.

'Disguise is a key that opens certain doors and keeps others shut. We wear masks every day. This one is just more honest about the lie. I'm sure you'll agree I wear it well.'

He brought the scent of cold air and something resinous with him: spirit gum, maybe, underneath the usual scent. He crossed to the easel, those heavy-soled shoes suctioning faintly at the boards, and stood over my painting without touching it. I watched him watching it, the way a patient watches the surgeon's eyes just before the anaesthetist pulls the curtain.

'Better,' he said at last, as though each syllable had been weighed before release. 'Much better. You know I've always admired your work, always. But even by your own exalted standards, this is something else entirely.'

He inclined his head, the movement small, the amber lenses of his glasses catching the light and throwing it back in a dull, impenetrable sheen. Whatever lay behind them, approval, calculation, or something darker, remained hidden.

'You've begun to let the edges unravel,' he went on, his tone softening into something that might have been reverence. 'That's where truth breathes in the frayed seams between the face we present and the secrets we can no longer contain.'

The warmth came even though I didn't want it. Recognition sinks its hook in quietly; you don't feel the tug until you move. I told myself it was relief that he approved, nothing else. Not pride. Not the old, dangerous loosening in my chest that said 'see me, see me, please'.

He suddenly turned from the canvas to me, beard bristling, wig hair blunt against the collar of his coat. The disguise made his mouth look unfamiliar, less expressive, so the smile he gave me was a suggestion more than a sign.

'Today's a big day in your ongoing development, Olivia. Your next mission.'

His voice carried that familiar cadence he favoured when he wanted me to absorb every syllable.

'The day of your first hunt. Another test you have to pass with flying colours.'

My skin prickled, the cold bite of instinctive dread crawling over me like the legs of something unseen. A foreknowledge I neither invited nor could dislodge coiled itself tight in my gut, a snake waiting for the strike. The answer took shape in the dark recesses of my mind before the question had even formed, pressing against me with suffocating certainty. Still, the words tore themselves free, ragged and reluctant, scraping my throat as they passed. My mouth was parched, every swallow an effort, my pulse pounding a brutal rhythm in my ears. And then unbidden, merciless, came the image of the dead girl. Her face. Her stillness. Thoughts that slid in like knives. Invasive. Unwelcome.

'Hunt?' I asked, my voice little more than a whisper. 'Will I have time for another painting?'

Charles had come alive, his earlier restraint stripped away, a restless energy sparking in his eyes. His voice carried a taut undercurrent, the kind of excitement that prickled against the skin, but there was calculation there too, a deliberate holding back. He wasn't about to give me the satisfaction of answers, not yet. He'd speak when it suited him, and only then. His terms. Never mine.

'You'll no doubt be pleased to hear I'll bring you some clothing a little later.' His tone was almost conversational, but the undercurrent was anything but. 'Not because you've any right to cover your nakedness; you haven't. But because it serves my purpose. Several previous guests discarded their attire before leaving for the afterlife. I'll choose you something suitable.'

He paused, eyes lingering in a way that made my skin tighten, a slow smile curling at the edges of his mouth.

'And we'll cut your long hair short. Change your appearance. That makes sense before we leave the house. We can't allow you to be recognised. Not now they've abandoned the search.'

The words settled over me like ice water, trickling down my spine. My mind caught on the words 'previous guests' and 'afterlife', and the images that came were blood-edged. I felt the phantom tug of scissors against my scalp, the cold certainty of his control closing in, piece by piece.

'Leave the house?' I asked.

'Oh, yes, after dark, we'll be heading to Bristol. The hunt I previously mentioned.'

His tone was matter-of-fact, but there was a glint in his eye that turned my stomach.

'Not too far to be inconvenient, given the inclement weather, but far enough for anonymity.'

He spoke with the calm precision of a man reciting lines long etched into memory, each syllable landing with a calculated inevitability.

'I've secured a suitable vehicle from a discreet criminal acquaintance

Alexander once introduced me to. Reliable, untraceable, and exactly what we need. False plates, naturally. We wouldn't want unnecessary eyes upon us.'

His lips curved into the ghost of a smile, but his gaze remained flat, detached, as if he were commenting on something trivial, a minor errand.

'It seems the world will never grasp the magnitude of my work,' he continued, his tone tightening with a flicker of grievance. 'True innovation is never understood at first. The body's convulsions, the mind's fracture, the exquisite collision of fear and flesh... such things demand sacrifices most are too weak, too cowardly, to make. It baffles me,' he said, the words laced with disdain, 'that any right-minded person would waste so much as a moment's thought on my guests. Pathetic creatures. Empty vessels staggering through their pointless little lives, blind to their own insignificance. In death, they finally serve an artistic purpose. They acquire a value they could never hope to claim in life. And for that, they should be grateful beyond measure.'

His mouth twitched at the corner, the parody of a smile, as if the very notion amused him. And the casual way he said it chilled me more than if he'd screamed and shouted. It was all logistics to him, distance, concealment, killing, disposal, the language of someone for whom the hunt was as routine as breathing.

He fell silent. And a crack seemed to open in the walls around me. My thoughts latched onto it, the possibility, sharp and bright as sunlight through a half-open door. Despite the horror. Was this it? My chance to break free, to run, to scream loud enough for someone to hear? I could almost feel the shift, the release of unseen restraints. But the image wavered, fragile and treacherous, a mirage in hostile terrain. One wrong move and that sliver of freedom would slam shut, locking me deeper in the dark.

The thought surged through me, heady and intoxicating, a jolt of something dangerously close to hope. I could see myself on the other side of it, away from him, away from this, a different future.

But even as my pulse quickened, a quieter voice threaded through the noise, insidious and persuasive. A small part of me had adapted to the attic, to the strange stillness of the room. I'd carved out a corner where I could lose myself in brushstrokes and colour, where the world outside felt distant and unreal.

The contradiction made my skin crawl. Freedom was there, gleaming just beyond reach, and yet... in that confined space, there was a semblance of control. I pushed the thought away, hard, forcing it back into the shadows where it belonged.

'Can I paint before we go?'

Charles nodded slowly, his eyes locking on mine with malignant intent.

'We'll choose a suitable target once we reach the city's red-light district,' he said, each word gleeful, as though savouring the plan aloud. 'And you'll help me capture her. Draw her in. Subdue her. Lock her in the boot. And then the creature will be ours to... entertain... at will, once we get her back to the house. Pass that test and I'll know you're the one. You won't have to die.'

I forced a quickly vanishing smile, brittle, the kind that falters before it ever takes hold.

'But make no mistake...' he hissed moments later, slipping the glasses from his face with care before leaning in, close enough for the heat of his breath to taint my skin. His eyes were flat, predatory things that reflected no hint of humanity. The words slithered from his mouth, alive, venomous. 'If I sense even a flicker of doubt, if you give me the slightest reason to question your commitment, I'll end you. I'll slice you open from ear to ear and savour the moment the light dies in your eyes. Never forget that. Not for a heartbeat. Not for a breath. You'll keep me satisfied, or you won't keep breathing.'

29

Time crawled once the darkness settled, each hour bleeding into the next. Every minute stretched until it seemed the night might never end. I lay awake in the attic room, pinned beneath the weight of my own thoughts, watching the shadows shift across the ceiling. They moved with a life of their own, circling, pressing in, relentless. And the silence wasn't silence at all. It was a living thing, broken only by the hammer of my pulse in my ears, louder with every heartbeat, a merciless reminder that Charles's arrival was creeping closer, inevitable, inescapable whether I was ready or not.

Bristol was supposed to equal salvation. I told myself it offered the chance of escape, an opportunity to breathe, without fear coiled tight around my chest. Freedom was what I wanted, what I had always wanted. And yet whenever I let myself picture leaving, the relief was tangled with something strange and uncertain. The attic, for all its claustrophobic confines, had become my sanctuary. My canvases stood sentinel against the walls, mute witnesses to my struggle. The air was heavy with the sharp tang of oils and turpentine, scents that had become as familiar as breath. Each brushstroke I'd laid down remained with me, etched into the room itself, binding me, comforting me, holding me together when everything else threatened to come apart.

And as crazy as it sounds even to me, the idea of walking away felt like tearing myself open. Freedom and loss twisted together so tightly I couldn't tell one from the other. My chest ached with the weight of it all, the impossible push and pull of conflicting truths. I wanted to go. I wanted to stay. I wanted both. I wanted neither. And still the hours dragged on, cruel and endless, as though taking pleasure in watching me unravel. I was a tangled mess of contradictions that made very little sense at all.

The attic door suddenly crashed open when I was finally drifting into fitful sleep, the frame shuddering with the impact, and he filled the threshold, a dark shadow. Charles's demeanour had shifted, urgent now, edged with anger. Draped over his arm was a bundle of rags, once-bright fabrics leeched of life, the colours bled to grey, seams frayed to nothing. They sagged in his grip like relics exhumed from the earth. The stench hit me before he dropped them, musty cloth steeped in iron, the unmistakable reek of old blood. A parody of freedom, a hippy's costume, he called it, long since rotted into something awful.

'Put them on,' he ordered, dropping them at my feet.

I stayed frozen, unable to move.

'Now,' he snapped, the word slicing through the room as he drew his arm back, slapping my face.

My hands shook as I fumbled with the clothing, pulling the fabric over my skin. The top clung where a bloodstain had stiffened. But I ignored it. Said nothing. And when I was finally done, I kept my eyes lowered, the shock of it all prickling my flesh.

'Hands out.' The next barked order.

This time I didn't hesitate. The cuffs bit cold and hard, steel locking bone to bone, the finality of it crushing. He tugged at my wrists, testing, and a cruel smile flickered at the corner of his mouth.

The clippers came next, the low growl of their blades filling the room.

'Turn your back. Sit. Keep your mouth shut. And don't so much as breathe without my say-so.'

He caught the back of my head, shoved it forward, and pressed the buzzing steel to my scalp. The vibration jarred my skull, my hair tumbling in lifeless clumps around me. Each strand stripped away felt like a theft, as if he was erasing me piece by piece.

'Yes, better,' he muttered, his voice thick with a dark satisfaction, the words rolling over me like a verdict. He stepped back a pace, slowly circled me, head tilting, eyes narrowing as if he were admiring a ghastly creation of his own making. As if I were a work of art. And he the artist.

From his pocket he produced a small, cracked mirror and held it up to my face. I barely recognised the reflection staring back. My scalp was ragged, raw where the blades had scraped too close, the shorn hair clinging in patches of sweat and dust. My eyes looked wider, hollow, as if the clippers had stolen more than my hair, they'd stolen the last fragments of myself. I looked like the ghost of someone I might once have known, a hollowed-out stranger wearing bloodstained rags. In the light of day, my appearance may have attracted attention. But there'd be nothing but dark in the early hours of the night.

He smirked, clearly satisfied with the devastation, then snapped the mirror shut and shoved it back into his coat.

'Better,' he muttered again, his voice low with satisfaction. Then louder: 'Up. Move. The hunt is on. No time for delay.'

He yanked me to my feet and dragged me towards the door. The stairs groaned underfoot as we descended, the air sharpening, colder with every step.

Outside, the night breathed against me, icy, merciless. Snow had begun to fall, a hush of white settling on the lawn, indifferent to my terror. He shoved me hard, the cuffs biting, my bare scalp stinging with each flake that touched it.

'Get in the van,' he ordered, gesturing towards a vehicle I hadn't seen before. It squatted on the gravel like some rusting beast, its once-white paint scabbed and peeling, the metal pitted and eaten through. A relic of neglect.

I stumbled into the bumper, the jolt shooting up my legs, the cuffs biting deeper with the impact. He shoved again, harder this time, driving me towards the passenger door. The hinges groaned as he wrenched it open, the dark interior yawning before me. There was no choice but to climb inside.

It took Charles three turns of the key before the engine coughed, spluttered, and finally roared into reluctant life. His frustration boiled over in a guttural scream, the sound tearing through the confines of the van before he slammed it into first gear and lurched forward towards the gates.

The shock of movement, of being carried back into the open world, struck me as almost surreal. Pavements, streetlamps, the faint glow of shopfronts, it was all there, so achingly familiar, and yet I no longer belonged to it. The windscreen might as well have been a wall of iron, sealing me in, keeping me apart.

Carmarthen unfolded around me in fragments I recognised: my old King Street bedsit, the curve of Castle Hill, the sweep down towards the river. Landmarks from a life I could barely touch. But the recognition brought no comfort. It only sharpened the distance. I wasn't part of any of it any more. I inhabited a different place now, a place of death and fear, where the world I'd once known could only be glimpsed through the smear of dirty glass.

Charles's demeanour shifted on the long drive, turning strangely jovial, as if the journey itself were a cause for celebration. For two and a half hours he played the part, whistling tunelessly and occasionally muttering to himself as the van ate up the miles, through Swansea, past Cardiff, and over the Prince of Wales Bridge into England. He broke the silence for the first time in over an hour as we left the motorway at junction 19, swinging the van onto the M32. Telling me it ran straight into Bristol, his voice almost casual, as though we were on some late-night errand rather than trapped in the nightmare he'd fashioned.

It was gone midnight by then. The snow had ceased, leaving the roads slick and glistening, the dark sky washed in shades of iron grey. A half-moon hung exposed above the city, no longer veiled by cloud, casting its pallid light across the tarmac.

I stole a glance at him as the glow of Bristol began to gather on the horizon. My body shook uncontrollably, the thin clothes offering little defence against the creeping cold, though fear played its part. Every turn of the wheels carried me closer to something I couldn't name but dreaded with every fibre of my being.

His voice cut through the drone of the engine as if he'd been turning the words over for miles.

'When we get into the red-light district, I'll pick out a suitable target,' he said, eyes fixed on the road, hands loose on the wheel. 'A vulnerable creature. Someone nobody will miss. She'll make the perfect guest. And then we'll have some fun.'

The words landed like blows, each syllable heavy with intent. I turned my face towards the window, the half-moon reflected in the glass like an indifferent witness.

He carried on, almost conversational.

'And when I've chosen, you'll play your part. Another test. You'll show me you're not just dead weight, that you're with me in this. On my side.'

My skin prickled, scalp raw beneath the thin fall of stubble, the handcuffs biting as I shifted in my seat. I wanted to scream that I wasn't his plaything, that I would never be on his side, but the words lodged like stones in my throat. The van rattled on, tyres hissing across the wet tarmac, carrying me deeper into his madness.

I forced myself to breathe, shallow and slow, though every fibre of me shook. The thought of another girl, some unsuspecting stranger, being dragged into this nightmare was unbearable. But his eyes gleamed in the glow of the dashboard, and I knew he was watching for weakness. He fed on it. Tested it. Waiting to see if I would break.

I didn't answer. I couldn't. Silence was my only weapon, pitiful though it was. The city lights grew sharper ahead, neon bleeding into the night, and I felt the weight of his words pressing down, binding me tighter than the cuffs on my wrists. Another test. Another descent.

Charles took one hand off the steering wheel and struck me with the back of his fist, causing my lip to spit.

'Use your words, Olivia. Tell me you understand.'

I spat blood from my mouth. 'I d-do.'

The red-light district announced itself in fragments, the throb of bass spilling from a club, the harsh laughter of men lingering on corners, the glint of neon signs bleeding against wet-black brick. Women stood scattered beneath the sickly glow of streetlamps, their faces painted, their smiles brittle, the smoke from their cigarettes curling like ghosts into the night.

And Charles slowed the van, his eyes flicking from pavement to pavement, the predator's appraisal clear in his gaze.

'So many to choose from,' he said softly, almost to himself, but loud enough for me to hear. 'But only the weakest will do. The most vulnerable. A creature who won't be missed.'

His words seeped under my skin. Each woman I saw blurred into the next: ridiculously short skirts, bare arms goose-pimpled against the cold, a defiance in their stance that masked the fragility beneath. I wanted to look away, but couldn't. My eyes locked on them, each a living reminder of what he intended, of what he meant me to be part of.

The van inched forward, the beams from the headlights slicing through the dark, catching on graffiti-scarred walls and the bent, hollow-eyed figures that stood on the kerb. Neon flickered and died in the wing mirrors, leaving only shadow. Somewhere in the distance a siren rose, thin and disinterested, before fading back into the night.

He kept driving, deeper into the city's underbelly, where the noise thinned and the streets grew meaner, stripped of colour and light. The van nosed into a narrow backstreet, its windows smeared with condensation, the buildings hunched and sagging on either side. He braked hard and killed the engine beneath a stuttering streetlamp that buzzed like an angry wasp, its sickly glow flaring and failing in uneven bursts.

And then he pointed. A girl stood framed in the doorway of a crumbling terrace, the yellow spill of light from inside cutting across her face. She couldn't have been more than eighteen or nineteen, still with the fragile air of youth clinging to her. Tottering on stilettos too high for the uneven pavement, she leaned against the brickwork for balance, her bare legs mottled blue in the cold. The skirt she wore was indecently short, hardly covering her at all, a thin scrap of fabric masquerading as clothing.

Charles opened the van's windows with an electric buzz.

'Look closely,' he murmured, the words low and intimate, his knuckles whitening as his hands clenched into fists on the wheel. His eyes never left the girl, but his voice was for me. 'I always know when the moment comes. She's the one. Call her over. Offer her money. Whatever she asks, you agree. No hesitation.'

He leaned a fraction closer, his breath hot against my ear. 'And I'll take care of the rest. I'll get her in the back, lock the doors. I've got a sedative ready, she'll be quiet soon enough. Won't make a sound.'

His tone hardened, the softness gone, replaced by steel. 'Come on. Do it. Before she moves on. This is your test, not mine. Show me you're part of this. That you belong.'

My throat was raw, the words sticking like glass, but I forced them out.

'Over here,' I called, my voice barely recognisable to me. Thin. Trembling.

The girl's head lifted at once, her painted smile faltering as she tottered forward on those high heels, legs unsteady beneath the flimsy skirt.

Beside me, Charles leaned forward, his breath quickening as if anticipation itself fed him. I could feel the heat of him, coiled, ready to pounce.

The girl drew closer, no more than a few steps away now. Her face came into focus under the stuttering glow of the streetlamp, young, far too young, eyes dulled by weariness but not yet hardened enough to conceal her fear. Vulnerable. Exactly what he wanted.

Something in me broke. I couldn't let it happen. As she neared the passenger door, her eyes met mine. And for a fleeting second the world narrowed to that fragile connection, two strangers bound in desperation. I silently mouthed the word, shaping it with everything I had left. *Run.*

Her scarlet-painted lips parted, confusion flickering across her face, but she'd seen it. She'd understood.

And all the while Charles shifted in his seat, oblivious, his hand tightening on the door handle, ready to spring the trap.

For a heartbeat the girl faltered, frozen in the glare of the flickering streetlamp like some startled animal, her eyes wide with disbelief. Then instinct won. She spun on her heels, the sharp clatter of them on the wet tarmac loud in the silence, and bolted.

Charles roared, the sound feral, as he unfastened my cuffs with a violent twist. In a blur, one cuff snapped back around my wrist while he locked the other to the steering wheel, the steel biting shut with brutal efficiency and tethering me in place.

'Stay put,' he spat, his voice shaking with rage.

And then he was gone, the van rocking as he slammed the door behind him, his boots hammering the ground as he tore after her.

I watched, helpless, as the girl stumbled at a doorway, hands scrabbling at the handle. Locked. She rattled it once, twice, panic flaring across her face as Charles closed the distance. In one desperate movement she kicked off her shoes, the heels skittering across the pavement, and sprinted barefoot into a narrow alleyway, the sound of her steps muffled by the damp.

Charles followed without hesitation, his shadow swallowing hers as the darkness claimed them both.

And then there was nothing. Nothing but the echo of their pursuit and the thunder of my own heart, chained, powerless, waiting for what would come next.

I sat tethered to the wheel, the cuff biting deep into my wrist each time I pulled against it. Five minutes passed. Or maybe more. Time bled in strange ways when fear took hold, each second stretched and as sharp as broken glass. I twisted, tugged, tried every angle I could think of, but the metal held fast. My skin stung where it cut into me, slick with sweat. Escape was a fantasy.

A shadow moved outside, and I froze. A dishevelled man, hood pulled up against the cold, hands jammed in his pockets, shuffled past the van. My heart leapt to my throat.

'Help,' I whispered through the open window, desperate, testing the word like it might explode. I couldn't risk more; Charles might hear, wherever he was, and I'd pay for it. 'Please. Help me.'

The man glanced sideways, the briefest flicker of eye contact through the dirty glass windscreen, and then he looked away. His pace quickened, footsteps splashing through the puddles as he hurried on, shoulders hunched. He'd seen. He'd known. And he'd chosen not to see at all. I tried pressing the horn, once, then again, harder the second time, but nothing. No sound at all.

The silence folded back over me, heavy and suffocating. I slumped against the wheel, every nerve braced for Charles's return. And then I heard it, the steady thud of footsteps approaching. The van rocked as the door yanked open, and Charles hauled himself back into the driver's seat. Alone.

He climbed into the van, panting hard, and the sight of him turned my stomach. His face was slick with sweat and streaked with blood that matted his hairline and smeared across his nose. And whatever had happened in the black maw of that alley hadn't dulled his hunger. It had stoked it. He wasn't finished. Not with me. Not with anyone.

He leaned across me without warning, the heat of him suffocating, and snapped open the cuff that chained me to the steering wheel. Relief flared for the briefest instant then died as he wrenched my arms together and forced both wrists into the steel. The ratchet clinked home, biting hard into raw skin, binding me even tighter than before.

Then, with brutal precision, he twisted the van into a three-point turn, tyres spitting water. Headlights flared across the crumbling street before he stamped the accelerator to the floor. The van leapt forward, rattling with speed, throwing me back into the seat, the cuffs cutting deep.

We tore back the way we'd come, the city flashing by in fragments, neon bleeding into shadow, and still he drove harder, like a man with something to prove.

'I had to kill the bitch far too quickly,' he said, his voice ragged, tears streaking through the blood on his face. 'Too much fight in her for such a scrawny little creature. Wouldn't lie down. Wouldn't give in. And then some interfering bastard shouted as he came into the alley from the opposite direction at the worst possible time. Left me no choice.'

He gave a twisted smile, lips wet, teeth stained red. Blood coated his mouth, dark and glistening, seeping between his teeth. His jaw worked as if he were chewing on the taste of it, savouring it. His eyes burned with a feral light, alive with something unhinged and ravenous.

'I bit into her neck one last time and ran,' he said, his voice low, almost reflective, as though recounting some trivial disappointment rather than murder.

'So disappointing. All too quick. No joy in it. No real satisfaction. Over before it even began. But unavoidable, I'm afraid. Needs must.'

He exhaled sharply, the sound breaking into a shudder that twisted at the edges into something close to laughter. His eyes glowed fever-bright, lips curled, blood still glistening at the corners of his mouth.

'We'll review and evaluate when we're back at the house,' he said, clinical, like a tutor delivering feedback. 'Learn from it. Adjust. Refine. And then... on to the next one.'

He glanced sideways at me, the look sharp enough to cut.

'I'll admit, your presence tonight was something of a distraction. But I won't hold it against you. Not yet, at least.'

A pause, heavy with intent.

'You haven't passed this test yet, of course. But you can resit, one final chance. I'll devise something suitable, give you the opportunity to truly prove yourself. You should be grateful for that.'

I swallowed hard. Said what he wanted to hear. He didn't realise I'd warned the girl. Tried to help her. And my relief was almost palpable.

'Thank y-you. It's appreciated.'

He smiled then, slow and joyless, eyes burning behind his lenses with feverish light.

'That's the spirit. Yes, that's it, try to look on the positive side. I like to think you can still claw your way back. Still save your life if you prove yourself worthy.'

30

The van rattled and groaned as it ate up the miles, every shudder of the engine dragging me closer to despair. My pulse throbbed in my throat, as though my body already knew the futility of hope. I stared out through the smeared glass, willing myself to hear the rising wail of sirens, the thundering certainty of pursuit. But the road remained empty, the silence unbroken, but for the drone of tyres and the uneven clatter of gears. Each passing mile stripped away another layer of belief. If the police were coming, they would have been there by then.

By the time we crossed back into Wales, dread had hollowed me out. My tethered hands trembled in my lap, knuckles white, nails biting into the fragile skin of my palms. Charles drove without another word, the tight set of his jaw an iron lock I dared not touch. And the further we travelled, the more the landscape closed in, a suffocating reminder that I was being carried away from hope, deeper into the dark heart of his control.

When the van finally ground to a halt in the gravel driveway, my chest tightened until I could barely breathe. The Georgian house loomed above me, its symmetry stripped of grace, every line rigid and unwelcoming. Once proud, its stone façade was weathered and cold, the pale render streaked with years of neglect. The tall sash windows stared down like watchful sentinels, their panes blind to mercy. The door, heavy and austere, seemed less an entrance than a barrier, holding its secrets tight. There was no warmth, no refuge in its architecture. A mausoleum draped in domestic disguise.

'Out,' he barked, his tone making me flinch.

I hesitated, my fingers clinging to the seat edge.

'Now!' His knuckles cracked against my face. 'Move yourself.'

I scrambled out, legs unsteady, warm blood dripping from my nose.

'Inside,' he snapped, pushing me forward with a shove. 'Move. Upstairs. Now. Don't drag your heels. You know exactly where you're meant to be. Even a half-wit animal would've grasped it by now.'

The familiar creak of the boards beneath my feet betrayed my every step as he drove me upward and into the attic.

It should have been a low point as he followed me in. The enforced return to my prison. And yet... now free of the cuffs, relief washed over me the moment I turned and my gaze fell on the canvases scattered across the walls. My work, my world, still mine, even there. The colours seemed to pulse against the faded wallpaper, small rebellions of life against his suffocating grey. The sight anchored me, calmed the storm.

I set a blank canvas on the easel, hands still shaking, and pressed the brush into the paint.

'That's it. Best keep yourself busy,' he said from the doorway, watching me with that familiar stare. 'Try not to be too disappointed. There'll be other hunts ahead. You can be sure of that.'

And then he was gone, leaving only the echo of his presence. The quiet that followed was a fragile reprieve, yet my world felt momentarily steadier, safer, as though the very walls exhaled in relief.

The bristles of my brush met the surface with a kind of desperation, each stroke carving out a space where he could not reach me. The rhythm steadied me, a bitter medicine that was mine alone. And with every line and shade I laid down, I reclaimed a fragment of myself. In the attic room, I could almost believe I belonged.

The days blurred into one another after that, a colourless cycle of confinement. Four mornings, four nights. The rasp of the key in the lock, the scrape of the tray across the floor, the stale scent of bread and water. Charles's voice always clipped, sometimes measured, drifted in and out of my world like a ghost.

'Eat,' he'd command, watching until I obeyed. 'Keep painting,' he'd add, his eyes flicking to the canvases as if measuring the edges of my mind.

And then the lock would click again, and I'd be left with nothing but silence and the whisper of my brush against canvas.

I lost myself in the paint, hours bleeding away as I clawed fragments of freedom from the colours. Strokes of defiance. Shapes of longing. Each canvas became a lifeline, a fragile thread binding me to the belief that I still existed beyond his will.

But on the fifth morning, the rhythm broke. The door flew open without warning and Charles filled the frame. There was something unfamiliar in his eyes, an edge that hadn't been there before. Urgency, sharp and restless, flickered beneath the surface, colliding with a raw agitation he couldn't disguise. His look darted and held, a restless current that unsettled me, as if he were teetering on the brink of something he could neither control nor contain.

'Up,' he snapped, his voice rising in pitch and tone.

I froze, brush still in hand, paint wet on the canvas. 'What's happening?'

He stepped into the room, keys rattling at his side.

'On your feet.'

My legs obeyed before my mind could catch up, fear propelling me upright.

'Why? What—?'

He silenced me with a glare, alight with a cruel anticipation.

'I've devised another little test for you, Olivia,' he said, savouring each word as if they were delicacies on his tongue. 'An opportunity to truly prove yourself. I'm confident you'll appreciate the chance, or at the very least, you'd be wise to try. I've gone to considerable trouble on your behalf.'

The word hung between us. 'Test'. My stomach lurched, acid clawing at my throat.

'A test?' I whispered.

He smiled then, thin and cruel, the kind of smile that had nothing to do with humanity.

'You've enjoyed your sanctuary long enough. Now we'll see what you're really made of.'

My pulse hammered in my ears, drowning out everything else.

'Move,' he ordered, stepping aside to clear the doorway.

I clutched the edge of the easel for balance, my mind screaming to resist, to cling to the canvases that had kept me whole. But the choice was gone. He had decided, and I was his to command.

'Don't make me tell you again,' he said softly, the menace worse for its restraint.

He led me from the attic room without the cold weight of steel around my wrists. And I clung to that detail, fragile as it was, forcing myself to see it as a victory of sorts. A hollow triumph, perhaps, but in a world stripped bare of hope, even the smallest fracture in his control felt like something I could claim as my own. I forced myself forward, each step dragging me away from the only refuge I had left, into whatever horror he had prepared.

Charles's shove sent me stumbling into the banister. I fought for balance, but his hand was already on me again, dragging me upright with brutal impatience.

'On your feet,' he spat, his grip like iron on my arm.

My legs threatened to buckle, next to useless, barely carrying me as he wrenched me down the stairs. The structure groaned with each forced step, the house itself complicit in my humiliation.

At the bottom Charles tightened his hold, his fingers clamping around my wrist until I thought the bones might splinter. Without a word he hauled me across the hall, towards a door I'd never seen before, half-hidden in shadow. The hinges creaked as he pulled it open, revealing a narrow flight of stone steps descending into darkness.

'Down,' he ordered, shoving me forward.

The air grew colder as I stumbled, damp and heavy, carrying the sour tang of rot. My heart battered against my ribs, each beat louder than the last, echoing in the cavern of my chest.

At the final step he shoved me hard, sending me sprawling onto the floor. My knees cracked against the concrete, skin tearing, palms scraping raw on its coarse surface. Pain shot up my arms, sharp and immediate, before the darkness fractured. A switch snapped and the cellar burst into blinding light, harsh, sterile, merciless. The glare seared my eyes, flooding every corner, stripping the shadows bare like an interrogation lamp trained on the guilty.

I raised a trembling hand to shield my eyes, the sudden electric glare stabbing into them like blades. Spots of white seared across my vision, the brightness disorientating. I blinked hard, again and again, until the shapes around me bled into focus. And then the breath caught in my throat and refused to move, a stone lodged tight in my chest. I stared, frozen, incapable of reconciling what I saw with any rational sense of reality, unable and unwilling to believe the evidence of my own eyes.

Joe. He was hanging, shackled to the far wall, arms and legs stretched wide in the shape of an X. Naked. Bruised. Bloody. His skin a map of suffering, every mark a story of horrors I couldn't bear to imagine. Blood crusted dark against fresh wounds, his body sagging against the irons that bit into his wrists and ankles. I asked myself how long he'd been there, and had no answer.

A plastic line snaked from a needle in his arm to a drip stand at his side, the clear bag above him mocking in its simplicity; life sustained only at Charles's whim.

The stench hit me then, sour, the mingling of blood, sweat and worse, soaking the concrete floor in dark, sticky patches.

I pressed a trembling hand to my mouth, fighting back the vomit that surged up my throat. My mind screamed denial, but my eyes wouldn't release me.

Joe's head lifted fractionally, a flicker of movement, his eyes searching, finding me through the haze of pain.

And in that moment the room seemed to close in around me, the walls pressing tight, the light itself becoming an instrument of cruelty.

Joe blinked, opened his bloodshot eyes, his lips cracked. And the sound he made was barely human, a rasp dragged from somewhere deep inside him.

'J-Joe...' The word slipped out, unbidden, jagged in my throat.

And behind me, Charles laughed, filled with evident satisfaction.

'Ah, yes, look, Olivia. A gift from me to you. Your great love. Though he wasn't much of one, was he?' His voice was a knife, prising open old wounds. 'I've been entertaining him these past days, breaking him down, piece by piece. And now it's your turn. How many times did he lie to you? How many nights did he find his comfort in someone else's bed while you cried yourself to sleep?'

'Stop...' My voice trembled, weak, barely a whisper.

And Charles's eyes glittered, triumphant. 'He betrayed you. Made you look a fool. And yet here he is, clinging to life like it matters. Pathetic. How could he ever believe he deserves to live?'

Charles moved closer, his footsteps echoing on the concrete. 'Your test is simple. You kill him.'

The words hung in the air, shameless. I stumbled back, but his hand clamped down on my shoulder, steadying me with brutal force.

'No. I can't. I won't.'

Charles kissed my neck, standing close behind. Then whispered in my ear. 'Oh, but you will. You certainly will. Because if you don't, your lovely foster mother, Eva, will be next.'

The sound of her name froze me. I turned, stared at him, shaking my head.

'Oh, yes,' he went on, savouring every syllable. 'I saw her. Morning television, after your apparent cliff dive. Tearful interviews, the nation hanging on her every word. She's been busy. Starting a charity in your name. Raising money for lost girls. For broken young people, just like you.'

Charles pressed the knife into my hand, curling my fingers tight around the hilt until the metal dug into my skin. And then he quickly jumped away, taking a yellow Taser from a high shelf and pointing it straight at me.

'Just a little self-protection,' he sneered. 'Until I can be entirely sure I can trust you with my life. So, here's your choice. Cut this faithless coward who spat on your love, or watch Eva take his place on that wall. I have any number of tortures etched in my mind.'

The blade seemed to burn in my hand, its weight unbearable. Joe's eyes locked on mine, pleading, broken, but still his, still the same eyes that once swore love and betrayed it in the same breath.

The cellar spun, the lights seared into me, Charles's words pinning me in a nightmare of impossible choices.

'Choose, Olivia,' Charles hissed, relishing the moment. 'End him... or he dies anyway, and Eva does too. Your choice. It really is up to you.'

Eva's lovely face rose in my mind, her smile, her warmth, the quiet strength in her eyes when I had nothing. She had been my anchor, my proof that not everyone was cruel. I could still hear her voice, soft with kindness, urging me forward when all I wanted was to collapse.

Then, unbidden, the shadows returned: men's hands, rough and unrelenting, stealing pieces of me I could never recover. Their laughter, their breath, their weight pressing me into silence.

And finally Joe. His smile, his promises. The way he held me as if I mattered. And then the lies, the photos. The betrayal that had shattered what little trust I had left.

The knife shook in my hand, slick with sweat. But my legs carried me forward, slow, heavy, as though each step dragged me deeper into a pit I would never climb out of.

I hesitated, trembling, internally begging myself to stop. But Charles's shadow loomed behind me, heavy with expectation, and Eva's face glimmered in my mind again, fragile, fleeting.

A scream tore from my chest as the blade drove forward, plunging deep into Joe's stomach. His cry broke the air, raw and animal, and still I struck again. And again. And again. Each thrust was chaos, grief, rage, and terror, exploding through me in a frenzy I couldn't contain.

Blood sprayed warm across my hands, splattered the concrete, ran in rivulets down his body. Joe sagged against the chains, gasping, choking, his eyes fading even as they pleaded with me.

And behind me, Charles howled with glee.

'Yes!' he roared, his voice booming off the cellar walls. 'That's it! That's my girl!' He danced across the floor, clapping, whooping, his mad laughter echoing. 'Congratulations, Olivia! You've passed! You've done it!'

The knife slipped from my hand, clattering against the concrete, crimson smeared across my fingers. My legs gave way, and I collapsed at Joe's feet, the metallic tang of blood heavy in my throat.

Charles's cheers rang above me, triumphant, deafening, as I curled against the floor, drowning in the enormity of what I had done.

My sobs tore through the cellar as Joe's blood pooled, warm and slick, seeping into my clothes, into my skin, into the very marrow of me. The knife lay discarded at my side, a shard of steel still wet with his life.

And Charles's laughter still echoed off the walls, manic, triumphant, before dwindling to something colder, sharper. He stood over me, breathing hard, eyes shining with the thrill of victory.

'Look at you,' he said, his voice stripped of warmth, the celebration already fading from his tone. 'A killer. My masterpiece.'

I pressed my hands to my ears, trying to block him out, but the words forced their way in, poisoning what little strength I had left.

'You see now, don't you? The truth of it. You're no different to me. The world carved us from the same stone, Olivia. You've just proven it. You are mine and I am yours.'

I shook my head, sobbing harder, rocking where I lay. 'No... no...'

He put the Taser in a jacket pocket, picked up the knife, then crouched beside me, close enough that his shadow swallowed mine. His hand brushed my shoulder, mockingly tender.

'Yes. And you'll remember this moment for the rest of your life, every thrust, every scream. You'll remember the way it felt to finally stop being the victim.'

I dragged my gaze to Joe. His head slumped against the chains, blood dripping steadily onto the floor. His eyes, glazed and unseeing, stared past me into the void.

'Enough,' Charles muttered, straightening. His triumph was already cooling, hardening into something more methodical. He reached for the light switch, his silhouette stretching tall across the cellar wall.

'I'll leave you with him for a while. You deserve that much. Grieve, pray, do whatever you need to do. But don't for a moment think about escape.'

I turned to him, my face streaked with tears and blood. 'Please... don't leave me here.'

'I'll be back in an hour or two,' he said, flat and businesslike now. 'With the tools. We'll need to dispose of him properly. As with the last one.'

The words fell like a hammer, final, irrevocable. Then the light snapped off, plunging the cellar back into blackness, the air thick with blood. The door closed behind him with a heavy slam.

And I was left alone with Joe's broken body, the stink of death, and the knowledge that my hands had put him there.

31

Each second stretched thin in the company of Joe's cooling corpse. The stench of blood and excrement clung to the air, suffocating, seeping into my skin until I could almost taste it. The weight of what I had done pressed down on me, a relentless tide I could not hold back. My hands trembled, my chest heaved, and the sobs came whether I welcomed them or not.

And yet even as the tears burned my eyes, I whispered the words I needed to survive. That it had been necessary. That there had been no other way. I forced myself to believe Joe had earned his fate. That his betrayals, his easy cruelties, had led him there. Punishment, not murder. Justice, not savagery.

The words no longer felt like a lie but a truth I could almost cradle. Better him than Eva. Better his body lying cold and broken on the wall than hers. I repeated it like scripture, let it seep into me, until the guilt dulled and the ache in my chest numbed.

Joe's blood was on my hands, yes, but for the first time, I wasn't sure that was wrong. He had lied, betrayed, taken what he wanted while I wept. Hadn't he earned his fate? Hadn't he brought it on himself?

The thought settled deep inside me, solidifying into something that felt close to belief.

Something in me had shifted, irrevocably. I wasn't the fragile girl I once was, the one who would have splintered beneath the weight of it all. She was gone, silenced by the blood on my hands. What remained was different. This new self could endure the unendurable. Could carry the weight and still stand. Could survive.

The fear that had once hollowed me out had given way to something fiercer, something primal. I felt it stir in my chest, hot and restless, no longer the quivering of a cornered mouse but the defiance of a roaring lioness with nothing left to lose. A creature that would bare her teeth, snarl at the darkness, and fight to the last breath if she had to.

And it seemed Charles had seen it too, the change in me, the thing he believed he'd fashioned with his own hands. His creation. When he returned to the cellar hours later, there was a different air about him. The menace hadn't disappeared. How could it? But it had twisted into something more insidious, softened by a grotesque cheerfulness that curdled my stomach and made me despise him all the more. Joe's death had shifted the ground beneath us, altered the balance in ways I couldn't yet fully grasp. Charles regarded me now with a glimmer of satisfaction, as though I'd finally crossed the invisible line he had been waiting for all along.

'There she is,' he said when he flicked the light switch, his voice low, almost affectionate. 'The Olivia I always knew was hiding beneath all that weakness. Not a victim. Not a frightened little girl. But something stronger. Something mine.'

He smiled then, smug, certain of his victory.

'Joe was necessary. You see that now. And look at you... finally becoming what you were always meant to be.'

That night Charles didn't merely bark commands from the shadows. He moved with me, over me, guiding my hands as though I were a child learning some macabre new craft. His presence pressed close, his breath warm against my ear.

'Steady now,' he murmured, calm and coaxing, every syllable sliding beneath my skin. 'Let me hold his head back. That's it... saw away. Not too fast. Precision matters. It always matters. One day, Olivia, you'll thank me for this.'

Together we carved Joe into something unrecognisable, each cut accompanied by Charles's low instruction, his measured approval. The sound of his voice steadied me against the tremors in my own body, even as my stomach churned.

When the time came to dig, the earth fought me with every thrust of the spade, the packed soil firm, each stab met with resistance that jarred up through my body. My arms ached, weak with exhaustion, the weight of it dragging at my shoulders until I felt myself falter, breath catching in ragged gasps. And then his hand closed over mine, firm, insistent, possessive, his strength driving the blade down through the stubborn ground as though the earth itself bowed to his will. The metal bit deep with a dull, final sound, and I realised with a sick twist that I was grateful for his touch. Not out of affection – shit, nothing could be further from the truth – but because his support lent me something I hadn't possessed alone. Power. The deluded fool was trusting me more with every passing moment. And I felt less a victim and more like a force capable of shaping fate.

'There,' he said softly, almost tenderly. 'See how much easier it is when we do it together? You don't have to fight it alone. You'll learn to rely on me. We're a team, you and I.'

Charles wanted me to see that moment as another binding, a covenant sealed in blood and earth, tethering me to him more securely than any chain. So I let him. I let my eyes linger on his, let my silence pass for agreement, allowed him to believe I had stepped willingly into the darkness he had carved out for me. If that illusion kept him satisfied, if it lulled him into lowering his guard, then so be it.

But inside, I recoiled. Every fibre of me loathed what he had made me, the hollow shell he'd reshaped to fit his design. He had chipped away at the girl I once was, stripped me of innocence, buried me beneath layers of blood and obedience until I scarcely recognised myself.

And yet beneath it all, beneath the fear, beneath the guilt, something burned. A fire that whispered of revenge. He thought I belonged to him. But he was wrong. I would bide my time, let him believe we were bound together. And when the moment came, I would break him with the same ruthlessness he had taught me.

It was only a matter of time.

32

Charles loosened the leash after Joe's burial. I was allowed out of the attic, permitted to cook in the cavernous kitchen, to shower, to move through the house as though I belonged there. Yet every door was locked, every window sealed, the illusion of freedom another form of torment. He thought himself generous, magnanimous, but I knew better. A prison dressed in comfort was still a prison.

'You've become like me,' he told me time and again, smiling with that fevered pride. 'A predator. Just as I planned. Now we're soulmates, Olivia. Destined to live, and to kill, together. I was right all along. A reflection of my genius. It was always meant to be.'

Charles's words struck like a curse, but I refused to let them take root. He wanted me to wear my sins like a second skin, to believe I was already lost. But I knew the truth. I was not his mirror, not his partner. He had forced my hand, nothing more. And though he'd chained me with blood and buried me in fear, a part of me remained beyond his reach, untouched, defiant, waiting. I was a killer, yes. That much was true. But I wasn't his. No, never his.

In the weeks that followed, my thoughts circled endlessly around a single obsession: how to end Charles's life and erase him from the world, as though he had never drawn breath. I pictured it in fragments, his body silenced, his shadow gone, his poison bled from my veins. The craving for it grew in me like a hunger, gnawing day and night, until every glance, every movement, every sound he made fed the need to see him finished and buried, reduced to nothing. Every breath I drew in his presence was poisoned by the knowledge that he had stolen my life and reshaped it into something ghastly. I owed him nothing but the grave. Pouring my torment onto canvas no longer dulled the edges. The colours, the strokes, the desperate rhythm of the brush, it wasn't enough. The fury burned hotter, demanding more than mere paint could offer. I needed to see him broken. I needed to watch the bastard bleed.

But wanting him dead and finding a way to make it so were two very different things. I repeatedly turned over various possibilities in my mind, each one collapsing under the weight of his strength. A knife from the kitchen? Too obvious. He'd see it coming, twist it from my hand, bury it in me instead. A hammer, even if I could find one? He was too quick, too sure of himself. One false move and I'd be the one bleeding out on the floor.

I trained myself to think as he did, cold, patient, cautious. Minute by minute. Hour by hour. Day after day. Survival demanded it. Revenge demanded it more.

And then, early one morning, while he worked elsewhere in the house, I opened a bathroom cupboard and saw them. A forgotten bottle, shoved to the back behind a rusting razor and half-used blister packs of painkillers. Small white tablets rattling in their brown plastic shell, the sound faint yet thunderous in my ears.

I turned the bottle in my hand. And for the first time since Joe's body had entered the earth, I felt it – a flicker of possibility, fragile but alive. These weren't just sleeping pills. They were a weapon, hidden in plain sight. A way to shift the balance. A chance to silence Charles forever. Real hope.

I gripped the bottle so tightly the plastic creaked in protest, the label swimming before my eyes with the tremor in my fingers. A plan stirred in the shadows of my mind, fragile, tentative, but alive. He trusted me now, or at least he believed he did. In his eyes, the chains had been replaced by devotion, obedience. And maybe, just maybe, that trust would prove the key to his undoing.

But it couldn't be rushed. I needed a plan that left nothing to chance, one that carried the weight of certainty and stripped away the risk of failure. Because failure wasn't an option. If I faltered, if I made even the slightest error, it wouldn't be Charles going into the ground. It would be me.

That afternoon, the idea took shape, sliding into place as though it had been waiting for me all along. The bottle of pills was hidden where he would never think to look, its presence pulsing at the back of my mind like a secret heartbeat. Every glance I stole in his direction was charged with a purpose he could not see.

I found him in his study, staring at his computer screen with a glass of red wine in hand, a self-satisfied smirk playing at his lips. He looked relaxed, almost human, and the sight curdled my stomach. Still, I forced a smile of my own, smoothing my voice into something softer, almost eager.

'I was thinking,' I began carefully, stepping into the room, 'we should mark... the day.'

His eyes narrowed, suspicion flickering and then fading into something else, something smug. He set the glass aside and leaned forward, studying me as though I were a puzzle he had finally solved.

'Go on,' he said.

'I could cook for us tonight. Something special.' I kept my tone light, coaxing, as if the suggestion came from devotion rather than design. 'A proper meal. Just the two of us. Like we did on that first night when I arrived. A celebration.'

Charles's lips curled, the kind of smile that made my skin crawl. He rose slowly from the chair, closing the distance between us until I could feel the heat of him, his presence suffocating.

'A celebration of what, Olivia?' he asked softly, his breath close enough to stir the hairs at my temple.

I met his gaze, steady, willing him to see what he wanted to see.

'Of us,' I said. 'Of what we are now. You and me. Together.'

For a moment he said nothing, weighing me, his eyes searching for cracks. Then he laughed, a low, satisfied sound that seemed to vibrate in my chest.

'Yes,' he said at last, nodding slowly. 'I like that. Cook me something special. It will be an ideal chance to discuss our next hunting trip. I have something special in mind.'

I forced myself to smile again, even as revulsion twisted inside me. He believed me. That was all that mattered.

At around seven that evening I set about my work in the kitchen, the wide counters gleaming beneath the light, the smell of cumin and turmeric thick in the air. I chopped and stirred as Eva had taught me so well, with a precision born of necessity, every movement planned. A chicken curry, rich, fragrant, layered with spice. Something warming. Something that would mask bitterness.

When it was ready, I ladled the curry into two bowls, white for me, blue for him. My hand trembled only once as I crushed the tablets beneath the back of a spoon, the powder fine and white against the porcelain plate. I scraped it carefully into his portion, stirring until it dissolved, swallowed whole by the dark sauce. A weapon hidden in plain sight.

I carried the bowls through to the dining table, forcing a brightness into my face, a softness into my voice. He was already seated, watching me with that smug curl of the lip that passed for a smile.

'Smells good,' he said, his eyes flicking to mine with a glint of amusement.

'Only the best for you,' I replied, setting the bowl before him with exaggerated care. 'You deserve it. A man like you... powerful, decisive, always in control.'

His smile widened as he leaned back in his chair, clearly savouring the words more than the food.

'Go on,' he said, his tone playful, but edged with command. 'Tell me more.'

I slid into the chair opposite, my own bowl untouched for the moment. 'You've changed me,' I whispered, lowering my gaze just enough to suggest submission. 'Made me stronger. Given me purpose. I'd be nothing without you. And my paintings have become all the more powerful because of it.'

He laughed softly, lifting the fork, letting the curry's steam rise between us. 'At last, you understand. You see who we are now. Bound by blood and truth.'

'Yes,' I murmured. 'Soulmates.'

I forced a quickly vanishing smile, though my stomach twisted into knots as he dipped the fork at last and raised it to his lips. My breath caught, suspended, while he tasted the first mouthful. The silence stretched, taut and suffocating, every second an eternity. My heart pounded with a single, unspoken question. Would he accept my offering, or spit it back in my face and damn me with it?

'Well?' I asked, my voice sharper than I'd meant. 'Do you like it? Powerful men deserve a powerful meal.'

He chewed slowly, his eyes fixed on me, weighing my reaction. For a heartbeat I was certain he'd spit it out, declare it bitter, expose me. But then he swallowed, set the fork down, and grinned. 'Not bad at all,' he said. 'It seems you have another talent.'

Relief surged through me, hot and dizzying. I leaned forward, urging, my voice low and coaxing.

'Have another mouthful. There's plenty more where that came from. I made it just for you.'

Charles obliged, a lamb to the slaughter, lifting the fork again and again, his appetite quickening as I sent more praise across the table like bait.

'You really do have refined tastes,' I said lightly. 'I've never cooked for anyone who appreciated food quite like you.'

And he kept eating. Each mouthful tightening the snare as I watched him closely, my pulse pounding as the minutes dragged by. When he yawned, wide and unguarded, elation surged through me. It was working. His lids grew heavy, his movements sluggish, the bravado slipping from him like a mask no longer held in place. He pushed back from the table, unsteady, dragging himself upright with a clumsy scrape of the chair.

'I don't... feel right,' he muttered, blinking hard, as if he could force the fog from his mind. His hand shot to the tabletop, fumbling, closing around a knife. His eyes fixed on me, wild, dangerous. 'What... the hell have you... done?'

I tensed as he lurched towards me, the knife quivering in his fist, his eyes fevered with hate. Every nerve in my body screamed at me to bolt, to shrink into the shadows, to vanish. But instead, I forced myself upright, retreating one step at a time. Terror pressed hard against my ribs, threatening to crush me, but I held his stare. I refused to flinch. Refused to gift him the satisfaction of tears.

Then I let out a loud cheer as his legs gave out. He collapsed to his knees with a heavy thud, the knife clattering uselessly to the floor. His words slurred into nothing, his eyes rolled back, and then he crumpled, lost to the chemically induced sleep. For a long moment I stood over him, chest heaving, listening to the silence. Then I moved.

It took every ounce of strength I had to drag his dead weight across the floor, his heels scraping against the tiles, his body slack and heavy as stone. Inch by inch, I pulled him down the hall, through the door, into the gallery I had come to think of as a killing room. The stench lingered there, still damp and decay, the memory of rot etched into the walls.

I stripped Charles naked, tearing away his clothes piece by piece until he lay exposed on the cold boards just as I once had. The reversal was stark, almost surreal: the predator reduced to prey, the master brought low. A fitting mirror of what he had made of me. He had always craved dominance but here, now, he was reduced to nothing.

I positioned him with care, dragging him into the exact spot where I'd first seen the corpse rotting on the evening of my arrival. The symmetry wasn't lost on me. It was fitting. Poetic, even.

My hands still shook as I reached for the cuffs, the same steel that had once bitten into my wrists. I snapped them shut around his, the metallic click loud in the silence, then shackled his ankles with equal precision. He was bound now, just as he had bound me. The predator caged. The balance reversed.

And for the first time since he had lured me into his world of horror, I felt something close to control. More powerful than I ever had in my life.

Charles came to hours later, groaning, his head lolling, before his eyes fixed on me with wild fury. The chains rattled as he strained against them, his whole body jerking.

'You bitch!' he spat, voice hoarse, eyes blazing. 'I'll gut you alive when I get free. I'll carve you open, watch you scream, watch you bleed out at my feet. I'll break every bone in your body and make you beg for death before I give it to you.'

He threw his weight against the cuffs, metal clanging against the floor, wrists tearing red as he fought the steel. Spittle flew from his lips as he raged, the veins in his neck straining, his face purple with the effort.

And I stood back, watching his frenzy with a calmness I hadn't known I possessed. Then, to my own surprise, the sound rose up in me, sharp, jagged, uncontrollable.

Laughter.

'Look at you,' I said, shaking my head, the laugh still spilling out. 'The great Sir Charles Fairfax. Reduced to nothing but noise and empty threats.'

The more he struggled, the louder my laughter rang in the room, drowning out his fury, turning his menace into something pitiful.

His voice broke into a ragged scream.

'I'll kill you, Olivia! I'll kill you slowly!'

'No,' I said quietly, the laughter fading into something harder, steadier. 'You'll never touch me again.'

His threats still echoed around the room when I stepped closer, the scalpel glinting under the bare bulb as I pressed it to his throat. His body went rigid, the fight bleeding out of him in an instant. The fury in his eyes faltered, replaced by fear.

'No... wait,' he stammered, his voice cracking as he pissed himself. 'You don't have to do this. Listen to me, Olivia. I'm a very rich man. You hear me? Not just money, real wealth. Millions. I invested in crypto years ago. It's worth a fortune now. I can make you richer than you ever dreamed, if you let me live. Just... set me free, and it's all yours.'

The chains rattled as he tried to gesture, his cuffed hands trembling. His voice grew shrill, desperate.

'Think about it! You'll never need any man again. You'll have real power, everything you ever wanted. I can give you that. Only me. No one else.'

And he was right, of course. But only if he died. I pressed the scalpel harder against his throat, just enough to let him feel the edge. His breath came fast, panicked, his eyes darting over my face as if searching for mercy.

'Prove it,' I said coldly. 'The accounts. The passwords. All of it. Or your money dies with you.'

He shook his head, lips trembling.

'No... no, I can't. If you have them, you won't need me. You'll—'

The blade moved before he could finish. A quick, precise slice across the ridge of his nose. He screamed, jerking against the chains, blood spilling hot down his face.

I left him chained and bleeding, his head bowed, his breath ragged with panic, while I fetched the laptop from his study. The machine was already warm when I set it on the floor before him, the screen glowing pale in the dim light of the room. I sat close enough that he could see every movement of my hands, the scalpel resting across my knee like a promise.

'The details,' I said, my voice calm, almost conversational, as though we weren't drowning in blood and madness. 'I might kill you anyway. Or I might not. That part's a mystery, isn't it? But you know as well as I do, it's the only card you've got left to play.'

Oh joy of joys. His words came thick and broken, but he obeyed. The sign-in details tumbled from his mouth, every letter, every number. Crypto, credit cards, bank account, the lot. I typed the details in, one by one, the clack of the metal loud in the silence. My heart hammered as the screen refreshed and then the figures appeared. Rows of numbers, striking in their enormity. Millions.

I turned my head slowly, meeting his desperate eyes. His face was streaked crimson, his lips trembling, hope flickering weakly in his gaze.

'See?' he rasped. 'It's real. We can—'

I smiled. Calm. Certain.

'Thank you,' I whispered. 'For making me rich.'

Then the scalpel moved in a single, decisive arc, slicing across his throat from ear to ear. His eyes widened, his scream strangled into a wet gurgle as the blood poured out, hot and fast, soaking his chest, the floor, my hands. He bucked once against the chains, then sagged forward, lifeless.

I set the house ablaze before I left in the early hours, the flames taking hold fast, licking greedily at curtains and timber, swallowing room after room in a roar of heat and smoke. The crackle followed me down the drive, a savage chorus rising behind me, as I slid behind the wheel of Charles's Mercedes. I drove without looking back, carrying the inferno with me in the rear-view mirror until distance turned it into nothing more than a glow on the horizon.

33

Five years have passed by since the night I opened Charles's throat and buried what was left of him beneath the lawn. Five long years since the chains fell away and the silence of that house became my own.

I began writing this in the attic room, scratching down words in secret, each line a plea. The first few pages were frantic, desperate, as if ink alone might unlock the door. But as days bled into weeks, I saw the futility. Words couldn't save me. Not then. And the risk of discovery was too great. So I stopped.

It was only much later, after the blood, after the burial, that I came back to the page. Not as a cry for help, but as a record. A testament. My truth, carved into sentences only I could shape. Not because I seek forgiveness. Not because I need saving. But because the world deserves to know what happened. What he did to me. What I became.

This book isn't a confession. And it isn't an apology. It is my story. At last, mine to tell. In the eyes of the world, I died. And I let them believe it. I welcomed it. Death gave me freedom. A clean slate on which to carve a new self.

I left Britain on a West Country trawler, no questions asked, no papers shown, the crew happy to take my money in exchange for silence. The sea swallowed my past, mile by mile, until the English coast was no more than a smear of shadow on the horizon.

I kept travelling after that. One country, then another. Now I live thousands of miles away, with a new name and face. The plastic surgeon's blade carved away the girl I was, leaving a mask the world accepts without doubt. And a false passport sits in my desk drawer, the key to a life that was never mine, yet serves me well enough.

My house is too big for one person, clinging to the cliff like it was built to keep watch. From the wide bay window I can see the ocean stretching into forever, its surface slick as oil under the night sky. Some evenings I stand there for hours, tracing the tide as it drags its broken body across the sand, a ceaseless, groaning thing that never rests. Eternal. Indifferent. A reminder that everything is exactly what it's meant to be.

I haven't killed again. Not yet. But the thought is never far. The darkness hasn't left me; it lurks like smoke caught in the rafters, restless, smouldering, an itch just under the skin. I tell myself I can control it, but the truth is more complicated.

I still can't quite believe how easily I was taken in by Charles. That soft voice, the careful flattery, the way he made me feel on that beautiful, sun-soaked island. And me, stupidly eager to believe. But I'd grown so used to change, used to moving on before the dust had settled, used to disappointment snapping at my heels. So, perhaps I forgive myself for that. Or maybe I don't.

Because when I think of Charles, of Joe, of all the men who carved their cruelty into me before I even understood what cruelty was, something shifts inside. The rage rises like a tide, sharp, corrosive, intimate, a familiar voice whispering promises I've heard too many times.

I tell myself I've broken free. That I've built a new life untouched by the past. But lies unravel in the small hours, when the sea presses its black weight against the glass and the silence leaves no room to hide.

That's when doubt seeps in. If the wrong man crossed my path, if I caught the sour reek of his power, the greedy heat of his eyes, would I turn away? Would I stop myself? Or would I reach for a blade? Only time will tell.

* * *

MORE FROM JOHN NICHOLL

Another book from John Nicholl is available to order now here:
https://mybook.to/BrandNewJohnNicholl

ACKNOWLEDGEMENTS

With heartfelt thanks to my editor, Isobel Akenhead, whose insight and patience helped shape every page, and to the entire Boldwood Books team for their unwavering support.

ABOUT THE AUTHOR

John Nicholl is an award-winning, bestselling author of numerous darkly psychological suspense thrillers. These books have a gritty realism born of his real-life experience as an ex-police officer and child protection social worker.

Download your exclusive bonus content from John Nicholl here:

Visit John's website: www.johnnicholl.com

Follow John on social media:

facebook.com/JohnNichollAuthor
x.com/nicholl06
instagram.com/johnnichollauthor
bookbub.com/authors/john-nicholl

ALSO BY JOHN NICHOLL

The Sisters

Mr Nice

The Cellar

The Student

The Cop

The Victim

The Bride

The Holiday

The Boyfriend

The Surgeon

The Girl in the Attic

The Carmarthen Murders Series

The Carmarthen Murders

The Tywi Estuary Killings

The Castle Beach Murders

The Dryslwyn Castle Killings

The Galbraith Series

The Doctor

The Wife

The Father

www.ingramcontent.com/pod-product-compliance
Ingram Content Group UK Ltd.
Pitfield, Milton Keynes, MK11 3LW, UK
UKHW041906300326
11592UKWH00001B/22

9 781806 564569